ALL OR NOTHING

A DCI HARRY MCNEIL NOVEL

JOHN CARSON

DCI SEAN BRACKEN SERIES

CALVIN STEWART SERIES

Final Warning

Hard Case

MAX DOYLE SERIES

Final Steps

Code Red

The October Project

SCOTT MARSHALL SERIES

Old Habits

ALL OR NOTHING

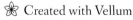 Created with Vellum

For the real Charlie Skellett.
And Carol.
And let's not forget Sir Hugo

ONE

She woke up in the dark, feeling cold and numb. She was on her back with her arms behind her. When she tried to move them, she couldn't. Something bit into her wrists, something hard and tight. She felt sick but fought the nausea. Something in her brain told her not to be sick in case she choked on her own vomit.

There was one more thing that got her attention. She was blind.

The cold made her shiver as her mind cleared more. It was at this point she realised her legs and head wouldn't move much either. Something was round her neck, preventing her from moving. The platform she was lying on creaked and groaned as she wrestled with the restraints.

It sounded like old springs from inside a mattress.

'A bed,' she croaked out loud.

'Exactly!' said a voice at her side and she jumped. She couldn't move to see who'd spoken, but no matter. She could feel her friend's warm breath on her cheek, like a gentle stroke.

'Sioux?' she asked, her voice still a croak.

'That's right, it's me, Sioux, your best friend.'

'What are you doing?'

There was a chuckle. 'We're going to have fun.'

This wasn't Sioux's voice. This version of Sioux was rough, like she had a cold.

Her brain was foggy still, her mind spinning, not quite able to grab what was just outside the periphery of her conscious thoughts. Who was this?

'Help me.'

'Help is long gone for you, my sweet one.' There was a harsh chuckle now, full of menace. 'I told you, we're going to have fun,' the voice said.

A hand ripped off the blindfold, but then a torch was shone into her eyes, blinding her even more. Then it was taken away and a strong hand grabbed her chin and forced her to look at the figure lying on the other bed. Then the blindfold was slipped over her eyes again and tightened.

Just before darkness took its hold, she knew that Sioux was dead.

And she was next.

TWO

Six months earlier

Victor McLean was on holiday with his wife, but they both had a different outlook on what a holiday was. His was lying by a pool in the sun in a far-flung destination, while his wife's was hiking through bushes on trails infested with beasties. Even now, on their second day, as they made their way into the hotel's dining room, he wanted to scratch his bollocks.

'What are you having for breakfast?' Cassidy asked.

'Fucking midges,' he replied.

'What?' His wife looked at him before side-eyeing the other guests. The dining room was heaving and surely somebody had heard Victor's complaint.

'I said, fudge and tatties.'

'Try and pretend you're enjoying yourself,' she admonished, and smiled weakly at an old couple who were sitting at a table near the door.

'Disgusting,' she heard the old woman say.

'Where's the bloody waitress?' Victor said, looking around for a young woman holding a note-book, but not seeing one.

'For Christ's sake, let's just find a table,' Cassidy said. She couldn't see one at first. 'I told you we should have come down earlier.'

'It's those bloody coach parties we saw pulling in last night. Bloody tourists.'

'I think there's a couple of seats over there,' Cassidy said, not making eye contact with the tourists at the table next to where they were standing.

'Oh, great. It's that pair of selfish bastards from the bar last night sitting alone at a table for four. Look at them, like butter wouldn't melt.'

'It's Ewan from work and his dad. Please don't embarrass me,' Cassidy said. 'Besides, your family members are taking up tables too. It's called "using the dining room for breakfast". Although some of them are acting like they've never drunk out of a cup before.'

'Oh, that's right. Have a go at *my* family. *Your* daughter was the one who didn't want to join us, remember?'

'I don't blame her,' Cassidy replied, but Victor was already blanking her out, his eyes fixed on the two men sitting at one of the few remaining tables.

'Hello, look around you: tables for two. Like they couldn't have snagged one of those. Now they're all full. Selfish dicks.'

'They're full of two people having breakfast. It's not their fault if there are no tables left. Where did you expect them to sit?'

Cassidy spotted a young couple heading for the dining room and hurried over to Ewan's table. 'Do you mind if we sit here?' she asked his back.

He turned to look at her.

'Oh, it's you, Ewan.' She feigned surprised and looked over to the old man sitting opposite. 'Joe! I didn't recognise you there.'

Ewan Gallagher was in his mid-thirties, with a nice smile and perfect teeth. He was smiling at her. 'Cassidy! Not at all. Please.' He indicated with one hand that they should join him and his father.

'I bet there was more room in the dining room on the *Titanic*,' Victor said, pulling out a chair and sitting down.

Ewan stood up and pulled out the chair next to him, and Cassidy sat down and he edged the chair in. If Victor noticed, he didn't say.

'Thank you,' Cassidy said, quickly looking over at her husband, but he had his nose in a menu already.

'How are you this morning?' Ewan asked Victor.

'Sore head. Only to be expected, though, after our wee sesh last night. You don't look as rough as I feel,' Victor said.

'Yes, those whiskies can kick you where it hurts if you're not used to it,' Joe said. 'Aye, I had one too many. But I had beer too. Good night, though, eh?'

Ewan smiled at the memory of the night before.

'It was indeed,' Cassidy agreed. 'Where are the others this morning? They been down already?' She thought back to the night before in the bar, when they had got talking and Ewan had ended up having quite a few with her husband. They liked whisky, but that was where the similarities ended. Ewan had class. Victor had none.

'I think Crawford said he would skip breakfast or just have a light one. I don't know about the others.'

The holiday was for members of the hiking club at the hospital where Ewan and Cassidy worked. Family members were welcome to come along too.

Suddenly, Victor slapped the menu down, like he had been trying to swat an errant midge that had dared to enter the establishment. 'Bacon, eggs and sausage,' he declared as if answering an unasked question.

'I think I'm going to have some bacon and eggs,' Cassidy said.

'I can thoroughly recommend the kippers,' Ewan said.

'She's not a fish person,' Victor answered for her, not bothering to look across the table but rather hunting for the waitress. Then he spotted her and snapped his fingers.

A minute later, she was at their table.

Victor rattled off the order. 'And keep the coffee coming.'

'Please,' Cassidy added, smiling. The woman smiled back and left.

'Fishers is the place to be, isn't it?' Ewan said, sweeping a hand around.

'I love this hotel. We've been here before, haven't we, Victor?'

'Hmm. What?' Victor's attention had been wandering again.

'It's nice to have a weekend break. Before duty calls on Monday morning.'

Ewan laughed. 'I hear you.' He took a sip of coffee and put his cup down.

'Me being retired, I don't have to worry about work on a Monday morning,' Joe said. 'Every day is like Sunday.'

'Listen to a lot of Morrissey, do you, Dad?' Ewan asked.

'You don't know the half of what I get up to when you're out,' his father replied, laughing.

A young man had come across to them. 'Refill, sir?' he asked Joe.

'Yes, please.' The waiter smiled as he poured from the silver coffee pot into Ewan and Joe's cups. 'Thank you.'

'Hey, chief,' Victor said. 'We haven't had our first yet.'

'Allow me,' the man said. He poured two coffees and a look passed between him and Ewan. The latter had already given the waiter a large tip to make sure his cup was filled quickly. Victor was on a hiding to nothing on getting a quick refill.

The waitress brought their food across.

'About fucking time,' Victor said in a low voice after she walked away.

'Victor, for God's sake,' Cassidy protested.

'What? Ewan there has heard swearing before, I'm sure.' He forked some sausage into his mouth. 'Haven't you, squire?'

Ewan looked at the other man and smiled. 'Once or twice.'

'See? He's not offended. The word's been in use for hundreds of years. In fact, King Harold the Second said, "It's all fun and games until somebody loses a fucking eye" when he got hit with that arrow.'

Cassidy closed her eyes for a second before opening them and looking at the man across the table. She loved him, but sometimes he could make her cringe.

'What are you up to today?' she asked Ewan. She was sure they'd had this conversation the night before, but the Baileys and ice had wiped most of the memories she had of their previous chat. She didn't like getting drunk, but the Baileys dulled the pain of having her husband climb on top of her after his session in the bar.

'We're doing some hiking. Up by the Falls of Bruar. It's not too far for Dad and the views are spectacular.'

'So are we! Why don't you join us?' Cassidy said, her smile bright. 'Victor's clan are here and we're all going up. Sisters and brothers with some of their kids.'

'Oh, no, we couldn't do that. I'm sure you and Victor want to hike in peace with the family. Be together.'

'You wouldn't mind, honey, would you?'

'What?' Victor said through a mouthful of bacon.

'You wouldn't mind Ewan and Joe coming along for a hike with us?' *If you can tear your fucking eyes away from the young German woman at the other table for two minutes and concentrate.*

'Yeah, whatever.'

Ewan finished his coffee. 'I'm sure we'll see you up there. Dad and I have finished breakfast, so we're going to head on up there after we've got our things from the room.'

'It's a nice place, and dense too,' Victor said. 'Especially if you need a slash.'

'Oh, Christ,' Cassidy said.

'I'll bear that in mind,' Ewan said, smiling. He pushed his chair back and stood up, then waited for Joe to do the same. The older man was slower.

Ewan and Joe headed for the dining room exit, the younger man quickly looking round before he left. Victor was looking over at the German girl again.

———

Up in their room, Joe shook his head as Ewan headed for the bathroom. 'He's a right arse,' he said.

'Who?' Ewan asked from the other side of the door.

'That Victor one. I told you earlier, I had to leave the bar last night or else I might have lamped him one.'

'You couldn't lamp your own shadow. Those days are long gone.'

'Where's Crawford?' Joe asked. 'I hope he's fit for the walk.'

Crawford Ingram was Ewan's friend and work-mate, and a member of the hiking club.

'He'll be there. People go up at their own pace. And then we'll meet up for lunch later.'

'I don't suppose your brother is going down for breakfast?'

'Room service,' Ewan answered. His voice sounded tinny coming from the small bathroom.

'Of course it is. He should try and socialise now and again.'

'He's got problems, Dad, you know that.'

'No need to shout. I'm in the next room, I'm not dead.' Joe sighed. 'Well, if that Victor one starts his pish, I'll tell him to go raffle himself. He's a loud-mouth. And now we're all going to meet up at the Falls of Bruar and sit round the campfire singing country music songs. Along with his family, who're probably a bunch of mutants like he is.'

'First of all, there will be no sitting. It's a hiking trail.' The toilet flushed and the sound of water rushing out of the taps could be heard.

'Just as well. Maybe we could go to another bar tonight?'

Ewan said something unintelligible while brushing his teeth.

'Where's your bloody couth? Talking when you're brushing,' Joe said.

More garbled conversation, and Joe could have sworn his son told him to go and have intercourse with his own person. He shook his head and started putting things into his backpack. He'd wanted to bring the machete and the kit for starting a fire if you got lost, but Ewan had said Joe would probably burn down half the Highlands if he went mental with the matches, so all Joe packed was his water-proof jacket and a roll of toilet paper. Unlike the last time, when he'd got caught short in the middle of nowhere and his son had suggested using leaves to wipe himself with and he'd blindly grabbed a bunch of nettles and used them before realising what they were and it felt like he'd set his arsehole on fire. So now it was toilet roll whenever they were out and about.

The running water was shut off and Ewan came out of the bathroom. 'Right, get in there and I'll give Crawford a shout, then we can get up the road ahead of those two and whoever else is joining them.'

'Two shakes of a lamb's tail,' Joe replied, scooting past and closing the bathroom door behind him. 'Christ, you might have lit a candle, manky wee bastard,' he said.

Ewan laughed and packed his own backpack as his father coughed dramatically and emptied a can of air freshener.

'Why is it fucking roasting in this car?' Victor complained. 'Why can't all cars have air con like in America?'

'I'm sure new ones do,' Cassidy replied. 'If you bought one, you'd find out. But no, you want to run about in this old Rover. At least your brother rented a nice new minibus. I bet that's got air con.'

'I'm not forking out hard-earned cash for a flashy tin box on wheels.' He wound the window down as he put the boot down on the A9 heading for the House of Bruar.

She looked at her husband. 'Did you remember your stick thingy?'

'Selfie stick. It's called a selfie stick, for God's sake,' Victor replied, and then spat out the window. 'Fucking midges. I hope stomach acid is enough to kill the little bastards. I've swallowed enough of them.'

'They can have a swim in all the beer you drank, then they'll all get pished and drown.'

Victor ignored her and wound the window up.

'You like to take photos on your phone with that selfie stick. I said you should buy a real camera.'

'I'm not forking out hard-earned for one of those overpriced Jap-crap things.'

'Well, that's not fucking racist,' Cassidy said. 'I hope you don't talk like that in front of Moira.' Their fifteen-year-old daughter was staying at Cassidy's sister's place with her husband and kids. She wouldn't be seen dead tramping up and down a manky dirt trail, especially if there was the slightest possibility that mobile phone service could go out. And the thought of spending time with people who were technically her cousins gave her the boak.

The traffic was busy on the A9, a mixture of tourists who had never driven on the left before and hot rod racers whose sole purpose in life was to make other motorists point and say, 'Look at that bastard!'

The House of Bruar was on the right. It was a country clothing store that sold a wide variety of Scottish goods, including preserves and whiskies.

'We can come and have a bite to eat in the restaurant after we've been up the trail,' Cassidy said. 'Your brother and the extras from *The Hills Have Eyes* are here,' she added, pointing to the silver minibus. 'He must have been booting it up here.'

'Bobby always was a bloody show-off. "I can get pished and still get up early. I can get a better-looking woman than you. I can balance a fifty-pence piece on my knob." Fucking twenty-pence more like.'

They got out of the old car and the driver's door creaked alarmingly as Victor slammed it hard. They got their backpacks from the boot and headed for the start of the trail behind the store itself, and walked along the path and through an archway that was more of a small tunnel.

Ten minutes later, they were in the woods on the pathway.

'Oh, jeez,' Cassidy said, stopping for a moment.

'What's wrong now?' Victor said.

'It's my knee. I felt a sharp pain.' She looked at Victor. She had partially dislocated her knee six months ago and it still wasn't a hundred per cent. 'I should have brought my hiking stick. I forgot it.'

'You'll be fine,' Victor said. 'The others are ahead. Just catch up.' He took off, marching.

'If that German girl from the dining room is here, she looks like she's twelve!' Cassidy shouted to her husband's back, but he wasn't listening. 'Bastard.'

She watched him walk away ahead of her and wondered if Ewan and Joe were already here.

'I need a pee,' Joe said. He had exchanged his normal walking stick for a longer hiking version.

'Oh, for God's sake, Dad. We've only just got here,' Ewan said, looking both ways along the path. There were some people ahead of them when they'd started out, but Joe couldn't move as fast as the others and the group had moved out of sight.

'You were rushing me. My bladder's sloshing

around. I told you we should have taken it a bit slower.'

'If we went any slower, we'd have been going backwards.'

'Aw, come on, help me find a quiet spot or else I'll pish myself.'

'Jesus. You do have that packet of baby wipes with you?' Ewan asked.

'And hand sanitizer. I'll never get caught out again. Remember that time when I pished in those bushes, not realising they bordered a caravan site?'

'I can still hear the screams.'

Joe chuckled.

They reached the stone bridge that looked over the gorge and waterfall below.

'That rushing water isn't helping things,' Joe complained.

They took a side path away from the bridge and walked up until they were out of sight.

'Right, keep a shoatie,' Joe said, taking his back-pack off. 'And get those wipes out so I can clean my hands.' He looked around. 'Where did your brother go?'

'Simon is being Simon. He and Crawford are probably away smoking something.'

'Don't be saying that.' Joe trampled into the

bushes off the path while his son rummaged about in the backpack for the baby wipes. These were the best thing ever invented when you were hiking in the middle of nowhere, he thought, taking out the bulky packet.

'You should have emptied half of them out to make the backpack lighter,' Ewan said.

Joe didn't reply but then came firing back out of the bushes in a rush. 'Bloody hell. I nearly went arse over elbow there.'

'I'll watch where I'm stepping.'

Joe laughed. 'Your bladder's a lot younger than mine. You shouldn't need to go until we get back down to the store.'

'It's you talking about it that's making me need it.' Ewan kept his own backpack on.

Joe wiped his hands and then his stick. Ewan climbed into the bushes, then the headache hit him like a hammer. 'Da...ad,' he started to say, his field of vision swimming. Not again. The doctor had told him he was fine. The last time, Ewan had thought he had a brain tumour, the headaches were so bad. But a new computer with a brighter screen and a new pair of reading glasses had sorted his problem. Or so he thought.

'It's just the divorce,' he told himself. 'She's long

gone. You're back living with your dad and you've moved on. Look forward, Ewan, not back.' The therapist's words rang in his head and he started to calm down again, the pounding receding. He hadn't seen the shrink in a long time and didn't want to go back to him again.

He realised he'd finished and zipped back up, and then he heard a commotion and a scream. When he came out of the bushes, Joe was gone. Ewan ran back down the path and saw a group of people in a tight line looking over the bridge. Joe was at the end with a man from the hiking group and they were all looking down.

One of the women turned and looked away, putting her face in her hands.

Ewan stopped running and walked slower and gave the line of people a wide berth, not wanting to startle anybody.

'Dad,' he said, just loud enough so the old man would hear him above the noise of the rushing water below.

Joe turned round, a wet wipe in his hand. He gave it to his son.

'What's going on?' Ewan asked his father, wiping his hands.

'Somebody fell off the bridge,' Joe said, his face white.

'Christ. Is it one of the hiking group?'

'Yes. You'll never guess. Have a look.'

Ewan looked over and his eyes went wide. Then he looked at Joe again. 'How did it happen?'

'I have no idea. I asked them, but they don't know.'

They both looked down at the man lying on the rocks below.

———

It was maybe five minutes later but it felt like hours when they saw the figure of Cassidy hobbling up the path towards them.

Somebody had called treble nine and been assured that help was on the way. Ewan knew they wouldn't have to hurry. The dead man wasn't going anywhere.

A fat bastard who looked like he got out of wind using an escalator was being held back by a few other men, one of whom was telling him that he couldn't help his brother now.

Cassidy reached the bridge and Ewan stepped forward, putting his hands out to grab her arms.

'Ewan! What's wrong?' Her voice was shrill.

'It's Victor. It looks like he fell off the bridge. I heard the commotion from further up the path.' *When I was having a piss in the bushes,* he thought. 'I ran down here and saw them looking over. Then I saw Victor. I'm really sorry. They've called an ambulance.'

'What happened?' Cassidy shouted to the others in the group, but they talked amongst themselves. 'Bobby? What happened?' she yelled again, panic gripping her now.

'He fell,' Bobby said simply, his voice sounding as distant as the rushing water below.

'He fell?' She shrugged off Ewan's hands. She looked over the side of the bridge, and after a couple of seconds she let out an ear-splitting scream.

Then Ewan was back, putting his hands on her arms, from behind this time, guiding her away from the edge. She crumbled, crouching down with her back to the stonework of the bridge. Ewan crouched too, putting an arm around her shoulders. He looked over at Joe, who just stood and looked at them.

They were still like that when help arrived.

Then one of the group stepped out from behind the others. A tall, gangly young man with a haircut that looked like he had done it himself in the dark without a mirror. He stared at Ewan and smiled an awkward smile.

'Come on, Brian,' an older woman said. She pulled his head onto her shoulder.

A man dressed in clothes that evidently weren't meant for walking up trails but more for walking round the aisles in Marks and Spencer stood with his hands held out.

'Ladies and gentlemen, my name is Detective Chief Inspector Dunbar from Glasgow Division. I'll take charge of this until the locals arrive.' He was holding his warrant card out. 'If you could step back from the bridge...'

He shepherded them away from the parapet and kept everybody away until the local force turned up.

Some of the group looked at Ewan as he stood to one side with Joe, before looking away again. Then nobody was looking at him, but he knew why. He couldn't explain it, he just knew.

One of Victor McLean's family was a killer.

The funeral was a busy affair. Victor had a lot of friends. Cassidy didn't know a lot of them, but they filled the chapel at Warriston Crematorium. It was a blur for Cassidy and Moira.

Ewan turned up, smart in a black suit and tie, almost like he was going to a formal dance. Joe was with him, wearing his wrinkled old suit and black tie he kept for 'saying goodbye to old friends' who popped their clogs before he did. He wasn't smiling this time. They joined the line of people shaking Cassidy's hand and telling her that they were sorry for her loss.

When it was Ewan's turn, he clasped Cassidy's hand and tried to speak, but the words wouldn't come at first. Then when they did, they were a rough whisper.

'I'm sorry,' he said simply.

'Thank you,' Cassidy said in a soft voice. 'Please come along to the wake. Victor would have wanted that.'

Ewan nodded and let her hand go. Watched Joe give his condolences.

And they did go to the wake, at a hotel around the corner.

Ewan told Cassidy he had gone off the main path for a few moments and had answered the call of nature. The same story he had told the police officer, Dunbar. The police had managed to get one of the

McLean group to tell them what had happened, and they'd confirmed that Ewan had turned up after they did. It was the scream that had alerted them.

Ewan hadn't heard Victor's scream because of the pounding pain in his head.

Cassidy told Ewan she wondered if Victor had fallen after he had tried to get a photo on his phone using his selfie stick while standing on the edge of the bridge. She would never know.

They never found his phone.

And never would.

THREE

Present day

'This is nice,' Morgan Allan said as Detective Chief Inspector Harry McNeil struggled to get his daughter out of her pushchair and fold the contraption without chopping off a body part.

He made a face like the surgeon had just told him that the operation to sew his willy back on had been a complete failure. Harriet.

Morgan laughed. 'Here, let me help you.'

'I was trying to impress you with my skills. I don't want you to think any less of me because I can't juggle my daughter with folding her pushchair.'

'Oh, I couldn't think any less of you, Harry.' She

laughed and collapsed the pushchair like she was paid to demonstrate such a feat in a baby store.

They had stayed over at the flat Harry still kept in Comely Bank. It was where he and his wife had lived when she died, and he had had plans to rent it out, but instead he paid a cleaning company to come in once a week and keep it fresh. Harry and Morgan had been for a quick walk to Inverleith Pond with Grace well wrapped up in her pushchair. It had given them rosy cheeks and frostbite in places they hadn't known existed.

'Thanks,' he replied, and he wasn't sure for what. Either helping him with the contraption or shooting his ego down in flames. Go with the pushchair thing then.

They were at the little café called Tattie Scones on the main road.

Grace had a dummy in her mouth, and she looked double her normal size with her puffer jacket on, and her woollen hat and gloves. For a little while they wrestled with coats and scarves and gloves, and Morgan lifted the protective hood on the pushchair and took off Grace's jacket and hat and scarf so she didn't overheat.

'Aw, what a cute wee yin,' said a woman with an order pad, coming over to them.

Harry smiled at her. 'I was surprised to hear you were open today. Usually, everything's closed on Boxing Day, isn't it?'

'Try telling that to the Gyle Centre.'

'Well, we certainly appreciate you, after having a walk round the pond.'

'I only close on Christmas Day.' She smiled and made a face at Grace, who was sitting on Harry's knee. 'Oh, wait, I'll get you a high chair.' She scuttled off and dragged the chair back to the table. Harry popped Grace in and shoved her jacket in behind her to prop her up better after strapping her in.

'What can I get you folks?'

'Tea, please,' Morgan said.

'Coffee and a bacon roll,' Harry said. He looked at Morgan. 'You want anything to eat?'

'Maybe I will have a bacon roll too, please.'

'Coming right up,' the woman said, leaving them alone. There was only one other person in, an old man sitting in a far corner of the small café, trying not to eavesdrop and failing miserably.

'This has been the best Christmas I've had in years,' Morgan said to Harry. 'I know it hasn't been for you, since this is...well, you know.'

'My first Christmas without my wife. I knew it was coming and a hurdle I had to get over. You said so yourself when we were having one of our chats in the pub.'

'I didn't know I'd be spending it with you back then,' she said.

Morgan was a psychiatrist who worked at the Royal Edinburgh. Police Scotland had insisted Harry go and see a psychologist there, to make sure he was mentally fit to lead a Major Investigation Team again. His psychologist, Dr Burke, was proficient at his job but could give watching paint dry a run for its money. Round the corner from the hospital was the Merlin bar and restaurant on Morningside Road where Harry went afterwards, just for a wee nip to take the edge off having to be mentally dissected and probed. That's where he'd bumped into Morgan one evening and they'd got talking. He had told her more about his feelings than he had told Burke. About how his wife had died the previous summer. About his seven-month-old baby daughter. They hadn't quite got to the stage of *What's your favourite colour?* yet.

Morgan looked at Harry, who was staring at his daughter. 'You don't regret inviting me over for Christmas?'

He blinked a couple of times before looking at her. 'No, of course not.'

'But?'

Grace was looking at him and then she smiled with the dummy still in her mouth. He smiled back.

'I was just wondering what it is we have here,' he said.

Morgan smiled at him. 'This is the point where we think, let's wait and see. I mean, we're not boyfriend/girlfriend.' She lowered her voice. 'But since we slept with each other on Christmas night, we're one step ahead of being friends. And no, I'm not going to be a friend with benefits. So we're somewhere in between. Like we're standing on either end of a seesaw; we can either keep the equilibrium, or one of us can jump off.'

'We can both jump off at the same time and go on the swings if you like,' he said, smiling at her.

'I'd like that.' She reached a hand over and squeezed his. Morgan's husband had been killed in a car crash on Christmas Day ten years before and she didn't have any family of her own.

They made small talk until the woman brought the rolls and drinks over.

'Thanks,' Harry said. He was hungry now that it was lunchtime. He had been about to get up and make breakfast when Morgan had pulled him back into bed.

'These are good,' she said. 'I don't often eat

bacon rolls, but sometimes you have to go over to the Dark Side.'

'Oh, yeah, I watch my figure too.'

'Sounds good to me.' She looked at him for a moment. 'Are you going to tell Jessica about me spending the night?'

'If it comes up in conversation.' He looked at her. 'Is that okay?'

'Are you asking me as a professional or your "friend with benefits"?' She used air quotes.

He laughed. 'As my friend.'

'Then yes, that's fine. I know Jessica is your sister-in-law and she stepped in to look after Grace when you had your sabbatical down in the south of Scotland, so she lives in the house with you. And I know you said it's strictly platonic. But she could still see me as a threat. That's why we stayed at your flat here in Comely Bank and not in your house in Murrayfield.'

'Flora wouldn't see you as a threat,' Harry said.

'Flora's your housekeeper. She doesn't live with you.'

'I don't think Mr Flora would be too happy if she said she wanted to live with me.'

'I can imagine.' She sipped some tea. 'How's the team doing? Nobody jumped ship yet?' she asked.

'Not yet. We've settled in fine. I already know a few of them, Frank Miller included. I haven't worked with Julie Stott before, but she has a good rep. And, well, you've heard me talk about Elvis.'

'Ah, yes, the inimitable DC Colin Presley. The man who was about to transfer through to Glasgow until he met DSup Calvin Stewart.'

'I tried to tell him that they're not all like that, but he won't listen.'

'Your son, Chance, would have kept him right, I'm sure, even though he's still in uniform.'

'Yeah, he's a good kid. He was gutted he had to work on Christmas Day, especially since this was... well, you know. I've said it a million times already.'

'I know,' she said.

He nodded. 'I feel bad that I had made plans to see Frank tonight.'

'I can stay with Grace if you like?' Morgan smiled at him and he felt like he was falling down a lift shaft.

'Oh, I wouldn't want to bother you. She can be a handful,' he replied.

'I understand. You don't know the real me and I might be a psycho in disguise and she's the most precious thing.'

'It's nothing personal, I promise you,' he said, the

detective in him kicking in. Truth be told, his daughter was everything and he wasn't going to leave her with just anybody. 'Besides, Kim really wants to see Grace.'

'Would you like me to stay tonight? I don't have a hectic caseload tomorrow, just two patients.'

'I'd like that, Morgan.'

'Good. Why don't you go and talk to Frank, take Grace with you, and I'll pop home and get a change of clothes.'

The words sounded strange to him. *Change of clothes.* He didn't want this friendship to be like a runaway train, but if he jumped off now, there might not be another one along for a while. *Go with the flow, Harry,* he told himself.

'That sounds good.'

'And when your heart stops jumping up and down like a pneumatic drill, we can have a nice stroll back round to your flat.'

'What are your plans for this week?' he asked, feeling like he was hinting at something.

'Work, work and more work. Rinse and repeat. How about you?'

'Same. Maria, my assistant manager at the nursery, is taking Grace this week since the nursery is closed.'

'What about New Year's Eve?' she asked.

'Celebrating it with young miss here.'

'If you don't think three's a crowd, maybe I could celebrate it with you?'

'Sounds good. And maybe if you're at a loose end before that, we could grab a coffee. I can't make it to the Merlin because Jessica is on holiday until the New Year.'

'Maria sounds like a godsend,' Morgan said.

'She is. They're all great at the nursery.'

'Vanessa must have really loved you to leave you her nursery business and her house.'

'She did. Us splitting up was all my fault. If I had pulled my finger out, she might have been alive today.'

Morgan had finished her roll and she reached over and put a hand on his. 'You can't blame yourself for what happened. It was a tragedy, out of your hands. You can't feel guilt for what somebody else did.'

His mind flashed back to when Vanessa died, but he mentally shook his head, feeling he was teetering on the edge of the abyss.

'I know.'

They finished and Harry paid the bill. Grace was yawning as they put her back in the pushchair.

They walked back round to the flat in air cold enough to make a brass monkey reach for his Y-fronts. They both lifted the stroller with a sleeping Grace up the stairs.

'I'll go and see Frank this evening,' Harry said.

'You sure you want me to come back here tonight?' Morgan asked.

Harry shook his head.

'Oh.' She smiled a sad smile at him. 'All good things and all that.'

'Listen –'

'No, it's fine, Harry. I had a good time with you and Grace. I wasn't expecting anything more, I promise you.'

'Listen to me, Morgan. I don't want you coming back here tonight. I want you to come over to Murrayfield.'

Her eyes widened a little bit. 'Are you sure? That's your main home.' She smiled at him.

'I'm sure. Fancy watching a film while Grace has her nap?'

'I'd love to.'

'Besides, there aren't so many steps there to lift the stroller up.'

He watched as this woman whom he felt comfortable with made sure Grace was okay before putting her pushchair to the side of the settee. He looked over to the carpet in the living room, to the spot where Alex had lain, the ruptured aneurysm in her brain slowly killing her. He couldn't put a finger on why he kept this place. It held some good memories, he had to admit, but there were ghosts here. Vanessa. Alex. Ghosts of Christmases past.

'Right, I'll get the kettle on,' he said.

'I won't argue with that,' Morgan replied.

FOUR

'Thanks for coming round so quickly, Ewan,' Cassidy McLean said, putting a hand on his arm.

Ewan Gallagher stood on the doorstep of Cassidy's house. 'I was surprised when you called, since I was coming round this evening anyway,' he replied as the woman almost yanked him into the house.

'It's Moira. She went out last night and was going to be staying at a friend's house. She never went. I tried calling her, but there's no reply on her phone. I'm worried, Ewan.'

Ewan gritted his teeth. *Fucking Moira.* '*Look at me, my dad is dead and now I want your attention.*' She was a pathetic creature.

'Listen, I'm sure she's fine. You know how

teenagers are. She just turned eighteen a few weeks ago and in her mind that means she can stay out however late she wants, talk to you however she wants and basically do her own thing.'

Cassidy nodded. 'I'm still worried. Moira never once fails to answer her phone.'

They walked through to the living room. Ewan looked around. *Messy cow.* This was a fucking hovel compared to how he kept his own house. Joe knew he was a neat freak and there was nothing out of place. His father had suggested they get a wee dog and Ewan had almost touched cloth. A fucking dog! That bastard would shed fur around the house when he was at work, and Joe had an allergy to the hoover. Not to mention Ewan's brother. Fucking Dracula came out more in the daytime than he did. Skulking about in his bed all day doing God knows what. Probably things he would be arrested for if Simon was doing them in public. Just picking up a can of furniture polish made Joe break out in a rash, so it was up to Ewan to keep the place clean, which he did with relish. You could eat your dinner off the carpet. Unlike this place.

Now, standing in Cassidy's living room, he thought an interior designer could improve the ambience of the room with a box of matches. He liked

Cassidy, but her idea of keeping a clean house was to make sure the cockroaches had a nice bed to sleep in. He hadn't actually seen any of the beasties, but there had to be *something* living in that fucking carpet, surely? Something far smaller than a cockroach, granted, but some form of life. He wasn't convinced that losing her husband had brought on the slovenliness. The stains on the arm of the couch looked like they had been put there when England had won the World Cup. Victor had probably been a manky bastard too.

'Look, she took it hard when Victor died. And the fact that you and I have become friends is probably wearing on her,' he said.

'Hardly just friends, though, are we?' She looked him in the eyes and he thought for a moment that she was going to lean in and kiss him, but she didn't, and he was glad he hadn't leaned in either, looking like a perv.

Ewan had slept with Cassidy a few weeks ago, months after Victor had gone diving off the bridge. The thought of that day still gave him the willies. That freak show nephew of Victor's, Brian, the one who had looked at him funny the day Victor died, made him shiver, and this young man was the reason Ewan now carried a Stanley knife whenever he came round to Cassidy's house. In case the bawbag decided to pop round to see if he could hurry along his aunt to the afterlife, just like he'd done to his uncle. All Victor's family looked daft in Ewan's eyes, but Brian was fifteen on a scale of one to ten on the daft-o-meter. It was the way the teenager had grinned at him that day before turning to his mother to be consoled.

Then there was Bobby, Cassidy's brother-in-law. He looked like he spent a lot of time in the woods with a plastic sheet and a shovel. He was in his fifties and had never married, 'because no woman will ever tame this stallion,' he had said at the wake after Victor's funeral. Stallion. Fucking donkey more like. It was nothing to do with the fact that the fat bastard looked like a hippie and would do well to use a bar of soap when he went into the shower.

Ewan hated Cassidy's family, but technically they weren't her family anymore, since Victor had fallen / been pushed to his death.

'Have you called Moira's friends?' Ewan asked, trying desperately to show some compassion. He had been invited round for some drinks tonight, and after having been told that the uppity little cow of a daughter would be going out, he had made sure to put on a clean pair of skids and brush his teeth.

When Cassidy had called, he had thought he was going to get the bum's rush. He was ready to tell her that she was a crap shag anyway and that he wished he hadn't wasted spunk on her, but the urgency in her voice had made his heart skip a beat. Was she still young enough to get pregnant, even though she was older than he was? Ewan had entertained the thought of being a father a long time ago, but as each opportunity landed, it was just as quickly whisked away again. His wife had told him she'd rather burn in hell than give birth, and he wished he had made her wish come true, but they had gone their own ways. After a while, he had given up on the idea of having kids.

He worked in a lab at the Sick Kids' hospital as an advanced biomedical scientist, and he liked to think of himself as the man on the front line who saved kids' lives. He would look at slides through a microscope and see if the samples contained cancer cells or not. It was he, Ewan Gallagher, who was the man at the top of the tree when it came to the little lives, not some overpaid prick in a hospital theatre. Any muppet with half a brain could do that shite. No, it was he who should have been given kudos for saving lives, not some smarmy fuck with slicked-back hair and a Porsche in his driveway.

'Yes, I called the houses of the friends I know. None of them have seen her. She said she was meeting Sioux, but I can't contact her either. Moira had been drinking before she left. We had words about it. Not a fight, but I told her to take it easy. She wouldn't listen.'

Ewan tried not to curl his lip when she mentioned Moira's friend. Sue Anderson spelled her name Sioux like the Native Americans. 'To be different,' she had told Ewan once. He had wanted to reply, 'Swearing like a truck driver and shagging around has the same effect', but had kept the thought to himself. The girl was weird. She even had the head of a Native American tattooed on the inside of her right wrist. She had proudly shown it to Ewan a couple of months back. Like he cared.

Ewan had given Cassidy his best advice: *have you called her friends?* It was what they said on the crime shows he and Joe watched. Beyond that, he was stumped. Maybe if he had some feelings for the impudent brat, he could have gone the extra mile, but truth be told she was probably off somewhere being pumped after getting blootered on a bottle of Thunderbird.

He just didn't have the contents in his mental

toolbox to deal with this situation. Also, he couldn't give a toss.

'Let's not panic, okay?' He pulled her in for a hug, more to hide the smile that was hovering about on his lips than from any desire to offer comfort.

'Okay,' she replied, pulling away from him.

Well, that was fucking rude. I wasn't finished offering the physical contact equivalent of a cup of tea.

'Would you like a cup of tea?' she asked, as if reading his mind.

'Thanks. That would be smashing.'

He watched her retreat out of the room, presumably to make her way to the kitchen. She would expect him to be seated when she came back, having put a folding tray table out for them to put their cups on. There was no evidence a coffee table had ever existed. Ewan had the feeling Cassidy and Victor had eaten off the tray tables, but there was only one that he knew of now. Maybe the other one had been burnt in the back garden along with Victor's skids after he was gone.

Ewan grabbed hold of the table, unfolded it and put it in front of the left-hand cushion so she would be forced to sit next to him. Not that he was going to pounce, but the last time she had put it in the middle

and he didn't even get a fucking kind look that time.
A quick peck on the cheek and 'I'll see you at the
weekend'. Just because the brat was upstairs looking
at willies on TikTok or something. He had been
disappointed that time, just a few weeks ago, but he
didn't whine to Cassidy or tell her that coming here
had been a waste of petrol. He kept that to himself.

It was after that that he had slept with her. And
their relationship changed. Not a seismic shift, more
like a little rumble in the jungle. She had told him
she was glad that they had taken their relationship to
the next level, although they were still going to take
things easy.

He had almost told her that he didn't want to be
trying on Victor's old slippers, and he was glad they
had been together but he too wanted to take it easy.
Then the daughter had given him the look. Moira
had glared at him one day as if she knew. Or maybe
she had arrived at the 'You're not my real dad!' stage
prematurely. Either way, there was no love lost.
They skirted round each other like members of the
Sharks and the Jets.

Ewan sat down at the rickety table. No matter
how tight he tried to put it up, the fucking thing had
a mind of its own. He didn't want the bastard
cowping the tea all over him. Cassidy being a nurse

was handy, but he didn't want her to shove an ice pack down his Y's.

'Here you are,' she announced, coming back into the room with two mugs. She placed them down and he looked into his and could see a brown line near the top where the dish-washing wand had failed in its duty. *That'll be the Salmonella-flavoured tea then,* he thought, but dug deep and took a sip.

'When should I call the police?' she asked, sitting down beside him.

'The police?' he said.

'To report Moira missing.'

'Has it been twenty-four hours?' he asked. His fun night was going to be anything but, so now he had to pick his time for getting out of there. There was a party going on later that he was going to. Ewan cursed himself for boxing himself into a corner. The table was in front of him and Cassidy was next to him. If he wanted to get out in a hurry, he would have to limbo dance between the rickety legs of the table and hope the bastard thing was wide enough so it didn't get stuck on him.

'Not yet. Close. Will the police take a missing person's report now?' Cassidy said.

'I'm not sure.'

Now he was itching to get away. Any prospect

of a romantic encounter had been blown out of the water. He would have to put the 'Get me out of here' protocol into play. Which he'd been intending to do later anyway, but things weren't quite going to plan.

'I need to use your bathroom,' he said.

Cassidy bumped along the cushion and he followed suit, until they were free and clear of having their privates burned off. Ewan didn't want to appear on an episode of *When Tray Tables Go Bad*. Booting a table over and spilling tea on his own carpet would have sent him into a frenzy of mopping it up and spraying carpet cleaner from fifty paces. But he thought a cup of char on this carpet would be an improvement.

In the bathroom, which was upstairs off a dingy landing that he was sure had been the model for many a horror movie, he took his phone out and called Joe.

'Listen, Dad, we need to put that emergency thing into play.'

'What emergency thing?'

'For God's sake. You know, the phone call you would make if I needed to get away from a woman quickly?'

'Why would you want to get away from a woman

quickly? You know they're not beating a path to your door. Besides, it's never happened before.'

'Can you just do it?'

'Why are you whispering?'

'Well, I can hardly fucking shout it, can I? I'm in her lav and I don't want her to hear. I thought that might have been self-explanatory.'

'No need to get snarky. For somebody who's in a pickle, you might want to try being nice.'

Ewan counted to ten.

'You still there?' Joe said. *'I mean, you wouldn't be doing anything while you're on the phone with me, I hope.'*

'That's nothing less than having you stand outside the bushes when we're hiking. But no, I was thinking.'

'Don't strain yourself.'

'Funny. But are you going to help me or not? Or do I have to start looking for a home for you?'

'Alright, don't get your skids in a twist. I'll make the call. You want me to do it now?'

'Not right now.'

'Obviously. I meant when you hang up.'

'You need to wait until I get back downstairs. Don't rush me. Give me five minutes.'

'What will I say?'

'You don't have to say anything.'

'What's the point in phoning then?'

'Fucking hell. Just so it makes it look like I'm needed back home. I just need to answer the phone in front of Cassidy so she thinks I'm needed else-where. I want to leave, but it has to be handled right. That's where you come in. Just call, and start singing "She'll Be Coming Round the Mountain" for all I care. Just make my phone ring.'

Ewan disconnected the call just as his father was starting to protest the song choice. He used the facili-ties and dried his hands on a towel that probably left more germs than if he hadn't washed his hands in the first place.

Back downstairs, Cassidy was on the phone again, either calling in to a radio show – long-time listener, first-time caller – or talking to one of the brat's friends again.

She hung up. 'Nothing,' she said. 'Nobody's heard from her.'

'What about Sioux? Have you tried calling her again?'

'I have. Neither of them have been heard from. Where could she be, Ewan?' Cassidy started sobbing and she rushed at him, throwing her arms around him. Then his phone rang.

Christ, he didn't want to answer it and have her hear his father belting out 'Saturday Night' by the Bay City Rollers. His old man went through phases of listening to music from different eras, and the latest was the seventies.

'I have to take this,' Ewan said. 'I'm on call.' Which wasn't a lie. Though being on call never stopped him getting pished. He had told Joe that if he ever did get a call to go into the lab, then the old man would have to come in with him and Ewan would talk him through what to do. Which had earned Ewan a suggestion of what he could do to himself, which was a physical impossibility, but he would roll with that if push ever came to shove.

He slipped the phone out of his pocket, gently prising Cassidy off him, and made sure the phone screen was away from her.

'Hello?'

'I was thinking maybe a bit of Les and the boys, or Ol' Blue Eyes. What do you think?'

I think I'm going to kick you square in the nuts. 'Oh no, what happened?'

'Nothing happened. You told me to call you.'

'Well, stay where you are. I won't be long. Try not to move.'

'I'm getting some moves going now, let me tell

you. "Bye-Bye, Baby" is up next and I've taken one of my pills. I'll be able to go all night.'

You're a fucking dead man walking. 'Just take it easy. I'm on my way now.'

Ewan hung up just as Joe was starting to belt out the lyrics to a song. He wasn't sure if Cassidy would have heard, but he wasn't taking any chances.

'Is everything okay?' Cassidy asked.

'It's my dad. He fell in the kitchen again. Bumped his head. I have to go.'

'I'll come with you.'

'What? Oh no, he'll be fine.'

'I'm a nurse, remember?' she said, about to walk past him to go get her coat. He grabbed her arm.

'There's no need. You need to stay here and wait for Moira. I can deal with this.' *I work in the medical field too, you know,* he was about to say, *and you may be a nurse, but I save fucking kids' lives.* But she wouldn't understand.

'I would hate for anything to happen to Joe,' Cassidy said.

Oh, there's something going to happen to the old bastard alright. 'I understand. But Moira needs you. We can do this again. We have all the time in the world.' He managed one of his charming smiles. The Plan B charming smile, the one he faked when he was really thinking, *Fuck that for a laugh*. He'd had good practice at it.

'I know. I feel I ruined our Christmas weekend.'

'It's fine, honestly.' *It's your daughter who ruined our weekend*. The thought stayed firmly locked up in his mental vault.

'You're a good man, Ewan Gallagher,' Cassidy said and kissed him, this time on the lips. 'I'll make it up to you.'

'I'm sure everything will be fine with Moira. They'll have gone off partying or something.'

'It's the *or something* that worries me.'

He shrugged into his jacket and left the house, and the cold air was literally a breath of fresh air. As he walked back to his car – which he was glad to see wasn't up on bricks – he had already made plans for how he could deal with the breakup.

Turned out, he wouldn't have to.

FIVE

'Sorry to ruin your Boxing Day,' Harry said as Kim Miller stepped forward to give him a kiss on the cheek.

'Don't be silly. Frank's playing with the girls. He bought them some cars and a Hot Wheels track.' She gently stroked Grace's cheek as Harry stepped over the threshold into the flat.

She led him through to the living room and took Grace from him, expertly taking her jacket and winter gear off.

'Thanks, Kim.'

'Of course. My husband will get you a beer while the girls watch some TV.'

Emma was sitting with her little sister Annie,

playing with the cars. Miller was lying on his side on the carpet, apparently having more fun than the kids.

'Now I see where you get your driving skills from,' Harry said.

'Hey, Harry. Grab a pew and I'll get us a beer.' Miller stood up.

'I've got the wee yin, so maybe just a soft drink for me.'

'Coming right up.' He left and went through to the kitchen. Harry looked at the kids playing with the toys, at the Christmas tree in the corner, and tried picturing his own Christmas and how it could have been with Alex. Having Morgan round for dinner had helped.

Miller came back in with a beer and a Coke, followed by Kim holding Grace.

'I'll keep hold of her,' she said, sitting down on the couch with the baby.

'Thanks. I think she's fed up of looking at my ugly mush anyway.'

Kim laughed and Grace looked at her, smiling.

'Cheers,' Miller said, clinking his bottle with Harry's can.

'Here's to us.'

'How's your friend?' Miller said.

'Morgan's fine. We had a good Christmas together.'

'Tell us more,' Kim said.

'I think I'm getting picked on now,' Harry replied.

'We just care about you, Harry,' Kim said. 'We don't want to see you get hurt.'

Harry nodded. 'I appreciate that.'

'When are you seeing her again?'

'Tonight. We stayed over at the flat. Now I want her to stay at Murrayfield.'

'Good man!' Miller said.

'Frank!' Kim said, but not too loud since she was holding Grace. 'This is not a locker room.'

'I know that.'

'Are you going to be seeing more of her after Christmas?' Kim asked.

'We're enjoying each other's company just now,' Harry said. 'Beyond that...who knows?'

'Good. Keep us in the loop,' Kim said. 'How are the new team settling in?'

Harry nodded to Miller. 'Spot on. I just feel funny about me being your boss when I've known you for so long.'

'You don't have to feel funny about it.'

'It should have been you leading the team,

Frank,' Harry said, taking a drink of the Coke and trying not to burp.

'No, it shouldn't. You're in your forties, Harry. Perfect for leading the team. I'm in my thirties. I have a while to go before I make DCI, and I'm comfortable with that. I'm happy to be working under you and not somebody I don't like or respect,' Miller said.

'Fair enough. I'm glad you're on board. You didn't have to be.'

'And work back in CID? No, thanks. Besides, did you hear they're closing the High Street Station?'

Harry's eyebrows raised in genuine surprise. 'I did not.'

'Hogmanay is its last day. They found some structural issue that's going to cost a lot of money to fix, so they're selling it and letting it be somebody else's problem. I would have been transferred to another station anyway.'

'No more falling out of bed and walking up the road,' Harry said.

'He'll be needing kicked out of bed,' Kim said. 'All I hear is, "Just another five minutes."'

'How are you getting on in your job, Kim?' Harry asked.

'I'm enjoying it. I work with Hazel Carter, and

we get along well. It's different working with my dad again, but it's a wee change from being an investigator with the Procurator Fiscal's office.'

'How's your mum liking retirement?'

'Just fine. She says her blood pressure is down now.'

'Being a PF herself wasn't always easy.'

'She's got it easy now.'

Harry stood up. The two girls were still playing with the toys, but they were yawning. 'I'd better be going.'

'She waiting for you?' Kim said.

'You're relentless.'

Kim laughed and got Grace dressed. Harry watched as she did it without fuss.

'See you down at Fettes,' he said to Miller and kissed Kim on the cheek. 'Watch that one, Kim.'

'Oh, I will.'

Harry took the lift down to the ground floor, Grace in her pushchair, and stepped out into the cold, dark air. Edinburgh knew how to do Christmas – the coloured lights strung everywhere. Alex had loved it. Then he pictured her face and suddenly he wished that Morgan wasn't coming round to the house. He hadn't sent her a text with his address yet.

He walked round to Cockburn Street, where he'd parked the car. He had just tucked Grace into her car seat and was about to walk round to the back to put her pushchair in the boot when his phone dinged.

Hi. How's your evening going so far? Smiley face attached.

He put the pushchair away, got in behind the wheel and started the car to get the heat going.

Fuck. Answer her, or give her a dizzy? Christ, no, he couldn't ignore her. Not that he felt sorry for Morgan or anything, but he wasn't one to mess women about. He felt the old panic grip him when he thought about another woman. Guilt complex. Frank Miller had told him it had affected him too when Carol had died. Deep breath.

Just got in the car. Give me a call and I'll give you my other address. I don't like to write it down in a text in case I lose my phone.

Harry started driving the car down the hill, and maybe thirty seconds later his phone rang, coming in through the car's speakers.

'Hi,' he said.

'*Hi. Did you have a nice evening?*' Morgan said.

Suddenly, he felt a jolt, like he was actually

cheating on Alex. This was something that he and Morgan had talked about in the pub one night, when they were just friends who sometimes bumped into each other.

'You're not cheating, Harry,' Morgan had said. 'You're moving on with your life. When you do eventually start seeing a woman, I guarantee you'll feel conflicted and think you're doing something wrong. And that's a natural feeling. It's like you're standing at a line drawn in front of you, waiting to cross. Some people never do, but if you want to cross that line and live your life again, then it is perfectly normal to feel the way you will.'

Her words made sense to him now as he turned left into Market Street and headed up to the Mound.

'It was business talk mostly, but yes, it was a good evening. How about you?'

'I packed some things, watered the plants and watched some TV. I didn't want you to think I was being impatient or anything. I was just...you know...'

'What's this? The mighty Morgan Allan lost for words? I'll need to mark that on my calendar.'

'If you think I'm taking a red face, then you're wrong, Harry McNeil.'

'I'm never wrong about that. In fact, I'll have to

turn the heat down in the car, it's so hot from your face.'

'You're such a funny man.'

'I am. So, do you have a pen handy?'

'I do.'

He told her his address.

'Great. I'll see you there in a little while.'

'I'll get the kettle on.' Harry didn't want to do the 'No, you hang up first' thing, so he hung up first.

He took George Street heading west, thinking about Morgan's house. When he'd invited her over for Christmas dinner, he'd put her name through the system and found out that she lived in a big house in Colinton. Nice place she had, a place she had shared with her husband before his death. Harry had left it at that.

It didn't take long for him to get to Murrayfield, and he saw that he had beaten her there. He got Grace inside, and no sooner had he got her jacket off than the doorbell rang.

He took Grace with him and found Morgan standing there with a small case. 'Don't worry, I'm not moving in,' she said, smiling.

'I actually thought you were running away to the circus,' he said and stood aside to let her in. She smiled at Grace and tickled her under the chin, making the baby laugh.

'I have been known to associate with a clown or two,' she said, laughing, as Harry closed the front door.

'Welcome to my home.'

SIX

'You're going to tell your girlfriend soon, aren't you?' Sharon Boyle said to her boyfriend, Ewan Gallagher.

'Of course I am. I already said, didn't I?' Ewan drank from the can of lager in his hand, which had turned nasty and warm. That was the whole purpose of going round to Cassidy's earlier. To let her down gently. That's what he had told Sharon. Besides, they weren't exactly going steady. He had jumped at the chance of going out with her pal Sharon when they had got talking in the canteen. She was younger than Cassidy, and didn't have any offspring or any baggage in the form of a daft nephew. He was ready to call it a day with Cassidy, but he had to pick the right time. He had been planning to do it earlier tonight, but Moira going missing had thrown the proverbial spanner.

Coming to his workmate Bingo's party had been appealing, but now it was starting to feel like he had pulled up to a Hells Angels meeting on a moped.

'You said that last week.' She was holding a cigarette and the smoke was burning his eyes. As a non-smoker, it was like sticking his tongue in an ashtray at times.

'Christ, Sharon, it's Christmas. What did you want me to do?' He was leaning in closer to her because the music was getting louder.

The more Bingo drank, the more outrageous he got. He'd already threatened the woman downstairs who had had the 'fucking audacity to knock on my door when she wakes up everybody in the building with flushing her fucking lavvy at three o'clock every night'. There had been another knock on the door, but nobody knew if it was the woman or the police, and Bingo had started raking about in his hall cupboard looking for his BB pistol. His girlfriend, Lexy, had told him that some filthy bastard was trying to tan his expensive bottle of whisky and that had diverted his attention. The night could have taken a dark turn if he had got hold of the gun, but his girlfriend had dumped it months ago, averting a lawsuit and possibly a hostage negotiation scenario.

'I want you to tell her that you're going out with me,' Sharon said. She drew in some smoke and blew it out the side of her mouth like a real pro. She knew how to blow smoke rings, and now blow it out the side of her mouth. What else? Blowing smoke out of her arse?

'I'll do it this week. I promise.'

There were a dozen or so reprobates dancing in the living room, or moving their bodies in a way that might have suggested they needed medical attention. Ewan's dance moves made it look like he was about to shit himself, but it was that time of night when nobody could give a toss.

Bingo made his way through the small crowd, either having greatly improved his own dancing skills with the aid of some Carly Spesh or he was going to the bathroom without leaving the living room.

'Great party, eh, pal?' Bingo said, his lips wet from sipping something in a pint glass and deciding it was too good not to share. Ewan blinked a few times, trying to remove the spit without resorting to putting the first aid lessons he'd learned to good use.

'It is,' Ewan said, and saw Sharon standing there shaking her head.

'You want a drink?' Bingo asked.

'I just had one.' *It nearly took my fucking eye out.*

'Get another one. There's plenty. Here, let me grab you a can.'

Bingo moved away, weaving through the crowd like a drunk boxer, and came back with a can of lager that he'd opened, foam pouring out the top like he'd just broken the world record for the number of shakes he could give a can in the shortest time possible. Ewan thanked him and sipped the froth, tilting the can back until some of the actual liquid reached his lips. He looked at the can and saw Bingo had grabbed supermarket lager and wondered if he knew some tight bastard had brought what could only be described as canned pish water.

'A'right, Sharon, darlin'?' Bingo asked, swaying about now that he had lost all of his momentum.

'Aye, I'm just dandy,' she replied, smiling at him, then the cigarette was in her mouth again, having the life sucked out of it. Just like Ewan was.

'Your boyfriend's a diddy,' Bingo said. He took a swig from his can.

'He *is* a diddy. Ken Dodd would have been proud,' Sharon replied.

Bingo sprayed the contents of his mouth across the wallpaper. He guffawed and wiped a hand across his mouth. 'I meant he's a fucking diddy.' Bingo looked at Ewan and laughed again. He put his arm around his friend's shoulders. 'You hear that, pal? Sharon thinks you're a fucking diddyman. I meant I thought you were a tit.'

'Well, I'm glad you're both amused and comfortable enough with me to openly mock me.' Ewan took one for the team and drank more lager, which should have been banned under the Trade Descriptions Act. Or used as toilet cleaner.

Bingo laughed. 'We are. Look, mate, you know I love you. Like a brother, mind. I also love that lassie there. Also as a brother. I just wish you would kick that dragon to the kerb.'

Christ. And there we have it, Ewan thought. Words of wisdom from a man who couldn't stand up straight, who had attempted impromptu Feng Shui by gobbing beer all over his living room wall and who wouldn't even know his own name when he woke up later that day. All it had served to do was rev up Sharon. It was like she had a key sticking out of her back and somebody just needed to give it a wee turn and she'd be off.

'I'm working on it, Bingo. Sharon knows that.' Ewan shot a look over to Sharon to see if she was in agreement or not. Even a wee nod of the head or the hint of a smile about to break out like a rash would serve as confirmation, but nothing. She was taking far too long with her lips to her glass, as if the wine too had been a product of the supermarket. Or avoiding talking to him.

Great. This was turning into a shite Christmas. All the whining and moaning from Cassidy and now flak from his new girlfriend. And Bingo wasn't helping matters either.

A young woman came over to Bingo and slid an arm around his waist.

'Bingo, love, let's have a wee dance.'

Bingo, looking through beer goggles, immediately smiled and Ewan saw his friend's face light up. He might literally light it up when he saw his dance partner on Instagram later on, but for now she was Shakira, right here in his living room.

Bingo put one hand up to the side of his mouth. 'Got to go, mucker.' Like he was about to leave on a secret mission.

'I have to go too,' Ewan said to Sharon.

'You know, my ex-boyfriend sent me a text wishing me a Merry Christmas. He said we should go out sometime. I told him I didn't have a boyfriend, because, you know, telling people your boyfriend is shagging an older woman invites all sorts of criticism, and a repeat of, "He'll never leave her for you". So if you're not interested in making a go of it, I might accept my ex's offer.'

'Who is he?' Ewan asked, halfway between nervous and angry. He knew she had an ex but didn't know anything about him except that he was a builder.

'Never mind his name. It's not for you to know.'

What should he do now? Shout at her and drive her away? Or plead like a sad bastard? Decisions, decisions.

'I need to pee, but I'll be right back,' he said instead.

'Don't hurry on my account,' Sharon said, curling her lip, and Ewan wasn't sure if her glass of wine really did taste like pish or she was still unimpressed by him.

He fought his way through the rush of sweaty bodies, the music blaring and the makeshift disco lights flashing like an electrical fire had started. He got to the lobby, where other couples were talking and drinking, and he squeezed past to make it to the lav.

He locked the door behind him and lifted the toilet seat until it clacked against the cistern.

'Oi!' a voice said from behind the shower curtain

when Ewan had started to use the facility. He sprayed the lino as he jumped.

'Fuck's sake,' he replied, looking down at the front of his trousers, but was relieved to see they were still dry. The floor and the side of the pan hadn't fared so well. 'Is that you, Crawford?'

The voice laughed. 'Aye. We're trying to have a wee moment in here,' Crawford Ingram informed him. 'If you could give me thirty seconds,' his work-mate implored.

'Thirty seconds? You going for a personal best?'

'Come on, mate.'

Ewan finished and flushed. 'You expect my bladder to explode while I wait on you finishing whatever it is you've started?' he said, washing his hands.

The shower curtain whished along the rail and a young woman stepped out, buttoning up her shirt. Stepping over the tub was easy in her short skirt. She smiled at Ewan as Ingram made himself look respectable again.

'Better luck next time, Romeo,' she said, laughing. She let herself out of the bathroom and closed the door behind her.

'You should have locked the door, mate,' Ewan suggested.

'I didn't want to draw attention, so we stayed in here with the curtain shut.'

'I think the groaning and squealing might have tipped the nod to somebody,' Ewan said. 'Who is that anyway?'

Ingram just shrugged. 'I don't even know her name. But that's the second time we got disturbed.'

'I don't know how you could perform with all the distractions. Usually, I have a shy bladder, but I was bursting.'

'Aye, well, all performances were cancelled.' He laughed and stepped out of the tub. Ewan made to open the door, but Ingram put a hand on his arm. 'That's going to look barry, us leaving here together. Let me go first.'

The door opened and a woman from one of the other labs at the hospital walked in and looked at them.

'So anyway, next time, just use the plunger and that'll help fire it away,' Ingram said to Ewan. 'Manky bastard.' He tutted and walked out, muttering something about 'a courtesy flush' and 'giving it a week' as he walked past the woman.

Ewan couldn't look her in the eye but suddenly found the pattern on the lino very interesting and had to stare at it as he walked out. He purposefully avoided Ingram.

'Ewan!' said a man in the kitchen doorway, grabbing his arm. Ewan knew the guy from the Sick Kids'; he was from another department. 'When are we getting a round in?' The man imitated using a putter to hit an invisible golf ball into an invisible hole, but with the drink he'd had, he made it look more like he was having a different kind of stroke. He guided Ewan further into the kitchen.

Ewan smiled and watched the man pour two glasses of whisky. Normally, Ewan wasn't much of a whisky drinker, but the label on this bottle had a name he couldn't pronounce and it was distilled in a place he'd never heard of but smelled like it should sell for a million pounds.

'Cheers.' He clinked glasses with the man. Andy was his name, Ewan thought. Or Benny. A name that ended in the letter 'y'. Maybe it was fucking Noddy for all he knew. That sort of sounded familiar. He was on the hospital golf team – there to make up the numbers, Ewan figured. He *did* know his name, he just couldn't remember what the hell it was.

'We can get something organised when the weather picks up.'

The man laughed. 'I meant some of the boys are

going on a golfing trip to Florida next month. I know we can't all get away, but seven of us are definitely going, and we need an eighth man. How about it?'

Ewan smiled and gritted his back teeth. 'Who pulled out?'

'What do you mean?'

'I mean, you're looking for an eighth man. That means everybody else knew about it except me. So now you're desperate and hoping I can go, so your wee holiday won't be fucked up. Sound about right?' Ewan chugged the whisky back.

He walked out of the kitchen.

'You know they call you The Undertaker at the golf club because of the way you walk!'

'Fuck off, Dick.'

'It's Roddy, ignorant bastard.'

Roddy! Fuck. Didn't matter. From now on, it would be *that arsehole from Radiology* anyway.

Sharon wasn't there. Ewan looked out the window at the dark, at the streetlights fighting it, and the blackness of the Water of Leith below. They'd had a few good nights in here recently, Ewan, Sharon, Bingo and Lexi.

'She left,' a voice said behind him. He turned to see Shakira had pulled herself away from Bingo for a moment.

'What?' he said above the noise of the music.

The woman leaned in closer. 'Your girlfriend just left while you were away doing some blow.'

'I wasn't doing...oh, never mind. Thanks.' Ewan saw that the DJ had put on the Gap Band and a line of people were now sitting on the floor singing 'Oops Upside Your Head'. He dodged the waving arms, twice narrowly missing getting punched in the bollocks, then reached the only bedroom in the flat, the depository for the guests' jackets. His was in there somewhere, so he started tossing them onto the floor. Then he saw it, a Berghaus.

He grabbed it, shoved it on and left the flat without so much as a by-your-leave to Bingo. He'd just tell the drunken sod he'd said goodbye and they'd had a laugh and one last drink before he shot off, and Bingo would nod and agree. By now, Bingo wouldn't even be able to spell his own name.

Take the lift or boot it down the stairs? He'd probably toss his ring if he tried the stairs, so Ewan stabbed the call button for the lift, and it took its sweet fucking time getting to the top floor, as if it knew what was coming from the hooligan's house.

Finally, it arrived and he got in and repeatedly poked the button for the ground floor, which apparently made the lift doors close faster. Had Sharon gone down in this or had she taken the stairs? No, she had to have taken this thing, which meant she was well ahead of him.

The doors slid open on the ground floor and he stepped out into the main lobby and rushed along to the front door. Outside, the cold hit him and he staggered for a moment, looking both ways along the Shore, a quiet street that ran parallel to the Water of Leith. The floating restaurants and the bars were to the north, across Constitution Street.

Where Sharon was heading. He saw her now. She was alone. At two o'clock in the morning. Christ Almighty, what the hell was she thinking?

Ewan started running but then felt the alcohol take over and he had to stop for a second and lean against the wall of the building. Just like in high school when the bastard PE teachers tried to turn them all into cross-country runners and Ewan could only manage a few hundred yards before he got the shakes and wanted to throw up.

He looked ahead. Sharon was at the traffic light, obviously trying to hail a fast black. He had a sickening feeling in his gut that wasn't just the alcohol; Sharon was about to leave his life.

He mobilised his feet again and tried to get a memo to his legs that it was full steam ahead, but

there was a breakdown in communications. He staggered into the road, only to have a black cab driver
blast the horn at him. It was the orange light on top
of the car that grabbed his attention – that and the
fact that the driver voiced his opinion that Ewan was
a female reproductive part and not a very bright one
at that. The suggestion that he suffered from macular
degeneration was thrown in for good measure.

If the taxi was coming towards him, then why
didn't Sharon see it? She had been up there and the
orange *For Hire* light was on, yet the taxi went on by
minus Sharon herself.

Then he saw why.

A white van had stopped by the side of the road
on the bridge and the passenger door was open.
What the hell? She wasn't that stupid that she'd get
into a van with a stranger, surely?

Then the truth hit him like a punch in the
bollocks. She hadn't been looking for a taxi. She had
called the one person she had threatened to rekindle
a romance with: her ex. The boyfriend who was a
builder and who had his own van.

The truth was, Ewan hadn't been sure he really
wanted to continue seeing her. Sharon was the bit of
rough, the rollercoaster ride after stepping out of the
teacups. But there she was, getting into a van with

her ex-boyfriend. Ewan had called her bluff and got burnt. Now she was leaving with the man, and they would go back to her place and spend the rest of the night...well, he couldn't think about what they would be doing. It should have been *him* going home with her.

'You want to have your cake and eat it,' a voice said behind him. He turned to see the woman from the party, the one who had danced with Bingo.

'Shakira,' he simply said.

She laughed, her breath blowing out like a steam train. 'Hardly. Denise.' She held out a hand for him to shake.

He took it and smiled at her. 'You're right. About the cake thing.' He started shivering, the cold trying to do some CPR on his system, trying to bring it back to life.

'There's a little café round the corner that's open all night. Near the Malmaison hotel but not quite as fancy. Grab a coffee?'

'Aye. Why not?'

They walked towards the traffic lights and crossed, Ewan's staggering now more under control.

'You from around here?' he asked her.

'No. You?'

'No. I don't know where the hell I'm from

anymore.' Denise slipped her arm through his. 'You a good friend of Bingo's then?' he asked her.

'Not as good as you. He's a good laugh.'

'You got a boyfriend?'

'No. You got a girlfriend?'

'Not anymore.'

They walked past the floating restaurants. It was quiet just now, just the sound of laughter in the distance. The pubs and the boats were closed.

They turned the corner, away from the boats, the river and the dead body.

Somebody's life had been turned upside down.

Just like Ewan's was about to be.

SEVEN

Harry walked into the Fettes Station, once again glad that Percy Purcell hadn't told him that the team would be based in the High Street. The parking here was better and he was a ten-minute drive away – two if he stayed at his flat round the corner – or fifteen minutes if he chose to walk and sweat like a bastard.

Frank Miller was at a computer, while DS Lillian O'Shea was at another one. Miller waved to him.

'Morning, sir,' Lillian said. 'Coffee?'

'I'll get it,' Harry said, hanging his jacket up. 'Where's everybody else?'

'Everybody else' was DC Colin 'Elvis' Presley and DS Julie Stott.

'They're on a wee errand.'

He switched the kettle on and shoved a spoonful of instant into a mug. He had brought his own from home after coming back here and finding that some bastard had choried his previous mug, after it had sat here for months on its own, desperate to get back to work and hold a brew. It was probably some dick from the housebreaking squad who'd pilfered it.

The incident room door burst open and the sound of laughter reached his ears.

Elvis was sitting on an office chair, simultaneously driving and guiding it with his feet.

'Morning, boss,' he said, grinning.

The dulcet tones of Julie Stott followed: 'Cheating bastard!'

'How did I cheat?' Elvis asked, coming further into the room and holding the door open. Julie appeared, and like her colleague was guiding an office chair by sitting on it. She gave the impression that this wasn't her first time.

'Oh, morning, boss,' she said. 'I didn't see you there.'

'Morning, Julie. Having fun?'

'No. I just lost ten quid to this cheater here.'

'What's all this then? You know, if you have too much time on your hands, my car needs cleaned.'

'Just fetching these new chairs, sir,' Elvis said, seemingly in no hurry to move his arse off his.

'Whose idea was that?' Harry asked.

'Mine,' a man said, hobbling into the room, leaning heavily on a walking stick.

'Jesus, Moonshine Charlie!' Harry said, smiling. He walked over to the older man and put his hand out.

DI Charlie Skellett shook it. 'I heard those yahoos in the drug squad had new chairs, so I decided to swap a couple, with the help of those two young detectives. One for you, being the boss, and I got myself one for going. Brand new they are, and right now my arse is needing a bit of coddling from a fine piece of cow.'

'What's with the stick?' Harry asked.

'Whoa, not so fast there, my friend; there are rules about asking somebody about his disability or medical condition. I'll get the forms for you to fill out.'

'Piss off, Charlie.'

Skellett laughed. 'Fell and buggered my back. Now my lower leg is numb, my knee feels like it's on fire and I walk worse than my old man, who's still kicking about in his eighties.'

'Jesus, that must hurt.'

'Not really. He's quite spry for his age.'

'Anyway, what are you doing here?' Harry asked.

'I got a call from Percy Purcell at home last night. He's still got a sense of humour that man. He said, "I hope I'm not disturbing your Boxing Day." As a matter of fact, me and the missus were on our private jet heading back from our villa in Tuscany.'

'But that's not what you said to him,' Miller said.

'That obvious?' Skellett said.

'You're here, aren't you, instead of signing on at the bru.'

Skellett laughed. 'I told him the wife had dozed off watching TV and I was sitting having a few tinnies on my own. Rock 'n' roll lifestyle, eh? Then he asked me if I wanted to join the team here. The last person to be chosen for the new MIT. It made me feel like I was back in high school and we were all having a kick-about at football. I used to be unpopular back then.'

'Nothing changed then, sir,' Elvis said.

'Bloody lip. I still carry some weight around here, son.' Skellett smiled at the younger man. 'Elvis and I used to work together in CID at Gayfield Square, before he was transferred down to Leith.' He turned to Harry. 'I hear you were down there too, and it was a bit rough.'

'Aye, they tried to batter me and Elvis. I wouldn't have classed them as true colleagues. But we rode it out together, didn't we, wee man?'

'We did that, sir.'

'Glad to hear it,' Skellett said. 'Shower of bastards. Word has it that they have a new team down there. But I'm not going to take any guff. Not that I'm going to be going out and about. I told Percy that: for the foreseeable future, I'll be desk-bound.'

'I'm just glad to have you on board.' Harry patted Skellett's arm.

Lillian had finished making Harry's coffee for him. 'Thanks, you're a star.'

Elvis and Julie had stood up from the chairs they had been racing in and Elvis put Harry's new chair in his office. The other one went in front of a computer and Skellett sat down heavily on it.

'Ah, that's better. That other one would have made me feel like my arse was on fire by lunchtime.' He bounced up and down a little bit on it, careful not to use his left leg. 'Now, if I could only get the hang of this computer shite, then we'd be laughing.'

'Julie can keep you right,' Miller said. 'Or Lillian. They're both the brains of the outfit.'

Elvis cleared his throat. 'Oh, crap,' he said. He was getting over being beaten up, and sometimes a wrong move or a cough could bring on a sharp pain in his bruised ribs.

'It's true, though, Elvis,' Miller said. 'No offence.'

'None taken, sir.'

'I heard about Paddy Gibb,' Skellett said to Miller. 'He was a good boss.'

'He's gone too soon,' Miller said.

'Aye, he is that. He was the first senior officer to call me an arsehole, way back when. I deserved it, so I took it on the chin. Just don't let that be an invitation for anybody else, though,' Skellett said.

Harry sipped his coffee and had to admit that Lillian was so good at making it. Just like Alex had been. But this was a different incident room they were in now. Fettes mainly housed different units here now, and the rooms had been shuffled around since he had last been here, back in the summer.

Before he had decided to chuck it all and had moved to the south of Scotland. But Percy Purcell had had his back and had made sure it was extended compassionate leave he was on. The fact that Harry's wife had been a detective had made things easier. Alex had been liked by everybody.

'...Leith,' Miller said to him.

Harry looked at him blankly.

'Sorry, I was going through the rota in my head.'

'We got a shout. Down in Leith. All hands.' Miller looked over at Skellett. 'Except you, Charlie. Since you've just got your foot in the door. As it were.'

'You're hilarious, Frank. Just leave me somebody in case I need help to work one of these damn machines.'

'I thought you said you were a computer genius, sir?' Elvis said.

'I lied. The only good computer is one sitting in a landfill.'

'I can stay if you like,' Lillian said.

'Magic. The rest of you, come with us. Two cars.' Harry looked at Skellett. 'Try and behave, and if you need us, give us a shout.'

'I'm in the capable hands of DS O'Shea. There will be no shouting or any other form of communication. Unless we need you to stop at Greggs for lunch, that is.'

'Christ, you're putting me in the mood for a sausage roll and I've just had my breakfast a wee while ago,' Harry said, putting his coffee down and grabbing his jacket. 'I knew you were going to be fucking trouble.'

EIGHT

Morgan Allan knew her first patient was waiting for her. The smell of his cologne, Eau de Drain Cleaner, was strong and pungent. It hit her nostrils before she rounded the corner to her office. The Royal Edinburgh always had an antiseptic smell anyway, but this man's cologne would strip wallpaper. She had given careful consideration to using chest rub on her nostrils, just like Harry had suggested.

She turned the corner and there he was in all his glory. Simon Gallagher. Dressed like he was a Quentin Crisp stunt double. Always the black fedora on his head, whether it was rain or shine. Or at this time of year, light snow. It sat atop his head just now like he'd taken a hair dryer to it. The thing was spotless. As was his long overcoat. And the cravat underneath.

'Simon,' she said, stopping before him.

'Tut-tut. And what did we say last week?'

She smiled, humouring him. 'Quentin.'

'That is correct.' He had a cigarette in a cigarette holder, held between two fingers. They belonged to a man who was much younger than Quentin Crisp had been when he'd been in the video for Sting's 'Englishman in New York'. This man was in his forties and underneath the exterior lay a strong physique and an even stronger personality.

'Let's get into my room,' she said.

'I like your boots,' he said, pointing with the cigarette as if he was trying to set fire to them.

'Thank you,' she said, unlocking the door to her patient room. He followed her at a distance. Morgan knew he didn't want to give *her* space, but himself. He was big on personal space.

He took his hat and jacket off and hung them on the coat stand. Morgan walked over to the side of her chair and took her boots off. There was nothing fashionable about them. They wouldn't be mistaken for Dr Martens, but they could dish out the same kick in the bollocks as those other boots. She slipped her flats on and felt relief flood through her. She wasn't one for heels, but comfy shoes weren't designed for walking on icy pavements.

Simon was skulking about near her bookcase again, like he was going to run a finger along one of the shelves.

'A new Stephen King, I see.' He turned round to look at her. 'You didn't tell me.'

'It was after our last visit. I liked his last one so I bought this one. I read in my lunch hour.'

'I know you do. You told me before, and despite what you might think of me, I do have the capacity to remember things.'

'I know you do. Come and sit down.'

He hesitated for a moment as if this was his first visit, but he had been coming for over six months. Then he moved like a poker had been shoved up his arse and made it over in a sort of stagger before plonking himself down in his chair. That was how he described it, *his* chair. She had to tell him it was just his chair and that some custodians came in and moved it after he left. It wasn't a lie but a shift in perception. She fully expected to come in one day and find him on his knees sniffing it, just to check. As long as he wasn't sniffing hers.

'Tell me what you got up to over the holiday period.'

'Christmas,' he said, correcting her.

'Christmas holiday,' she said.

He chewed a fingernail. She wasn't sure if the real Quentin Crisp had chewed his nails, but this was a reaction from Simon when he was stressed.

'Christmas*time*,' he said. 'Holidays are when parents take their kids to the caravan park at Pettycur Bay.'

'Is that where your dad took you and Ewan?'

She met his stare. It was important not to back down. It had taken her a long time to reach this stage and he expected it from her now. Backing down would be seen as a sign of weakness and she would no longer be his equal but merely a puppet. Just like the other patients.

'Yes,' he said. 'Ewan and I had fun. Dad took us down to Burntisland beach. There were boat trips. We went on one once. I remember he had bought me a little bin lorry. I held it above the water as the boat moved out to sea and I debated whether to drop it into the water or not.'

She kept her pen poised above her notebook. Ready to write with it or ram it into his fucking eyeball if the little switch in his brain overloaded and he decided to see if he could defy gravity and fly through the air towards her.

It hadn't happened yet, but she knew people it had happened to. Simon would get a swift lesson on how to sew one of his testicles back on after she ripped it off.

'How would you have felt if you'd dropped it?' she asked. The pen was steel with a flat bottom where her thumb would sit as she used it like a knife. She'd watched YouTube videos on how to rip somebody's spleen out with a knitting needle. Now all she had to do was learn how to knit and bring the ugly sweater with her every time she came to work.

'I would have felt sad.'

'Why?'

Simon shrugged. 'I liked the small truck. It was a little Matchbox size, and it was a good truck. And Dad had bought it and I knew if I lost it, I would have felt bad.'

Morgan nodded and wrote something on her pad. Dropping his truck was all part of the self-destruction Simon had gone through growing up after his mother left. It symbolised a connection to his father – buying the toy – and it would be another thing that he didn't have in his life. It would be gone and it would be Simon's fault. Just like he blamed himself for his mother leaving.

'How was Christmas Day?' Morgan asked.

Simon looked at her, then sucked on the cigarette in its holder even though it remained unlit. 'It was uneventful. And by that, I mean a fat man in fancy dress didn't come down our chimney. Ewan would have pissed himself if that had happened. Not in fright but for the mess; he always has the hoover on standby. I dropped a little piece of turkey on the floor and he looked at me like he wanted to rush round and pick it up before getting the carpet cleaner out.'

'How would that have made you feel if he had done that?'

'I would have stabbed him in the eye with my fork.'

'What does Joe have to say about this?' It was the same question she had asked before trying to get him to reach an acceptable place where the anger didn't come out.

'My dad is Switzerland when it comes to his sons. He does a lot of things with Ewan, hiking and stuff like that, and to give him his due, he does invite me along. But who wants to go walking through bushes where somebody like me could be hiding?'

'Do you mean, big?'

Simon looked at her like he was expecting to see a smile, but there wasn't one.

'I think you know what I mean. Somebody who

isn't all there. That's how Ewan describes me. I used to threaten him a lot, but then he got as big as me and told me he would take my head off if I touched him. Really, the boy needs to come and see you.'

'You said he does go to a therapist,' Morgan reminded him.

'Yes, yes, he did, after his divorce, but not one as good as you. He needs to go back. She kept him on track.'

'We're all doing that, Si...Quentin. Keeping our patients on the right track. Maybe Ewan just needs guidance like you.'

'He didn't talk about his sessions. Whoever his therapist was, I hope she talked to him about his God complex.'

This was a new one on Morgan, hearing about Ewan this way. 'What do you mean?'

'The way he walks on water. Didn't I tell you this before? Every time I have a glass of wine, I think it came out of the tap.' Simon put the cigarette holder down like it was boring him now. 'I told you that he thinks he single-handedly runs the Sick Kids'. Yes, he's good at his job, but only the other day he was bragging about how he had saved the lives of several kids in one day. He had spotted cancer in their pathology samples.'

'That's a good thing, though, isn't it, Simon?'

'I suppose so, but does he have to make me and my dad feel so incompetent?'

'How does Joe feel about this?'

'I think he tunes it out. He's retired, he doesn't need this grief. Yes, we know Ewan is the big hero, but he doesn't need to throw it in our faces.'

Morgan knew that Simon was on disability, and at his age he was about as employable as the Yorkshire Ripper in a hammer factory.

'Some people find it hard to switch off from work when they get home, so they recap their day to their loved ones,' Morgan said. 'It might come across as bragging, but maybe it's just shop talk.'

'You don't live with him. And yes, I do appreciate the fact he brings in decent money and that helps us keep a roof over our heads, but it feels like there are metal shavings flowing through my veins sometimes instead of blood.'

This was a new one on Morgan too.

'I did something stupid too,' Simon said.

'Okay. Are you comfortable talking about it with me?'

'Of course.' He took a deep breath, as if he was about to tell her he had been running about Princes Street in his underpants. 'I crashed Ewan's work's

Christmas do. He was telling our dad where he was going, and as you know I look like the Phantom of the Opera's younger brother and the chances of me being invited anywhere are slim to none. So I decided to go along anyway. They were having a meal and then going to a pub. A public house. The operative word there being "public".'

'How did that go down with Ewan?'

Simon stared off into space as if reliving that moment. 'He wasn't happy. There he was, getting pissed with his so-called friends from work, when in walks his brother, the one with half a face. You would think I was on a shooting spree. The others looked uncomfortable but smiled through it, like how you want to punch your dentist in the nuts for causing you pain. You know, you're lying back and the bastard is standing right there and you really want to reach out and squeeze his balls and say, "We don't want to hurt each other, do we?" But you don't, and you act like he's your best friend, because he's one of two people you don't want to piss off – him and your hairdresser.'

'Were they uncomfortable because they didn't know you, do you think?' Morgan asked.

'I'd met some of them before. When I worked at the hospital. At the hike back in the summer. A few of the guys I know. Crawford Ingram especially. He was the one who was smiling the most. I met him and a few of the others a long time ago, when Ewan actually invited me along to have a drink with them. Before I got burned. Back when I was normal. The time Lauren came.'

'Who's Lauren?'

Simon looked at her like he was now in fact staring at Lauren.

'She was nice. Lauren was the new girl in town, as it were. She joined the pathology lab at the Sick Kids'. Everybody thought she was the bee's knees, and they were right. She was wonderful. Beautiful woman. Her smile was worth a million dollars. She should have been on the cover of a magazine instead of working with those cretins. I couldn't believe a woman so beautiful would even glance at me, never mind have a conversation.'

'She boosted your confidence,' Morgan said. It wasn't a question.

'Oh, yes. The others were chatting among themselves while Lauren stood next to me, just having a normal conversation. She was funny and witty and had a great sense of humour, just like I had. When I was a normal man.'

'You're still that man, Quentin.' *If you would only stop hiding behind the mask, as it were.*

'That's very kind of you to say so, Morgan. Lauren and I had moved away to another standing table without really thinking about it. It was so comfortable talking to her. We chatted all evening, about books, about our love of science fiction. It was so refreshing.'

'How did Ewan take this, you talking to his colleague?'

Simon shook his head slightly as he remembered. 'Ewan was fine. This was just before his marriage ended. He was unhappy with his wife at the time, and I think having Lauren join them for a drink made him feel happy. He wasn't bothered that I was having a good time. I think he was actually pleased for me. Not everybody else was, though.'

'Really? Were the others unhappy?'

'Not all of them. Just one. Ben something, Ewan's colleague, was getting drunker as the night wore on, and more obnoxious. He started making comments to Lauren about how she'd better watch out or I might pounce on her. Ewan and Crawford told him to quit it, then Ben fell onto the table where we were standing. It was one of those tables you stand at to save space. The drunken bastard fell over and swiped the glasses off it. The others were raging, and Ben went home after that. It didn't faze Lauren at all. She was nice about it, but Ben was being a total prick!' Simon was talking faster and faster, like at the end of a mortgage advert on the radio where they don't want you hearing the small print but by law have to read it anyway, so the guy reads it out like he's on drugs and had a suck of some helium.

'Just relax, Quentin.' Christ, she hated calling him this. He was always hiding behind some façade, and she was trying to get him to come out of his shell, to let the world see the real him, but it was slow progress. Maybe after another ten years.

He took a deep breath. 'I think Ben wanted her for himself. He was married, but it was obvious he was jealous of me talking to her. Later on, Ewan said that Ben was always talking to Lauren in the lab, and she had a laugh with them all, but Ben was starting to get creepy. He kept asking her out to have a drink with them all, and she eventually agreed, and that was the night I met her. Ben wasn't happy. We thought he had gone home, but he was waiting outside. I had left with Lauren. We were going somewhere else for a nightcap, and he approached and started getting wired into me, telling me not to come back out with my brother again. Ewan told him to fuck off and they started wrestling in the street. Ewan didn't want to hurt him and he punched him in the guts, winding him. Afterwards, Ben got up and walked away without another word.'

Morgan looked over at Simon. There were tears in his eyes then. She hadn't heard this story before. He wouldn't ever say why somebody would throw acid in his face.

'Did you and Lauren continue your relationship?' she asked.

Simon nodded. 'Yes. She was a good-time girl, and boy did we have a good time. We even found a hotel where we could spend an afternoon. That was the best fun I've ever had with a woman, let me tell you. She said she felt comfortable with me and wanted me to be her boyfriend. I didn't argue with that. Everything was going fine. Ewan was over the moon. He said he liked Lauren but she wouldn't go out with him even if he did ask her. He isn't the most confident of men. But he was happy for me. Then the attack happened.'

Simon wiped a hand over his eyes.

'Are you comfortable carrying on?' Morgan asked.

'Yes. Of course.' He took in a deep breath before speaking again. 'It was a dark winter night. I had borrowed Ewan's car from the hospital. He said he would get a bus home. I didn't have my own car at the time. I told Lauren I would meet her in town. She hadn't been working that day and I told her I'd drive her to a restaurant outside of Edinburgh. When I parked up near Stockbridge, there was a knock on the driver's window. I wound it down, thinking it was a homeless man looking for money. That's when he threw the acid. Luckily, I saw it coming and moved my face slightly and it didn't hit me full on.'

'Did they get the man?' Morgan asked.

'Yes. It was Ben. After attacking me, he went home and killed himself. He had already killed Lauren in her own flat. He left a note telling police he was jealous of me and Lauren. He hadn't been to work that day, but they had CCTV footage of him sitting in his car, waiting for me.'

'How did he know you were borrowing Ewan's car?' Morgan asked.

'The day before, in the lab, Ewan had mentioned that I was coming to pick up the car. It was easier for Ewan to take it to work, then I would just come along and pick it up. I had the spare key. Ben must have planned to follow me and disfigure me.'

'That must have been a shock for not just you but Ewan as well.'

'It was,' Simon agreed.

The truth of the matter was, Morgan had known about Simon long before she met him. She had worked in the Royal Infirmary a long time ago and had known Ewan Gallagher quite well. A young, charming man, he had known her husband, David. He too had worked in the Royal Infirmary, that hospital having the only accident and emergency department in Edinburgh. Even though surgeons wouldn't normally mingle with lab staff, David and Ewan had played golf at the same golf club, Baberton, and they both played on the hospital golf team.

Ewan had gone to David's funeral and had attended the wake afterwards. He had sat and talked with Morgan and told her tales of David on the golf course. Ewan was genuine when he said he was going to miss her husband.

It was shortly after this that Simon was attacked, but it had taken Ewan's brother a very long time to seek the mental help he needed. Ewan had recommended Morgan, and by then she had moved away from the Royal Infirmary, feeling she couldn't work in the same building that David had.

This was the first time Simon had been able to speak in detail about his attack.

'You miss Lauren,' Morgan said matter-of-factly.

'I do,' Simon agreed. 'I think we could have hit it off. We could have had a future together, if Ben hadn't stolen it from us.'

Morgan nodded and wondered, not for the first time, why Ben hadn't killed Simon like he had killed Lauren. Was it because he wanted to make sure Lauren was gone for good, and to punish Simon by not only taking his girlfriend away but ensuring he never had anyone again?

She looked at the clock. Their time was up. Forty-five minutes, then fifteen for her to make up her notes and prepare for the next client.

'I want you to work on telling me more about Lauren and then we'll help you move forward. I'll see you next year, Simon.'

He stood up, put his coat on and picked up his cigarette holder. 'Have a good New Year, Morgan.'

She stood up. 'You too. My best to Ewan and Joe.'

He nodded and left the office.

Outside the Royal Edinburgh, Simon walked across the car park, making his way towards the main road. Morningside was a posh area, filled with expensive houses. It didn't stop some lowlifes coming to the alcoholic clinic in another part of the hospital. They drank a few cans of Carly Spesh on the bus so they were half-jaked when they went in to see their counsellor, their breath honking of booze. Then they got assessed as still being an alcoholic and got whatever handout they were getting from the government.

Two unfortunate jakies were walking out of the clinic behind Simon when they spotted him.

'Hey, nice fucking hat,' one of them said. 'Gie's a fucking shot.'

Simon ignored them and walked on.

'Hey, are you fuckin' ignoring us, ya fuckin' ponce?' the second one said.

Simon kept on walking and reached the end of the car park before crossing over. He heard the footsteps getting faster and then they were right behind him. He felt a hand on his shoulder as he reached the tall wall of somebody's garden.

'I said, gie's a fucking shot of yer hat,' one of them said, and Simon didn't know if it was the first or second one, but it didn't matter.

He turned, grabbed the man's hand, twisted it and brought his Stanley knife out in one swift movement. The other man was about to step forward.

'Don't fucking move, or I'll cut your fucking

bollocks off after I'm done with this prick.' Simon turned back to the man who had yelled and was now bending sideways, trying to take the pressure off his arm, which was going in a direction that nature hadn't intended.

'This is what's going to happen: I'm going to let you walk. I'm going to walk in front of you, but if I even so much as think you're too close to me, I'll cut your fucking face off.' He hadn't extended the blade but used the pointed edge to draw a circle round the man's face.

'We were just having a laugh, mate,' the second one said.

'You think it would be funny if I cut into your nut sack, then?'

He shook his head at Simon.

'I didn't think so,' Simon said, turning back to the other man, who was doing a fair impression of how a wee lassie would squeal if she was unwrapping a new doll on Christmas morning. 'Do I make myself clear?'

The reply was a cross between 'please don't hurt me' and 'I've just pissed myself'. The man may or may not have spilled a can of the extra-strong lager in his front pocket, but his jeans didn't look big enough to hold a can.

'I'm sorry, I didn't catch that.' Simon dug the body of the knife into the man's cheek.

'Yes! Fuck me, yes.'

'Good.' Simon let him go. 'Remember, you'll look worse than I do if you ever touch me again.'

He walked away, not looking back, knowing he didn't have to. He started whistling, 'An Englishman in New York'.

NINE

'I would recommend hypnotherapy, sir,' Elvis said as he guided the car down Leith Walk. 'I've been hypnotised before. It's nothing.'

'What, you were on the stage with your willy out when the hypnotist brought you back round?' Harry said. He was sweating now and turned the heating down in the car.

'Not exactly. I went to a hypnotist who specialised in helping people to stop smoking. It worked for me. You could see one about being a nervous passenger.'

'I could have helped you stop smoking in thirty seconds.'

Elvis looked over at him.

'Eyes on the road,' Harry said.

'How could you have stopped me smoking in thirty seconds? With a shotgun? Then have written on my headstone, "I told him I could get him to stop smoking"?'

'No. I'd have clamped your balls up to a car battery every time you lit up. Trust me, after the first time, you'd have stopped every bad habit you have.'

Elvis contemplated this little nugget. 'I suppose that would have worked.'

'Would have cost you less too. And you could have kept the battery as a spare.'

'I don't have a car, remember?'

'Amy does, though.' Harry had very kindly been driven home when the team had stopped off for Christmas drinks one night after work, and while he hadn't been three sheets to the wind, he had been bordering on winning a three-legged race all on his own.

'She's thinking of installing sick bags after the debacle at Christmas.'

'Listen, son, you were the one who was sucking the shag pile in the back. You couldn't even keep your arse on the seat.'

'That's because it's a small car.'

'Bollocks.'

'But I get the distinct feeling you're trying to change the subject.'

They turned into Great Junction Street and took a right into Henderson Street, heading down to the Shore.

'There's no subject to change, Detective Constable. I am not a nervous passenger.'

'I beg to differ, sir. It's all a control issue; you've handed control of your life over to me. I'm driving and could literally get us both killed, and your brain is screaming at you, *Grab the wheel! He's going to get you killed!*'

'Where did you read that pearl of wisdom? In your Christmas cracker?'

'It's nothing to be ashamed of. There are groups you can go to. You know, they all sit in a circle telling stories of how they turned into being a Jessie in a car.'

'Do they sit and talk about how they snapped and killed a colleague who was asking for it?' Harry unbuckled his seatbelt before the car had fully stopped, as if to prove the point that he wasn't the least bit worried as a passenger.

A patrol car was blocking the road, along with other emergency vehicles. They stepped out into air that laughed at long johns and promised to suck the living breath out of anybody who dared to mention sun, sea and sand.

'Morning, sir,' said the uniform who was guarding the street.

'Morning, son,' Harry said. Elvis nodded his thanks to the uniform, who held up the tape.

There were more uniforms along by a boat, as if they were waiting on it opening up to go get a cuppa. Miller was already there with Julie Stott and they were standing outside of a forensics tent.

'She's still in place in the Portaloo now,' Miller said. 'Jake Dagger was waiting for the forensics to finish taking photos before he squeezed in there.' Dagger was one of the city pathologists. They heard him banging about in a toilet that was smaller than a wardrobe.

'She's in a bad way, sir,' Julie added. 'It's the worst thing I've ever seen.'

'Where exactly was she found?' Harry asked.

The largest floating restaurant, *The Blue Martini*, was moored across from tenements that were having roofing repairs. Materials were sitting outside of the boat.

'I'll show you,' said Miller.

They entered the tent and Harry saw it had been

hiding the Portaloo. The new head of forensics in Edinburgh, Callum Craig, was in the tent.

'She was found in there by one of the workers,' Craig said, nodding to the Portaloo. 'I just finished taking the photos. I'll have one of my younger staff do the fingerprinting. One who's eager and keen to learn.'

'Is she going to fill her wellies with vomit?'

'Oh, yes.' He grinned.

Harry looked at Miller. 'There's no doubt that it was murder?'

'Absolutely none.'

Harry saw that whatever blood had been in Julie's face had now gone south.

'Jake Dagger's gone in for an initial inspection,' Craig said. 'She looks young. And very messed-up.' He was a tall bloke in his forties, balding and with fashionable glasses.

'Street worker?' Harry asked.

'I would hazard a guess at not, but some of them are decent-looking women. But I didn't think they operated down here nowadays. Do they?' Craig answered.

'What are you looking at me for?' Harry said as the others looked at him too. 'Seriously. You think I

come down here to find a woman to play Dungeons
and Dragons with?'

'You play some D and D for R and R on the
QT?' Elvis asked.

'GFU,' Harry answered.

'What does that mean?'

'Goblins, fairies and urchins. Guess which one
you are.'

Elvis looked at Julie for help. 'Maybe all three?'
she suggested.

'You're no help.'

'Who found the body?' Harry asked.

'Roofers starting work this morning,' Miller
answered.

'Doesn't Robert Molloy own one of these
restaurants?'

Robert Molloy, an Edinburgh businessman who
was a gangster by any other name.

'He does,' Miller confirmed.

'Maybe you should have a talk with him later,
Frank. See if we can get access to his CCTV.'

'I will.'

'Julie, you and Elvis get the door-to-door organised. DI Miller and I will have a word with the
pathologist. Get more uniforms drafted in, and make

sure they speak to the guests in the hotel. It's a long shot, but you never know.'

'Yes, sir.'

'Elvis? Go with her.'

'On it, sir.' The two younger detectives left the tent.

The pathologist opened the toilet door and they got a brief glimpse of the victim inside. 'Christ, that's tight,' he said to nobody in particular.

'Jake,' Harry said, nodding to the doctor.

'Harry. Did Frank here fill you in?'

'He gave me the synopsis. Why don't you fill me in?'

'This is gruesome, and I've seen some bad stuff in my time.'

'And that's just looking in the mirror first thing in the morning,' Miller said.

Dagger stared at him for a moment. 'I feel there's been a shift in our professional relationship.'

'I knew you missed Andy Watt slagging you off. I was just trying to wean you off.'

'Thank God. I thought you'd bumped your head or something. Kate's been keeping me in the loop, but she's been having some time off, trying to help Andy recuperate.'

DS Andy Watt had been deliberately run over

and had been healing in hospital until his recent discharge.

'He's taking early retirement,' Miller said. 'He was on the fence, but now he's decided. Too old for this shit, he said.'

'I don't blame him. The more I see stuff like this, the more I want to retire, but I'm not even into my fifties yet,' Dagger said.

'If it wasn't for us, bastards like the person who killed this lassie would roam the earth doing it whenever they felt like it. At least there's a chance we'll catch them,' Harry said.

'True,' Dagger said. 'The victim was placed in there after he completely disfigured her.'

A wind whipped at the walls of the tent, flapping them about. Dagger opened the toilet door and they looked in at the girl who sat on the manky toilet seat, slumped over to her right. It was her face that everybody focused on immediately. It had been completely destroyed.

'I'll have to examine her, of course, but looking at her, I'm pretty confident that the blunt-force trauma was the cause of death. There are a couple of round marks on her face which would suggest a hammer did this damage.'

Harry couldn't remember when he'd been to a

more gruesome crime scene. The female was completely unrecognisable. 'Any ID on her?'

They looked at Craig. 'Yes. Her name is Moira McLean. Eighteen years old. There's an address on her driving licence.'

Harry nodded. 'Can you get me the details, please, Callum?'

'Coming right up.' He left the tent, his camera still hanging from his neck.

'She wasn't killed in here,' Dagger said. 'There's blood but not enough from those injuries. It looks like she hadn't been dead that long when she was put in here.'

Harry shook his head. 'All these flats round here, hopefully somebody saw something.'

'Aye, there were times when somebody would have said something. People living round here were a different breed back in the day,' Miller said. 'Now with all these expensive flats getting thrown up, everybody's a stranger. Leithers were a close community, but not now. All this gentrification is killing the neighbourly spirit.'

'They wouldn't turn a blind eye to this sort of thing, Frank,' Harry said, not wanting to believe it but having to admit to himself that his friend was probably right.

Callum Craig came back in with a piece of paper. 'That's her address.'

Harry took the piece of paper. 'Thanks. We'll see if there's a next of kin here. Catch you later. Let me know when you're doing the PM.'

'I'll make a start now,' said Dagger. 'I don't have anything serious going on, just a sudden death that can wait.'

'Great. You want to go to the mortuary with Julie?' Harry asked Miller.

'No problem.'

'I'll have to get some DNA samples or dental records.'

Dagger shook his head. 'Teeth were smashed. It will have to be DNA. Unless there are some identifying marks on her.'

'Right. Keep me in the loop.'

The combined smell of death and a manky portable toilet was putting Harry off tomorrow's breakfast. He left the tent and saw Elvis standing with Julie as she instructed a uniformed sergeant. He waved Elvis over.

'I have an address. We're going to talk to the next of kin.'

'Okay.'

'Give me the keys to my car. You can sit and look

out at all the pretty colours in the sky.'

Elvis looked up. The sky was the colour of *the wind'll make your face stay that way.*

'I have to make a phone call first,' Harry said.

'That's fine. I can stand outside in the freezing cold while you sit in the car with the heat on.'

'I knew you'd understand. And before you start any of your pish, Glasgow is just as cold as it is here, so transferring there would have been like swapping deckchairs on the *Titanic*.'

'If you say so, sir.'

'I do,' Harry said, ending the conversation as he got in the car and started it up.

The phone was answered on the other end after an annoying amount of time had passed.

'Fuck me.'

Harry thought he'd connected with a sex line. 'Hello?'

'Jesus.'

Or a Find Religion helpline.

'Charlie?'

'I'm going to kill that bastard!'

'Charlie, that you?'

'Yes! I just banged my fucking leg on that stupid bastarding desk.'

'That inanimate piece of furniture?'

'I swear it moved. All by itself.'

'That would make sense. I mean, how else would it move?'

'Maybe it was me being a clumsy bastard, I'm not sure. What do you think, Lil?'

'Clumsy bastard,' Harry heard Lillian agree.

'Aye well, that's just an opinion that wasn't asked for.'

'You did just ask me,' Lillian countered.

Harry jumped in before Abbott and Costello made an appearance. 'I need you to do something for me, Charlie.'

'Fire away.' Then, to Lillian: *'Find me a box of matches, then we'll have a wee bonfire with this bastard thing. Imagine leaving the fucking corners sharp. I ask you.'*

'You got a pen?' Harry wound the window down and saw Elvis talking to a uniform. He was wondering if the young man would stand with his hands in his pockets or take the initiative. He had done well. He honked the car horn.

'I'm coming, Harry. Some bastard stole my pen. Lillian? Fire us one across if you don't mind.'

Harry listened as the writing implement apparently missed its intended target but pretty much landed in another.

'Christ, that could have taken my eye out. I said pass me a pen, no' disembowel me with the fucking thing.' The sound of grunting and what sounded suspiciously like Charlie shitting himself, but could equally have been the air being squeezed out of the office chair cushion, filled the inside of the car through the speakers.

'Good God. That feels good. Oh yes, that hit the spot.'

'Right, Charlie, if you're ready, and you clearly are, can you write this name down: Moira McLean. Find out any details about her.' He rattled off the address in Baberton.

Elvis walked over and Harry held up a finger, indicating for him to wait.

'Got that, Harry. Anything else?'

'That's about it. Now go and play with your matches and let me know if you find anything.'

'Will do.'

Harry heard the DI asking Lillian if she knew where he could get an axe before there was dead air.

Harry wound the window down. 'You're doing a good job there, Elvis. Organising the door-to-door. I'm assuming you were doing that and not organising a piss-up for after work. Or during it.'

'Let's just go with the door-to-door thing, sir.'

'Right. I've changed my mind. I'm going to talk with the victim's next of kin, if one is available. Call me if you need anything.'

'A hot cup of coffee wouldn't go amiss, if you're offering.'

'Good idea. I'll stop and pick up one for myself.'

'Not quite what I had in mind, boss.'

'See? You're full of good ideas when you try.' Harry wound the window up and turned the car round and waited for the uniform to lift the tape.

As he drove away, he was sure the name Moira McLean was familiar to him. And somehow, it was involved with another death.

TEN

DI Charlie Skellett pulled up his trouser leg and pulled a knitting needle out of his desk filing cabinet.

'I'll have a new scarf, if you're asking,' Lillian O'Shea said from her own computer.

'Don't think I couldn't rustle up something if I had a pair. You can find anything on YouTube.'

'It doesn't have to be a Dr Who scarf.'

'Trust me, I can put my mind to anything. Except my phone. I always have to call up my daughter and ask her how to do stuff on the bastarding thing. Then she'll tell me to do something on the screen, and then I'll ask her how I can do that if I'm talking to her. Use the house phone, she says. Like I'm a daftie.'

'I hate to ask what the knitting needle is for then, sir.'

'Watch and learn.' He stood up and rolled up his left trouser leg to reveal the leg brace he was wearing. 'I just slip this thing in for a quick scratch. Like you would do if you had a plaster cast on. Saves me having to drop troo and take the damn thing off for a scratch. Besides then, being up on a disciplinary charge, I might very well find my name on the sex offenders' register.'

Lillian laughed. 'Not to mention I might go blind.'

'Watch it.' He bent over and somehow managed to shove the needle up his brace without poking it into an artery. 'I can't even imagine having a cast on and having to do this a million times a day.'

'It's no fun,' Lillian agreed. 'I had a cast on my wrist when I was younger.'

Skellett opened the cabinet and fired the needle into the first folder. 'Right, let's see what we have on that young lassie,' he said, banging his fingers on the keyboard and managing to tap into Google, which would have been handy if he had wanted to find out ways to kill a man using only a knitting needle and a banana skin.

'What are you looking for, sir?' Lillian asked.

'Harry asked me to check up on something and I seem to have gone off on a tangent.' He looked across to her. 'Like when you're on YouTube and start watching videos about electric cars and somehow end up watching college girls gone wild. I told my wife that somewhere a college girl must have been driving a Ferrari and that was the crossing point.'

'And she fell for that flannel?'

'It was the truth.'

'You need a hand finding something?' Lillian asked.

'Aye. He gave me the name of the murder victim who was found this morning, Moira McLean. Young eighteen-year-old girl.'

'Let me have a look.' Lillian brought up the intranet for Police Scotland and typed in the name. Then she poked her head up above the computer. 'There's a Moira McLean linked to the accidental death of a Victor McLean.'

'Really? Spill.'

'Up in Pitlochry, back in the summer. A man was hiking with a group of his family, and he was walking to catch up with them when he fell off a little stone bridge onto the rocks below. It says here DCI Jimmy Dunbar was there on scene.'

'What was a detective from Glasgow doing working in Pitlochry?' Skellett asked.

'He wasn't there officially. He was on a break with his wife. He happened to be there and took charge of the scene as the highest-ranking officer until a local detective showed up.'

'Why was a detective needed?'

'McLean's face was completely smashed in.'

'Protocol, under the circumstances,' Skellett said. 'DCI Dunbar did the right thing. But what was the outcome?'

'The only people near him were his family and a couple of men from a work outing, a father and son. Joe and Ewan Gallagher. It was ruled an accident by the PF here in Edinburgh. McLean was brought here because he lived here. He left behind a wife and daughter. And that daughter is Moira McLean, who was just found murdered.'

'I'd like to see the report on that case,' Skellett said.

'I'll fire it over to your email.'

'Or we just do this the old-fashioned way and you do a printout. Which I would be able to read if I could find my bloody reading glasses.'

'Maybe they're beside your knitting bag.'

'That's not even funny. But you can make it up to me by buying me a coffee.'

'Buy you a coffee? For what? You *do* have a knitting bag.'

'Needle. Knitting needle. There's a bloody difference and fine well you know it. I only have one.'

'That's not how I'll put a spin on it.'

Skellett drew in a deep breath and blew it out. 'You've been working with Harry McNeil too much.' He fished a tenner out of his wallet and slapped it on the desk. 'Just milk. My wife says I take in too much sugar, so now I take my coffee without it. People think Big Pharma rule the world; I say it's the sugar cane owners.'

Lillian got up from her desk and walked over to snatch up the money. 'Don't worry, we'll be getting a kettle soon. The old one blew up it was on that often.'

'It'll save us a fortune. But meantime, I need to call Harry. He'll want to know about a potential second murder.'

ELEVEN

Harry had driven up to Baberton Mains, on the west side of the city, bordering the city bypass. He had thought about calling Morgan, but looking at the clock in the car, he had realised she might be in with a patient.

It might look fucking desperate too, he told himself.

He got out of the car into a sharp wind and was approaching Cassidy McLean's house when a nosey old bastard opened his door from the house next door. They were semi-detached, so the old boy was close, and he probably held up a glass to the dividing wall in the living room, if not upstairs.

'She's not in,' he said. Harry looked at him. He was balding with glasses perched on top of a beaky nose. Tall, skinny, wearing a sweater with a golfing logo on the front.

'I'm sorry?' Harry said.

The man gave him a look that he probably practised in front of the mirror, one reserved for double-glazing salesmen, which would then turn into a snarl with a threat of 'I'm going to call the fucking police!' if said salesman made to come towards him in a threatening manner.

'You heard. Now bog off. You pond life come round here expecting people to fork out their hard-earned on your shitey windows and doors when you can clearly see she has them already. Now sling your fucking hook.'

Harry walked back down the path towards the pavement, and the man stood taller, like he'd just ripped into the Yorkshire Ripper with one lash of his tongue and was relishing the prospect of inserting his size tens into a body cavity. But then his face changed into uncertainty when Harry started walking towards the man's pathway.

There was a driveway at the side of the house, with a detached garage at the end. A wooden gate joined the end of the house with the edge of the garage.

'I've got a golf club here that I'm not shy about

using, fucking scum of the earth.' The man did indeed have a putter in his hand, which up until now had remained behind its owner's leg, either waiting to play a round of golf or go into battle with a wide-boy salesman.

'Steady there,' Harry said, reaching into his pocket.

'You'll never reach me with a knife, little bastard. I'll break this fucking putter over your head before you have a chance to even get it near me. Don't believe me? Come and have a fucking go.'

Harry brought out his warrant card. 'DCI McNeil, Police Scotland.'

'Oh.' The man's face was flushed with anger. Harry wondered if the man had practised those words or if he'd actually used them before. He was sure this would have been a first. Coming out into the cold and beating the shite out of some arsehole salesman was a step up from watching somebody do it on TV.

'Now, let's see where we're at, shall we? Threatening a police officer with a deadly weapon for starters. Breach of the peace for seconds, and a whole slew of other things I can think of. But threatening to break the putter over my head is threatening to murder me. I don't like your chances in court when they find out you threatened to kill a police officer.'

'Oh, that. It's an old one that I use in the back garden,' the man said, smiling the way he would if he'd got caught shoplifting, in a sort of *How did that get there?* way.

'Threatening bodily harm with an antique won't get you a lesser sentence.'

'I was just joking. I mean, I know it didn't sound like it, but you should see some of the hippie bastards we get round here trying to sell all sorts of shite. Any one of them could be a bloody maniac.'

His mouth was starting to run off now.

'Besides, I was one of you lot, a long time ago.'

'Really? Where were you based?' Harry had got closer but was keeping a distance in case the old man was a nut case and decided to charge at him after all.

'Corstorphine, many moons ago.'

'Is that what they taught you, back in the day? Threaten to batter somebody's brains in?'

The old man looked like he had let one go. 'Come on, you know what it's like. These fucking scallywags run riot all over the city, sticking two fingers up at the polis, laughing at them and goading them to raise their hands. I'd kick their arses, the lot of them.'

'Right, we can start by you telling me your name.'

'Jock Forrest. Why don't you come in and have a coffee and I can fill you in on why I think Victor McLean next door was murdered.'

TWELVE

Harry looked at the older bloke for a moment. This street was one of many in Baberton Mains that was a dead end. Did Forrest not get out much? Had being stuck in a street where nothing much went on driven him to become a curtain-twitcher?

'I've got Tunnock's teacakes,' Forrest added, as if that would seal the deal, which it pretty much did.

'Put the putter away, Mr Forrest,' Harry said. *Before I ram it up your arse.*

'Oh, aye, no problem.' The entrance was made up of a glass-panelled door and another half that was also glass. Harry saw Forrest put the putter in amongst some umbrellas, where it would hide until the next unsuspecting salesman came calling.

Harry walked up the rest of the way to the front

door and up the few steps into the man's small lobby. Harry took his overcoat off and Forrest hung it beside the putter. He then ushered Harry into the living room on the right.

It was sparsely furnished but well kept. A gas fire was on the opposite wall, and the house was warm.

'I'll get the kettle on. Won't be a mo', Forrest said. 'Have a seat.'

There was a chair next to the gas fire and a settee opposite it. An older-model TV sat in the corner by the front window. Harry sat as Forrest went through the archway that led into a small dining area next to the kitchen.

'How do you take it?' Forrest shouted through.

'Milk,' Harry replied. He heard Forrest banging about and he looked around. There was a bookcase behind the chair, with photos in front of the books. There was one with Forrest standing next to a woman – probably his wife, Harry thought.

A few minutes later, Forrest came back with two mugs and set one on the side table next to Harry. He scurried away and came back with the unopened box of teacakes, like he had been keeping them for this particular scenario. He opened the box, took one out and handed it to Harry with a paper napkin.

'I love them, but they're messy wee bastards,' he

explained. Harry agreed and hoped they weren't foosty. He unwrapped it and wondered if he should wait and see if Forrest ate his first, in case he had been through in the kitchen with a hypodermic syringe and a bottle of cyanide. But it had been ages since he had had one, so he bit into it.

'You know what some bastard said to me once?' Forrest said, sitting down in the chair. 'He had dished the teacakes out and he said, "You're very trusting. I could have poisoned them."'

Harry stopped eating his and looked at the man, a piece of cream filling stuck on the side of his lip.

Forrest laughed. 'Don't worry, son, the only harm that'll come to you after eating this is clogged arteries and eventually having a massive stroke. Otherwise, fire into it.'

Harry took another bite and washed it down with coffee. 'Who made that comment about the poison?' he asked.

'Some smartarse. Retired copper he was an' all. He's deid now, I heard, but I don't think many people shed a tear over him.'

Harry wondered if the unknown man had succumbed to the putter. When he was finished, he sat with the coffee in his hands and looked over to the photo again. 'You married?'

Forrest looked at the photo as if reading Harry's mind. 'Was. She's been gone for a couple of years now.'

'Sorry to hear that.'

Forrest smiled. 'Oh, don't be, son. I mean she fucked off with one of the members of the golf club. Good riddance. But I met a nice woman. Ruby's her name. And she's Victor McLean's auntie.' He looked at Harry. 'I met her when she came to visit one day and they were having a barbecue next door. Cassidy, Victor's wife, invited me over. She felt sorry for me, I think, because Boot Face had left me. I went, and Ruby and I just clicked. Then she invited me along to the family weekend away up in Pitlochry. And I jumped at the chance. There was a whole group of us, including Victor's brother, Bobby, and his other brother, Dan.'

'Why do you think Victor was murdered?' Harry asked.

'The brother, Bobby, has a son who I swear is not human. He's like something out of a horror movie.' Forrest drank more coffee and Harry wanted to keep him focused.

'How old is he?'

'About twenty-two. Something like that. Victor and Cassidy were always grilling out in the garden on a Sunday, and sometimes Dan would come over with the offspring in tow. Sometimes both Bobby and Dan would be here.'

'Brian is Bobby's son?' Harry asked.

'Aye, he is. Brian looks like...well, have you ever seen the film *Full Metal Jacket*?'

Harry nodded. 'I have. Years ago.'

'Right. The actor Vincent D'Onofrio plays the chubby soldier who's struggling. I can't remember the character's name. But anyway, before he shoots the drill sergeant, he has this look on his face, like he's totally fucking doolally. Brian was like this one day. I had been invited round to join the family; I had been seeing Ruby for a few weeks by then. Before I went round, I went out into my back garden to lock my lawnmower away in the shed and I could sense somebody looking through my hedge. It's a fairly tall hedge that you can't see over, but I could make out the shape of somebody standing there. I went inside and upstairs to one of the bedrooms and looked out, and there he was, that nut job, Brian. Just standing staring into the hedge. Then he slowly turned his head and looked up at the window. He couldn't see me because I was behind the nets, but fuck me, I'll never forget that look. With the wee smile. Then he slowly turned around and went back to his mother. I was so spooked, I called Ruby and told her I felt sick and wouldn't be joining them.'

'How did that go down?' Harry asked.

'Ruby was fine about it. So were Victor and Cassidy.'

'What happened at Pitlochry?' Harry knew he would have to keep the older man on track.

'Oh, aye. Pitlochry. That was a disaster. They go on hiking trips and they invited me along. I went and it was a good time, until we went up to the Falls of Bruar. We were in small groups, me and Ruby doing our own thing. The clan was following behind us. Victor and Cassidy were behind them. We heard screaming and walked back down the trail as fast as we could and they were all staring over the bridge. Somehow, Victor had taken a heider over the bridge. Christ, his face was smashed in. From hitting the rocks, so they said. But Brian was there and the wee bastard was smiling.'

'Was it just family or were there other people there?'

'There was a guy there with his dad. Ewan, I think. Turns out he works in the Sick Kids' hospital. Cassidy's a nurse in the Royal, and now the Sick Kids' is there, they see each other.'

'Did Ewan get invited along on this hiking trip?' Harry asked.

'I'm not sure. I don't think so, or else Ruby would have mentioned it. I think maybe Cassidy and this Ewan had talked about it, and since Ewan went hiking with his dad, he might have just invited himself along. There was a copper there too, and he took charge. A detective from Glasgow. Dunbar his name was. I remember that because it's the same as the town.'

'Jimmy Dunbar?' Harry asked.

'Yes! That's him. He took charge of the situation while the locals turned up. It turned out they classed it as an accidental death.'

'Why do you think it was murder?'

Forrest sat silently for a moment, as if picturing the scene back then. 'I saw Brian McLean's face. You didn't. It was full of menace. If he didn't kill his uncle, then I don't know who did. But that man didn't die because of a fall.'

'Have you seen this Brian again?' Harry asked.

'Oh, yes. I've seen him around here just recently.' Forrest looked at him. 'Can I ask, are you here about Moira? Ruby told me Cassidy is worried about her.'

'Yes, I am. I'm sorry to tell you that somebody with Moira's ID was found dead this morning. But

I'm going to have to ask you not to tell your girlfriend just now. I need to find Mrs McLean. Is she at the hospital?'

'Probably.' The colour had left Forrest's face. 'I bet that bastard did it.'

'I just said she was dead, Mr Forrest. I didn't say anything else.'

'You didn't have to. Just like her dad died "accidentally",' he said, making air quotes.

Harry stood up. 'Thanks for the teacake.'

'One more thing before you go,' Forrest said.

'What's that?'

'How do you know I didn't poison 'em?' He grinned as Harry left.

THIRTEEN

Detective Superintendent Calvin Stewart was sitting in his office in the incident room. The last week he would ever be sitting in there.

There was a knock at the door as he was busy carving his name into the wood on top of the desk.

'Come!' he said. He looked up as the door opened and a young uniformed officer entered.

'You wanted to see me, sir?' PC Chance McNeil said.

'Aye. Come in and take the weight off.'

Chance closed the door and sat down opposite Stewart. The other detectives were in the incident room, none of them looking in.

'You might have heard I'm retiring at the end of the week. Or you could have read it on the lavvy wall, along with some other nuggets of wisdom that might suggest I perform some acts of self-degradation on myself.'

'I did hear somebody mention something about you leaving, in the canteen,' Chance confirmed. He looked at his watch.

'You in a hurry, son? I mean, I'm no' keeping you from that lassie you're wenching, am I? Young Katie.'

'No, sir, it's not that. It's just...well, it doesn't matter.'

'What doesn't, Chance? Speak up, son.'

'Look, I don't want to drop anybody in it, obviously, but my sergeant said he'll give me a hell of a hard time if I...' He hesitated.

'If you what?'

'If I spend more than five minutes with you.'

'Did he now? And who the fuck does he think you're coming down to see? The janny? I'll boot his baws so far over the top o' his fucking heid, people will think he's wearing a new toupee. That wee fuck. And a sergeant, no less. Well, guess what?'

'What?' Chance answered, not realising that the question had been rhetorical.

'I might only have a week left here, but I leave behind some people who won't stand for some little baldy prick throwing his weight about. I know who you're talking about and he couldn't put his own fucking skids on without googling how to do it first. He's making my blood boil now. But you know what?'

Chance didn't answer this time. Instead, he watched as Stewart picked up the phone from the desk. He dialled a number and spoke into it. 'Get me Sergeant Short on the phone.' Stewart covered the mouthpiece. 'Short by name, short-arse by nature.'

Then the voice came on at the other end.

'Short. It's me, Calvin Stewart. Listen, pal, I might only have a week to go before I head off to pastures new, but I can fuck your career well and truly before I go. There are a few people in this station who owe me a favour, and I will call in every one of them to kick you back down to constable for the rest of your career. Are you hearing what I'm saying?'

'Yes, sir, but I don't know what this is about.'

'It's not about anything. I have one of your uniforms in here and I need him on special assignment. You got a fucking problem with that?'

'No. Did he tell you I have?'

'Of course he didn't, ya mangy wee bawbag. I know what a fucking whining wee lassie you are when somebody takes one of your pals away. You start greetin' like somebody's choried your fucking ball. Well, I've just choried this ball you have on your team. So if I hear any pish about you going behind my back and talking shite, or giving this young laddie a hard time, I might not be in this station or on the force anymore, but I have fucking long arms and you will find that they can stretch all the way back in here. Plus, you know who his faither is, don't you?'

'No, sir, I don't know who his faither is.'

'Well, Shortie Boy, you will find that out the hard way if you start any of your bollocks. Now fuck off back to work. And don't count on seeing this laddie again this week. When I'm not here, DSup Lynn McKenzie will be in charge and she'll make sure Chance here is taken care of. And if you think I'm a tough bastard, just get on the wrong side of her, son.'

'Please feel free to keep PC McNeil as long as you like, sir.'

'That's very kind. Now, back to work, skiving bastard.' Stewart hung up the phone by clattering the handset back onto the cradle. 'I don't feel like I've warmed up for the day unless I chew somebody out. Now, I want you to work undercover, in plain clothes. How does that sound? You do want to get into CID, don't you? After your probation?'

'I was hoping to, yes, sir.'

'You'll get there, son. I've heard good things about you. And trust me, Jimmy Dunbar's got your back. Katie will get on just fine too. Now, this is going to be a simple undercover job. Nothing too big, just a wee taster of life in the fast lane, and it will look good on your record when the time comes for your CID interview. And for back-up, you'll be working with your girlfriend, Katie.'

'I appreciate you thinking of us, sir.'

'No problem. You'll be working with Jimmy Dunbar, Evans and me. Dunbar and Evans will be going through to Edinburgh to liaise with your dad.'

'Does my dad know about this, sir?'

'Not yet, but then again, I don't exactly have to ask his permission. If I don't go through to Edinburgh, then I'll be sitting on my arse here making a ball of rubber bands, just before I go around smacking people. Starting with your sergeant.'

'Great.'

'Jimmy will fill you in, but basically there's been a murder through in Edinburgh and it's very similar to a death that happened up in Pitlochry six months ago. Jimmy will talk to you and Katie and let you know what we want. Oh, and in case you're wondering, this job is a voluntary one. You can walk away if you want.'

'No chance, sir. I mean, there is a chance. This Chance, if you see what I mean.' He was grinning.

'If your idea was to twist my fucking melon, job well done.' Stewart picked up a pen and threw it at the window that faced the incident room. It clacked off the glass and Evans looked over. Stewart made a 'come here' motion with two fingers. Evans looked away.

'Fuck's sake. Daft bastard thinks I was giving him the vickies.' Stewart shook his head and sat back in his chair for a second, taking in a lungful of air, and then lunged forward as if he'd just lit a fart and it had gone awry.

'Evans!'

Evans turned round again and this time Stewart used his whole hand to indicate a meeting was requested. The young DS got up from his chair and walked over to the office and came in.

'What, you forgot how to fucking knock?' Stewart asked.

'You just waved me over, sir.'

'And? Did you have a fucking brain fart in the time it took you to get your arse off your chair and walk over here?'

'No, sir.'

'Well, you did a damn fine impression of it.'

Stewart shook his head. 'This young man here is going to be working with MIT for this week, along with his girlfriend from Edinburgh, Katie. Jimmy knows all about it. I just briefed him a wee while ago. Something's gone down in Edinburgh and it's been booted up the chain of command. And I'm sitting at the top of that particular tree. Jimmy Dunbar knows the details, so he'll tell you, instead of me having to write it down in fucking crayon just for you.'

'Very good, sir.'

'Right, the pair of you fuck off to the canteen. Jimmy's waiting and there's a rumour going around he's buying the coffees. But don't put any weight into that. The last time he bought coffee, Scotland was in the World Cup.'

Chance stood up and Evans led him out. 'Come on, pal, let's go and get that coffee. You don't mind paying, do you?'

'Evans!' Stewart shouted. 'Knock that shite right on the fucking heid!'

FOURTEEN

'This is mince,' Harry said as he skirted round the hospital car park. Then a pair of coffin dodgers walked up to their car, laughing and giggling and taking their sweet-arse time.

Parking at the hospital was a joke. Why there wasn't a multi-storey car park was beyond him. He was just glad he didn't have to work here. He put his hands deeper into his pockets and headed over to the hospital entrance.

The uniformed patrol was waiting for him, a young man and woman. He showed them his warrant card. 'Let's get inside,' he said simply, and they followed him inside.

Inside, a sign on the wall welcomed him to the Royal Hospital for Children and Young People.

'Is this the Sick Kids' hospital?' he asked a young man behind the reception counter.

'It's not called that anymore,' he informed Harry, who pulled out his warrant card.

'Be a good lad and see where Cassidy McLean is.'

The man worked the keyboard. 'I can give her a call.'

'Or you can tell me where she is.'

The man looked at the uniforms for a moment before telling Harry where he could find Cassidy. They walked away and found a lift, and took it to the first floor. They walked along to a ward and Harry asked somebody to point out Cassidy, and she did.

'Cassidy McLean?' Harry asked, showing his warrant card.

'Yes?' It was that 'deer in the headlights' moment when she saw the man in the overcoat with the two uniformed officers behind him. 'Have you found Moira? I reported her missing.'

'I'm sorry to tell you that we located a body this morning, and we found identification on her that leads us to believe it's your daughter.'

'Oh God, no.' Harry saw the woman stiffen up before she looked him in the eyes. 'Wait a minute, what identification?'

'Her driving licence.'

'What did she look like?'

Harry hesitated. 'Is there somewhere more private we can talk?'

Cassidy nodded. 'There's a family room here.' She led them down the corridor and into a room that had a small settee and a chair with a side table. On the walls hung cheap prints that were meant to seem comforting, Harry supposed. He wondered if parents would forever associate such prints with receiving bad news about their child.

It smelled of antiseptic, just like the mortuary did. Not his favourite place on earth. Harry followed her in and was in turn followed by the two uniforms.

'I'm sorry to have to inform you that identifying the female we found will be difficult. We're going to have to ask you for a DNA sample and ask you if she had any identifying marks on her body.'

Cassidy's mouth dropped open and her eyes went wide. 'Christ, no. They had to confirm my husband by doing a DNA test. His face was so...he fell onto rocks by a river from a height. Please don't tell me that happened to Moira.'

'There's been trauma to her facial area. That's why I need to ask you if she has any identifying marks on her. Tattoos for example.'

Cassidy started crying. 'No. Moira doesn't have tattoos. She's too scared of needles to get a tattoo.'

'Are you sure she didn't just tell you that? Could she have maybe bent to peer pressure and had one done anyway?'

'Oh no. You don't know Moira. When I say she hates needles, I mean she hates them.'

Harry noticed she was talking about her daughter in the present tense, which a lot of people did when they first found out their loved one was dead.

'The female we found looks to be around sixteen or seventeen. She has a tattoo on her right arm.'

Cassidy snapped her head up. 'A tattoo? Oh God. What kind of tattoo?'

'The head of a native American. Full headgear. You know, like you would see on TV.'

'Jesus. That's not my daughter. That's her friend, Sue Anderson! She spells her name S-I-O-U-X, like the tribe. Hence the tattoo. Oh my God. What was she doing with Moira's licence?'

'I'm sorry to tell you this, but this female was murdered and her facial features were obliterated to hide her identity. We're assuming that whoever killed her placed your daughter's ID on her.'

'Oh no.'

Harry could hear relief and panic in Cassidy's voice: relief that the victim wasn't her daughter but panic at knowing that her daughter was still missing.

'Is there somebody we could call to be with you?' he asked her. Standard protocol.

'Yes. Ewan, my boyfriend. But I'll call him. He works here, in the lab downstairs.' She took her phone out and dialled his number, then started crying.

'Oh, Ewan. Can you come up to my ward? There's a policeman here.'

FIFTEEN

Crawford Ingram walked into the pathology lab in the Sick Kids'. He walked over to Ewan Gallagher and put an arm around his shoulders.

'Hell of a night,' he said, grinning.

'I have to admit being invited along to a last-minute party was a lot more exciting than I had thought it would be,' Ewan said. 'Apart from Sharon dumping me.'

'It was great, eh? Bingo was blootered.' Ingram took his arm off Ewan's shoulders and looked across at a little man on the other side of the lab. 'Eh, wee man?'

Bingo, wearing black sunglasses, looked over at the two men standing staring at him. 'Put it this way, my liver's still hanging on the washing line, drying out.'

Ingram laughed. 'That's m'man. I couldn't believe how much peeve you put away. I'm proud of you, my friend. Is that why you're wearing sunglasses inside?'

'I can't see out of my left eye and the right one rolled backwards. My pish was burning this morning and I think my willy fell off. Apart from that, I'm fine, and thanks for asking.'

A woman in a lab coat walked over to Ingram. 'I'm sure Christmas was fun, opening up your wee toys, Mr Ingram, but that was two days ago and now we're back in this big playroom we call "work". Maybe you can join in and play with the others. Even Bingo made it in and he's rougher than a badger's tadger.'

Ena Stubbs was the boss of the pathology lab. Rumour had it that she was a Gemini and under a certain moon she could almost be human.

'Right away, boss,' Ingram said.

Ena looked at her watch and kept looking at it until Ingram walked away to the locker room and fetched his lab coat. Only then did she move away. The others in the lab didn't look at her for fear of getting their own tongue-lashing.

Once he had his coat on, Ingram walked back over to Ewan. 'I take it that old Ena didn't get asked back to anybody's place after getting blootered at a party?'

'I don't think Ena goes to those sort of parties,' Ewan answered.

'Maybe she should. Getting a good seeing-to would do her the world of good.'

'Next time you have a party, invite her round. She might surprise you.'

'Aye, right.' Ingram laughed. 'How did it go with your girlfriend?'

Ewan shook his head. 'She's not my girlfriend. She's just a friend. Who's a girl.'

'You've spent the night with her, though, right?'

'I have. But we're not at that boyfriend/girlfriend stage yet.'

'Uh-oh. I sense there's trouble in paradise already.'

Ewan looked at his friend. 'Not exactly that. I went round yesterday for a few drinks while her daughter was out. But it turned out the girl's missing.'

'Missing? What do you mean, missing?'

'I mean, nobody knows where she is. She hasn't called her mother.'

Ingram was still smiling. 'How old is she now? Nineteen? Twenty?'

'Eighteen.'

'There you are then! You know what lassies that age are like. She probably hooked up with some guy and stayed out all night getting blootered. She's probably lying on somebody's couch trying to sober up.'

'I think you're right, but her mother won't hear of that. She thinks something's happened. I think Moira's rebelling now.'

'I know. *We* know. We were eighteen once. But on another note, do you think you and Cassidy will make a go of it? Her old man's been pushing up the daisies for six months now, and life goes on.'

'She still misses him a bit, I think.'

'What? Pish. Yes, I'm sure she misses him, but if she's slept with you, she's ready to move on. But you don't sound like you're ready to move on with her.'

Ewan looked at his friend. 'This is between us, okay?'

'Of course it is. If you tell me something in confidence, it stays with me and you.'

'What are you pair of sweetie wives gibbering about now?' Bingo said, coming up behind them.

'Christ's sake, Bingo, I nearly shat myself. Why are you creeping about?' Ingram said.

'I'm not earwigging.'

'Of course you are, wee earwigging bastard.'

'Well, if you spoke up instead of whispering, I wouldn't have to stretch my ears so much. Is it about the Hogmanay party?'

'No. But don't worry, you're still invited,' Ingram said. 'Or we could have it at yours. You have a sister, don't you?'

'She's off limits,' Bingo said.

'Listen, if she's not daft like you, she won't be off limits.'

'She's perfectly normal like me. In fact, she writes her own songs. She wants to be a singer.'

'What does she play? The banjo?' Ingram asked.

'Funny. I just thought Ewan was updating us about what happened with Sharon last night. She was in a real strop because young Ewan here won't kick the cougar into touch.'

'She's hardly a cougar.'

The lab's phone rang, and Bingo answered it and then shouted Ewan over.

'Who is it?' he asked.

'Your friend, the nurse,' Bingo said, grinning. 'Rarr,' he said, doing a fair impression of a cat clawing.

Oh, Christ, Ewan thought. He hoped this wasn't

the start of Cassidy calling him at work just because they worked in the same hospital. He wished he had kicked her into touch last night when he had the chance.

'Cassidy?' he said.

'*Oh, Ewan. Can you come up to my ward?*' She was crying, her voice thick. '*There's a policeman here.*'

SIXTEEN

Ewan Gallagher had just saved the life of another child. 'Funny how many kids' lives I've saved, but I don't have any of my fucking own,' he said to Bingo as they walked out of the lab. The smaller man was heading for the canteen, having regained some sight in his left eye. He wasn't ruling out getting a guide dog.

'I'm sure you've sown your seed in many places, resulting in little ankle-biters that you don't know about.'

'Christ, don't say that. Can you imagine the child support? I'm not going to be forking out my hard-earned for some slapper to be sitting on the settee watching daytime TV, eating a box of chocolates and letting the little sod run about with his nappy full of shite.'

'Me either. That's why I told Lexi I'm not interested in kids. Good luck with the fuzz.'

Ewan shook his head. Fuzz. Bingo had told him that he had bought himself a *Starsky and Hutch* DVD set for Christmas. Next thing, he'd have a fucking haircut like Huggy Bear.

Ewan took the lift up to Cassidy's level. His dad would have lectured him about taking the stairs to keep fit, but hiking was about as much effort as he wanted to put in. He knew people who ran marathons. At the end of the day, they were guaranteed a hundred per cent to die just like he was.

He stepped out into a ward full of people and sick kids who were on the mend, thanks to him. *You're fucking welcome,* he thought. Cassidy was in a room with the polis. This had to be about the attention-seeker, he was sure. Whatever the stupid lassie had got herself into, Ewan didn't want any part of it. Cassidy was toast after this. Dealing with her brat was not what he'd signed up for. In fact, if he remembered correctly, it was his father, Joe, who had thought his seeing Cassidy would be a good idea.

He approached the door and knocked. Then walked in.

Two in uniform and a tall man in an overcoat, unbuttoned now because it was like a fucking sauna in here. *And of course the Oscar goes to...Cassidy McLean!*

'Oh, Ewan, thank God you're here,' she said, getting up from a small settee that looked like somebody had nicked it off the display at Ikea. He put his arms around her and dug deep.

'What's wrong? Is it Moira?' *Don't smile now, for fuck's sake, or else the boy in the suit and boots will have you in handcuffs before you have time to say Happy New Year!*

'It is. Sort of,' she said, prising herself off him.

'Sort of' didn't sound good. 'What's happened?' He kept a straight face and looked at the detective.

'I'm DCI Harry McNeil. A friend of Moira's was found murdered this morning. She had Moira's driving licence on her.'

The shocked face was real, no need for acting. 'Sioux?' Ewan asked Cassidy.

She nodded.

'Do you know her?' Harry asked.

Ewan made eye contact with him. 'Yes. She was at Cassidy's house a few times when I went round. Nice girl. But what about Moira? What's happened to her if Sioux had her driving licence?'

'We're still working on that. We want to know if the girls were meeting anybody.'

The two in uniform was standing over to one side, like they were having a race to see who would fall asleep first. Ewan's money was on the lassie, who was bored out of her crust and hadn't yet managed the art of not showing it. He looked back at Cassidy, waiting along with the coppers to hear the answer.

'They were going to a party. I think. Moira was supposed to be staying over at Sioux's house. But they didn't make it there.'

'Where does Sioux live?' Harry took out a notebook and waited with the pen poised over it.

'In Clovenstone. Not far from us in Baberton.'

Baberton Mains, Ewan wanted to say. Baberton was in Juniper Green, where he lived, and he literally – and figuratively – looked down on her. His bungalow looked out across the rooftops of the Baberton Mains houses below, right across to West Lothian.

'Not far from Ewan too,' Cassidy added, and Ewan cringed inside.

Why the fuck did you tell them that?

Harry looked at him like he wanted to take out his baton right now and make him eat it.

'Is that so?' he asked in a tone he might have

reserved for a man who had just torched a nursing home.

'I didn't know where she lived,' he said.

'Where were you on Christmas night?'

There it was, the thinly veiled accusation. 'At home with my father and brother. We had dinner, then settled down to watch some TV. I can give you their contact details.'

'Go ahead.' Harry still held the notepad. 'We might ask you to submit a DNA sample in the near future.'

'Fine. Joe's my dad, he'll confirm. But my brother's special needs. He won't know what day it is.'

'Understood. Give me your dad's number, then.'

Ewan rattled it off.

'I'd appreciate it if you didn't contact Sioux's parents. We'll need to break the news to them,' Harry said.

Cassidy laughed, but there was absolutely no humour in it. 'Parents? Her dad's dead and her mother's got her head in a pill bottle all the time. That's the reason why she was over at my house so often. We all looked after her. Brian, too, was fond of her.'

Ewan watched as Harry locked on to this fact. 'Brian?'

'Victor's nephew. My late husband. I would say

he's my nephew too, but I've been estranged from that side of the family since Victor died; it was Ewan who helped me get through it. They're mucky bastards, the lot of them. Especially Dan, one of Victor's brothers. He's Brian's dad. Brian's a good lad, though, isn't he, Ewan? In fact, he just moved in with me,' Cassidy said.

'When?' Ewan asked a little too quickly.

'Christmas Eve,' Cassidy said. There was no apology in her voice, just a simple explanation.

'I didn't see him when I was round yesterday.'

'He was out.'

'Where's he sleeping?' Ewan asked, trying to keep his voice if not exactly singsong then not quite accusatory.

'On the couch.'

Ewan pictured the young man trying to fuck around with the tray table and the wooden bastard snapping closed around his neck. He would pay to watch that happen. Sit with his feet up and dig into a big old bucket of popcorn to watch *The Battle of the Tray Tables* and see Brian get his arse kicked. It would be better than *Robot Wars*.

'He there now, is he?' Harry asked.

'I don't know. Maybe,' Cassidy said. 'He might have the clinic to go to.'

'The clinic?' Ewan said, now not holding back his disgust.

'Not that kind of clinic. The alcohol-abusers' clinic.' She looked at Harry. 'He's getting on top of it, despite his father giving him a hard time. He goes to AA and everything. He just needed a roof over his head. What was I supposed to say?' This was directed to Ewan.

No. You could have said no. That's the answer for that psycho. 'You had no choice. He's family after all.' *But I'm not.* He looked at his watch. 'I have to get back. I hope they find Moira. I'm sure I'll hear about it through the grapevine.'

He turned and walked out, closing the door behind him.

SEVENTEEN

Harry spent more time with Cassidy, assuring her that everything would be done to find her daughter. He would send somebody round to try to talk to Sioux's mother. They would need DNA, maybe from a hairbrush.

He went back down to the ground level, leaving the uniforms with Cassidy.

Back at the reception desk, the dour young man had been replaced by a young woman. 'Can you point me to where the biology lab is?'

'Yes, of course. Turn right there and head back. I'll buzz you through.'

He approached the door and the woman did as she had promised and hit whatever it took to unlock the door. Harry walked along the corridor and it still smelled like a hospital, even more back here.

He found Ewan in the lab, now wearing a white lab coat. He was standing talking with two men when he saw Harry approaching.

'Inspector,' he said, taking a step forward. 'Did you forget something?'

Harry looked around. Two men were still looking at the floor show.

'I just wanted to talk to you.. Ask you a couple of questions.'

'In front of my friends, if you don't mind. Crawford Ingram and Bingo.'

'Sake,' Bingo said. 'I'm having nothing to do with whatever you've got yourself into.' He walked away.

Harry watched the small man walk over to his work bench. 'How about you, Mr Ingram?'

Ingram smiled. 'I'm fine. Only too happy to help the long arm and all that.' Then he held up a hand. 'Not that I get asked on a regular basis, you understand.'

'Good.' Harry turned his attention back to Ewan. 'I just wanted to ask your opinion on Brian McLean. You seemed upset when his name was mentioned upstairs.'

Ewan shook his head and made a face that would

normally be reserved for trying a new dish in a restaurant and finding out it tasted like shite.

'Fucking Brian. The guy's a nut job. You should have seen him the day Victor died. He actually smiled at me. Fucking freak.'

'You were there when Victor died?'

'I was. My dad and I like to go hiking. We go all over. I was talking to Cassidy one day in the canteen and we got onto the subject of hiking, and she mentioned that she, Victor and Victor's clan were going to Pitlochry for a weekend with the hospital hiking club. She suggested I should come along. You remember that, don't you, Crawford?'

'I do. She asked us both. So we said yes. But she said something strange; she said, "Don't let my husband know I told you about the trip. It would be nice to have a friendly face to talk to when we're there." Like she was admitting she thought her husband was an arsehole.'

Ewan nodded, agreeing with his colleague. 'That's what she said. We met in the hotel bar the night before Victor died. It was a good night. Joe, my dad, was with me and Crawford, and we had a good time in the bar, but Victor was a bit of a knob. Loud and proud.'

'Was there anything going on at the time between you and Mrs McLean?' Harry asked.

'No, of course not. She was just one of the nurses I speak to every day. We just happened to have the hiking connection.'

'We talk to a lot of nurses here. Both sexes. Even Bingo gets his opinion in there too. Eh, Bingo?' Ingram said.

Bingo looked away like the place was about to be raided.

'But you're an item now?' Harry asked Ewan.

'Not exactly. I just sort of...comforted her. We fell into each other's arms, as it were.'

'You went round to comfort her and you fell into her,' Ingram said, grinning.

Harry ignored him. 'Brian was there with the family. What happened up there?'

'My dad and I said we'd meet Cassidy up on the trail. To be honest, I wasn't in the mood to listen to Victor's bragging about how good at golf he was.'

'Aye, because Ewan's just as good as anybody. Me too. We play on the hospital team,' Ingram added.

'What golf club do you play at?' Harry asked him.

'It used to be the Merchants of Edinburgh,' Ingram answered. 'Then we joined Baberton.'

Harry nodded. 'You were up the trail with Joe. What happened next?'

'We went across the stone bridge and then veered off to a path on the right,' Ewan said. 'We could see Victor's family way ahead, and they were a right noisy bunch of bastards. But anyway, my dad and I were going up this path and then we heard a scream. So we carefully made our way back. It's a bit rougher, that path, so we took it easy so Dad wouldn't fall.' Ewan left out the crucial part where he was having a piss in the bushes.

'What did you see when you got back to the bridge?' Harry asked.

'His family looking over the bridge, crying and shouting for Victor. I looked over and there the poor bugger was, lying on the rocks below. It seemed like a thousand feet down, but it wasn't. Nobody knew what to do. Then Cassidy caught up with us.'

'She wasn't with Victor?' Harry asked.

Ewan shook his head. 'No. She partially dislocated her knee earlier in the year and she couldn't walk fast. She said that Victor had wanted to catch up with his family, so she'd told him to go ahead.'

'He walked up the trail and...then what?'

'His family were ahead, me and Joe were off on the other trail, so I don't know exactly what happened. It appeared that Victor liked to take photos with his phone on a selfie stick.'

'Do you know if any photos of that scene were on the phone?'

'I don't know. What I do know is, the selfie stick was on the ground at the bridge, but his phone wasn't. I asked myself the question: if he was standing on the edge of the bridge wall taking photos using the stick, how come it was left behind and the phone wasn't?'

'It could have fallen off, mate,' Ingram said.

'Have you ever used a selfie stick?' Harry asked.

Ingram shook his head. 'Nah. I'm not into taking photos that much with one of those things. I usually just use my phone to take photos of my...' He grinned. 'Dog.'

'They're usually on there tight. And plugged in to the phone with a cable.'

'Ah, right.' Ingram shrugged his shoulders like Harry had just tried to explain that using a balloon is *not* the same as using a condom.

'Maybe he was standing on the wall trying to put it on and that's what caused him to overbalance,' Ewan said.

'That's not what you believe, though, is it?' Harry said.

Ewan shook his head. 'No. I think that daft bastard Brian slipped away from the pack and saw his uncle on the wall and pushed him.'

'What makes you think that?' Harry asked, thinking about what Jock Forrest, Cassidy's neighbour, had said about Brian.

'He's just a weirdo, that's all. If you saw him, you'd know what I mean. He looked at me after his uncle died and then he smiled before looking away. And now he's living with Cassidy? No wonder Moira's gone missing. I'm not going back to Cassidy's house. No way. Next thing you know, I'll be missing.'

'No way,' Ingram echoed. 'I don't blame you. He might do you in as well.'

'That's what I just said.' Ewan shook his head.

'Mrs McLean said that Brian was out when you were round yesterday. Do you know where he goes?'

'I know nothing about him. Except he's an alcoholic. I mean, he looks like he's twelve, but he's twenty-three. I bet he was getting drink for Moira. I saw her hungover a few times.'

'She's an adult, though, isn't she?' Ingram said.

'She just turned eighteen, so technically he was

buying drink for somebody who was underage at the time.'

'That doesn't mean anything,' Ingram said.

'It would certainly have a bearing in court, if he's done something to her,' Harry said.

'If you want my advice, you should track him down and talk to him,' Ewan said.

'I will. Thank you for your time, gentlemen.'

Harry left the lab, planning to talk to Jimmy Dunbar about his wee hooly to Pitlochry.

EIGHTEEN

Harry and his team were in the incident room when Calvin Stewart, Jimmy Dunbar, Robbie Evans and Chance McNeil came in.

'No, no, don't stand to attention just because a fucking senior officer enters the room,' Stewart said.

Charlie Skellett looked at the newcomer.

'Glad you could make it, sir,' Harry said.

'I'm just glad we made it in one piece. Jimmy was driving, so it was acceptable. If Heid-the-baw had been driving, we'd have been up the arse of a tractor. While it was in its field. But enough fucking chitchat, I'm assuming you have a kettle here? Or do you all drink that poncy overpriced pish water from the coffee shop?'

'I just brought a kettle in, sir,' Lillian said. 'Brand-spanking new.'

'Don't just stand there gibbering about it then, get the bastard switched on.' Stewart smiled at her. Lillian was an officer he liked and he knew she would go far.

'This is a new face,' he said, looking at Skellett.

'Sir, this is DI Charlie Skellett. Newest member of our team.'

'Christ, if it isn't Moonshine Charlie. I thought I recognised the ugly mug. It's been a long time, son. How's things?'

Skellett grinned. 'It has indeed.' He stood up, leaning on his walking stick and holding out his hand. 'This is how things are right now.'

They shook.

'What happened here? The wife catch you diddling some young DS?'

'Yeah, right. You'd be putting flowers on my grave if that happened. No, I fell. My leg's fucked-up because my back is injured. They're working on a solution.'

'Good man. Maybe we'll get a drink while we're here.'

'You're staying in Edinburgh?' Harry asked.

'We are,' Dunbar answered.

'Hey, son, how's things?' Harry said to Chance, meaning, *Why aren't you in uniform, pounding the beat in Glasgow?*

'He's doing a bit of undercover work for me,' Stewart answered.

'I'm doing a bit of undercover work,' Chance confirmed.

Harry looked at Stewart. 'Nothing dangerous.' It wasn't a question.

'Not at all. The lad's getting some valuable experience. He'd be in more danger on a Saturday night in the city centre. I just want him and his girlfriend to check somebody out.'

'Oh aye. You mind if I ask who?'

'Not at all, Chief. Brian McLean. Let's sit down at the conference table and have a coffee. My body thinks I'm deliberately starving it of caffeine and it's about to make me start throwing tables about.'

There was a table at one end of the room where they sat and brainstormed, so the Glasgow team sat down there with Harry.

'The others can listen in,' said Harry.

'Where's Elvis?' Robbie Evans asked.

'He's attending the PM with one of my other DS's, Julie Stott. It's our murder victim, who's a friend of a missing person. Another teenage girl.

Frank Miller's dealing with the scene down in Leith.'

'Christ, so what are we thinking?' Dunbar asked. 'That the other girl's dead too?'

'If not by now, then maybe she's next,' Harry said.

'You mentioned on the phone that the murder victim is the daughter of the man who fell when I was at Pitlochry last summer. Victor McLean.'

'Turns out his daughter, Moira, is missing. Her friend, Sioux Anderson, spelled like the Native American tribe, is the one who was found in a Portaloo. Her face was like hamburger, not to put too fine a point on it.'

Lillian made a face just as the kettle switched off.

Stewart looked at Harry. 'Well, thanks for putting us off fucking hamburgers for dinner, Harry. Fuck me. It's enough to make young Lillian there go vegan. If you did eat something with a face before, then you sure as fuck won't now.'

'You've seen worse, sir,' Evans said. 'Being the most experienced and all that.'

'You make it sound like you're taking the pish out of me when you talk like that, but you're right.' Stewart looked at Harry again. 'Tell us more about this lassie you found.'

Harry looked at them all around the table. 'It seems that her mother is an alcoholic as well as a pill popper, so young Sioux spent a lot of time round at Moira's. Moira's mother, Cassidy, has a boyfriend, Ewan Gallagher, though when I spoke to him earlier today, he made it sound like she was just a friend with benefits. He found out just when I was talking to both of them that Cassidy's nephew, Brian, is now staying with her.'

Dunbar looked at him. 'His name keeps cropping up.'

'I heard about what happened at Pitlochry.'

'Aye. I was there with Cathy. My daughter had the dog. We were having a weekend break and were in the House of Bruar shop when somebody started shouting there had been an accident. So I went up the trail while we waited for an ambulance, and I took control of the situation. That's when I saw Brian McLean. By Christ, I've met some fucking weirdos in my time, but that boy takes the biscuit. He stared at me, his head tilted slightly, and had a wee grin on his face.'

'You thought the bastard was special, you said,' Stewart added.

'Aye. Special wasn't the word I used, but in this official capacity, let's say special.'

'There would have been an enquiry, I take it?' Skellett said.

'There was,' Dunbar confirmed. 'It was ruled an accident. They found out that Victor McLean had done this kind of thing before, climbing up on things to take photos with his selfie stick. That was the end of the matter. Until now, when Charlie there made the connection on the computer between Moira McLean being missing and her old man falling to his death.'

'To be fair, the hard work was done by DS O'Shea there. I just communicated it.'

'It was a team effort,' Lillian said.

'What are you wanting Chance to do exactly?' Harry asked, not sure if he was going to like the answer. He felt like a dad who didn't want his wee laddie to play football with the older boys.

'We found out through the enquiry that this Brian twat is an alkie,' Stewart said. 'Jimmy found out that he goes to AA meetings. I want Chance and his girlfriend, Katie, to go to the meetings and befriend him. He might reveal something to them.'

'Like where he's keeping his cousin?' Harry said.

'Something like that.' Stewart nudged Evans. 'Go and help the lassie with the coffees, son, before my fucking mouth starts to taste like a camel's arse.'

Evans got up from the table and went over to where Lillian was pouring the coffees.

'None for me, thanks,' Skellett said. 'I don't need to be running for a pish every five minutes when I can hardly walk.'

'Just be like Calvin and pish your pants,' Evans said in a low voice to Lillian, who tried not to laugh.

'I'm no' fuckin' deef, Evans. I wish you'd get that into your misshapen heid.'

'I wasn't talking about you, sir, I was talking about another Calvin I know.'

'Daft, ignorant *and* a fucking pathological liar. I hope Vern takes a lot of pills, that's all I'm saying.'

'If I ever need a wee pill, I know who to get one off,' Evans added, grinning.

'One fucking week until I'm off, but in those five days I can make your life hell. Don't forget that, son.'

'I meant I'd get it off...' Evans looked at Dunbar, who stared back at him. '...a fella I know in my local.'

'Fucking thin ice, boy,' Stewart said.

They dished out the coffees and Stewart smacked his lips. 'I think you could do with coming to work alongside me in Muckle McInsh's office, Lily.'

'As a tea lady?'

'Not *just* a tea lady. Your detective skills would shine through.'

'Maybe one day.'

'Where does this Brian go for his meeting?' Harry asked before the conversation went off-topic altogether.

'A small church in Juniper Green. St Mungo's,' Dunbar said.

'Where did he live before he went to live with Cassidy McLean?' Harry asked.

'Clovenstone,' Evans answered, sitting down with his own coffee.

'Clovenstone?' Harry said. 'That's where Sioux Anderson lived. I wonder if it was close to her.'

'What's Clovenstone like?' Stewart asked.

'It's a council scheme. Not a bad place. There's a rough element of course, but mostly good folks.'

'That rough element being the fucking McLeans,' Stewart said. 'The nut job and his family.' Then he looked over at Lillian. 'Wee bit of sugar for my coffee, Lily?'

Lillian looked at him with her eyebrows raised.

'Please,' Stewart said.

'Certainly, sir.' She walked over to the table where a box of packets of sugar from a cash and carry lived. 'There you go.'

'Ta.' He tore a couple open and poured them into the brown liquid. 'You would get on well with Lynn McKenzie, let me tell you.'

'I'm assuming that's a compliment,' Lillian replied.

'You know what they say about assume, Lily. And could you toss me a spoon?'

She waited again.

'Fuck me, you're making me work for this, aren't you? Please and thank you.'

She tutted and walked back over to the table.

'I heard that,' Stewart said.

'You know what they say about earwigging,' Lillian said, grabbing a teaspoon.

'No, I don't actually.'

'You might hear something you don't like,' she educated him.

'I've never been bothered by tossers talking about me.' Stewart stirred his coffee and laid the spoon down. 'Right, between us we've established that this wee prick Brian McLean was up hiking in Pitlochry, or he was there for a fuck-about, but either way his parents could keep an eye on him. But did they? There's a chance he slipped away from the crowd and offed his uncle by giving him a good shove off the bridge. For some reason, he's staying at his aunt's house in...' He looked at Harry.

'Baberton Mains, across the road from Clovenstone. They're on opposite sides of the bypass.'

'Baberton Mains. While he's living there, his cousin goes out with her pal, the pal is found murdered and the cousin is still missing. That sound about right?' Stewart said.

'It does,' Harry confirmed. 'I called Charlie to enquire about Cassidy McLean's boyfriend's alibi. It checks out. Ewan Gallagher was at home Christmas Day with his father and his brother. None of them went out.'

Stewart made a face. 'Why didn't he go round to his girlfriend's house? Because Brian the axe murderer was there?'

'That's the thing; he didn't know Brian was staying there. He only found out earlier today when I was talking with Cassidy. She called him to the family room in the hospital for support. They both work in the Sick Kids', she as a nurse, he as a lab rat.'

'That must have come as a shock,' Dunbar said.

'It was. Especially since he knows Brian. Or rather, saw him that day in Pitlochry. Also, I spoke to Mrs McLean's next-door neighbour, Jock Forrest, and he's been seeing one of Brian's aunties. He says

Brian will stand about in the back garden, just staring.'

'No law against that, unless he was in his Y-fronts and chasing somebody about with a chainsaw,' Stewart said.

'Jesus,' Skellett said. 'He sounds like a candidate for a straitjacket.'

'There's definitely a cog missing,' Dunbar said.

'What's the plan?' Harry asked.

'We'll go over it, don't worry. We have to fine-tune it yet,' Stewart said.

'You can stay at my place,' Harry told his son.

'Thanks, but I'm staying at Katie's.'

'The flat's available, if you boys haven't booked in to the hotel yet.'

Stewart mulled it over for a minute. 'Smashing, pal, thanks. You got any scran in it?'

'I think there's some milk.'

'That's hardly fucking haute cuisine. What sort of an Airbnb is that?'

'It's not an Airbnb.'

'It is now. Accounts will want to know who to make the cheque out to. But we'll need it stocked with some scran. Evans!'

Evans looked on in disbelief. 'Shopping?'

'Aye. Take somebody with you. Here, I'll give

you the cash and I want my fucking change. And none of your fancy shite either. Get enough breakfast stuff for a good few days. We'll be here for the duration. Or at least until Hogmanay, when we'll have to get back through to file some paperwork.'

'What's her name?' Lillian asked.

'Never you mind that, ya nosey wee nebber. It's my last day, that's what.'

'Won't they question why you're staying here when Glasgow's just an hour's drive away?' Skellett asked.

'Charlie, how long you been on the force, son?'

'Long enough to get my boots under the table.'

'Exactly. We'll be up at the crack of dawn, working until God knows what hours, then we'll be knackered and have to drive back home then back here before the milkmen get up? I don't think so.'

'Milkmen?' Evans asked. 'Been watching Benny Hill recently, sir?'

'Shut your hole. I'm explaining to a senior officer the logistics of why we're staying here.'

'Easier for a piss-up as well,' Dunbar added.

'I didn't hear that. Officially.' Stewart turned back to Evans. 'Go and get the scran. Harry, you got a couple of spare keys?'

'I always have them on me,' Harry said, fishing

out his keys, taking two off the keyring and handing
them to Stewart.

'Baw-heid. Take one of these keys and get the
scran loaded.' Stewart took his wallet out and
handed over a pile of notes. 'I want to see the fucking
receipt as well.'

'Permission to help Robbie, sir?' Lillian said.

'Aye, off you go. We'll be having a meeting with
Katie. She should be here shortly. I told the wank of
a sergeant to release her into the team and to shut his
pie hole.'

Harry looked at his son. *Did he do that to your
sergeant too?* Chance nodded slightly. Harry closed
his eyes for a moment, sure that somewhere down
the line, when Stewart was long gone, this would
come back to bite him in the arse.

Evans left with Lillian.

'When's the first AA meeting?' Harry asked.

'Tonight.'

'Okay.'

The phone rang and Skellett answered it. He
spoke to the person on the other end for a couple of
minutes. 'Interesting,' he said. 'Thanks for letting me
know.' He hung up and looked at the others.

'What's up, Charlie?' Harry asked.

'A woman's been reported missing. The thing is,

she was at a party down at the Shore. Near where the victim was found this morning.'

'Is that right?' Stewart said. 'Right, Harry, get along there and have a chat with whoever reported it. Take Jimmy. You got an address there, Charlie?'

Skellett ripped off a piece of paper. 'Oxgangs.'

'Go then, lads. Me and young Chance here will go over the plans for tonight.'

The incident room door opened and Katie, Chance's girlfriend, walked in. She was still in uniform.

'Glad you could join us, young lady,' Stewart said. 'Now, your future father-in-law is leaving, but me and Charlie will keep you youngsters entertained.'

Chance was pulling a beamer. But Katie just smiled.

'Good to hear it, sir.'

'Keep them all in order,' Harry said as he and Dunbar passed her.

'Yes, Dad.' She laughed.

'Don't encourage DSup Stewart. It'll only go downhill.'

NINETEEN

Oxgangs Avenue was an arterial street that joined Greenbank with the main road that ran through Oxgangs on the way to the Pentlands.

'It's about here somewhere,' Harry said. 'Can you see the numbers on the outside of the blocks of flats?'

'I think your eyesight is better than mine, mucker,' said Dunbar. 'I'd need a pair of binoculars and a torch to make out any of those bastard numbers if I was a taxi driver. That would go down well at night, eh? There's a fucking peeping Tom with a torch and binoculars creeping about in the dark. Explain that one away when they're putting you in handcuffs. "I was looking for a stair number, honest."'

'Aye, that one might get your name on a list

somewhere, right enough.' Harry stopped the car at a bus stop. 'Is that it there?' He pointed to the stairway entrance and the number painted on the left of the door.

'I think it might be, but since I don't have telescopic eyesight, it could also very well be Holyrood Palace.'

'Look at the window, second up on the right-hand side. There's a woman standing looking out and she isn't hiding behind the curtains.'

'Naked?' Dunbar asked, squinting.

'I think she might be wearing a skin-coloured sweater.'

'Thank fuck for that. Although I have to be honest, I've walked into worse situations.'

'You and me both.'

Harry had called ahead to make sure the woman who had made the report would be home and she had assured him she would. He assumed this was her since there was a green wheelie bin sitting outside the stairway with the number painted on it.

They got out into the cold. The sky was the colour of *Go on, say it again. One more fucking time.*

'What's this area like?' Dunbar said.

'Well, there's not many Rolls-Royces get parked around here. Working class.'

'Like you and me then?'

'Exactly. With a sprinkling of ne'er-do-wells.' Harry locked the car and looked up. Both were relieved to see the woman was indeed not putting on a DIY burlesque show and was wearing a sweater. She stared at them like her granny might have stared at the rent collector, but Harry thought many, if not all, of the flats here had been bought.

Many moons ago, the stairway might have smelled of pish and fish suppers, sometimes at the same time. Harry had known many a drunk to have acquired a skill that meant he could relieve himself while keeping the open fish supper perfectly balanced. He'd not tried it himself, and it was spoken of only in certain circles.

They walked up to the first level and the woman who had been looking out the window was standing there with the door open. On closer inspection, it was clear the cardigan had a flower pattern. Red, like the woman's eyes.

'Mrs Boyle?' Harry asked.

The woman nodded.

'I'm DCI McNeil. We spoke on the phone. This is a colleague of mine from Glasgow, DCI Dunbar. Can we come in?'

'Yes, of course.' She stepped aside and let them in, closing the front door behind them.

They stood aside and let her show them to the living room at the far end of the hall. Harry mentally worked out the floor plan and figured that the woman had been watching from a bedroom window.

'Thank you for coming,' she said, standing in the middle of the room, wringing her hands.

'Of course,' Harry said. 'Why don't you sit down and you can tell us about your daughter.'

Mrs Boyle looked behind her as if to make sure her chair was still there, like they had been playing musical chairs and one of the detectives was waiting to whip it away. It was still there, so she sat down.

'It's my daughter, Sharon. I haven't heard from her since she went to a party last night. I've tried calling her, but it goes straight to voicemail.'

'Where does she live?' Harry asked.

'Here, at home. She's quite happy living here. She wouldn't stay out and not tell me.'

'This is unusual then?' Dunbar asked.

'It is. I mean, she's stayed out before. I'm not one of those mothers who's possessive. I let her live her life. She's even had a boyfriend stay the night. I don't mind, as long as they're respectful, which they have been.'

'I have to ask you this, Mrs Boyle,' Harry said. 'Has Sharon had many boyfriends recently?'

Mrs Boyle shook her head. 'No. She started seeing somebody from work, but he's in sort of a relationship already and she didn't want to be the one who broke it up. She was wanting him to finish with the other woman, but he was taking his sweet time.'

'Do you know this man's name?' Dunbar asked.

'Ewan something,' she answered.

'Does Ewan have a second name?' Harry asked, then thought he'd sounded condescending, but it was too late now, the words were out. If Mrs Boyle noticed, she didn't comment.

'I'm sure Sharon told me, but I can't think straight.' She looked at them both in turn. 'I've been worried sick.'

'Where does Sharon work?' Dunbar asked.

'She's a nurse. At the Sick Kids'. She was supposed to be working today, but she's not there. I told her about staying out too late then getting up for work, but she said she wasn't due to go in until twelve and she wouldn't be drinking much. But when I called the ward, she wasn't there.'

Harry looked at Dunbar before asking the next question. 'Is Ewan's last name Gallagher?'

Mrs Boyle's head snapped round so fast, Harry

thought she'd just caught on about what he'd said earlier. 'Yes! It is. Ewan Gallagher. He works at the hospital beside Sharon. Why? Do you know him?'

'I've spoken to him regarding another matter.'

'Oh my God. That's why two senior detectives are here instead of some plook in uniform. This has something to do with that murder I heard about on the news, hasn't it?'

'I can't comment on any individual case we're working on. I'm sorry.'

'It is, though. I'm not stupid. Do you think he's taken Sharon?' Her eyes were wide now and spittle flew through the air, landing on the carpet some-where. She snapped her fingers. 'That other lassie's missing. That young one. I heard that on the news too. What the hell is going on? Do you think that's connected too?'

She was starting to talk faster and both men recognised the signs. This was the pre-emptive strike before a full-blown panic attack, where the shouting and screaming would start.

Harry stood up. 'I don't want you jumping to conclusions, Mrs Boyle. Is there a neighbour we can get in to make you a cup of tea?'

Mrs Boyle was breathing hard now. 'Sadie across the way.'

Dunbar got to his feet quickly and headed for the front door and a woman called Sadie who might be the key to helping Mrs Boyle off the ledge. Harry heard him opening the front door and knocking on another front door. Low voices, then the other door closing.

Sadie appeared, an older woman like Mrs Boyle. Harry told her what was going on and asked if she would mind sitting with her neighbour for a little while.

'This might be nothing,' he assured Sadie, 'and it's early days. We're hoping Sharon had more to drink at the party than she'd planned and is sobering up now as we speak.'

'Where was this party?' Dunbar asked.

'Down at the Shore.' Mrs Boyle looked at a pad on the table next to her chair. 'I told her to give me the exact details, just in case.' She read them out to Harry, who wrote them down.

'We'll go and talk to the person who threw the party.'

'Wait a minute, the Shore. Isn't that where the girl was found murdered?'

'It is. But there's no reason to believe there's a connection just now,' Harry assured her, though he didn't believe his own words.

Sadie was rustling about in the kitchen.

'We have your number, so we'll keep in touch, Mrs Boyle.'

She nodded. 'Thank you for coming round.'

'Of course.'

Harry and Dunbar left the flat and walked down the stairs. They both knew not to discuss anything just now, in case the walls had ears.

Outside, the wind was challenging them to a fight and Harry was glad to get back in the car.

'Ewan Gallagher. His name keeps popping up,' Dunbar said.

'We'll have to go and have a talk with him. I have his address. We can go and talk to him on his home turf, if you like? After he's finished work.'

'I'd like that more than anything.'

TWENTY

'I swear to God, I'm going to become a vegetarian,'
Elvis said, coming out of the mortuary's bathroom,
wiping his mouth with a paper towel and then
shoving it in his pocket where the other half dozen
were. His eyes were red, like they'd been dipped in
vinegar.

'What is it with you men?' Julie Stott said. 'DI
Miller said Harry McNeil is just the same way. Big
babies.'

'What? Away with yourself. I just ate something
that was off, that's all.'

'Nothing to do with the fact that the girl's face
looked like it had been through a wringer.'

'A what?'

'A wringer. It was something that was attached to

the side of a sink in the old days. Two rollers with a handle, and you put clothes through it to squeeze out water. Before the days of washing machines. It looked like that girl's face had been put through a wringer. Poor thing.'

'Jesus.' Elvis turned round and ran back into the bathroom, where he did a good impression of somebody trying to disembowel himself the hard way.

Julie's phone rang. She looked at the screen. Miller.

'Hello, sir.'

'Julie. You finished at the PM yet?'

'Five minutes ago. I was going to call you and see if you wanted us back at the Shore or back at the station.'

'I was going to tell you to head back, but I got a call from Harry. It's about another female who's gone missing. There's a connection. I'll explain when I see you. Can you meet me at the Shore, but at this address?' Miller rattled it off for her.

'That's fine, sir. We'll head down there now. Elvis is just using the bathroom.'

'I'll wait outside. We've been doing the house-to-house and there's not been many hits. It ranges from people seeing Bigfoot to Lord Lucan. I think some of

them are taking the piss, but there's a few leads we
have to check. I'll see you shortly.'

'See you soon.'

Elvis came out of the bathroom. He held up a
hand as Julie started to speak. 'I don't want to hear it.
No disrespect, but I don't think I have anything left
to chuck up.'

'I was going to say, Frank Miller wants us down
at the Shore for an interview. He got a call from DCI
McNeil.'

'Oh God. I hope my breath doesn't stink.'

'Not any more than usual.'

'That's a relief.'

DI Frank Miller was skulking about in his car
outside the block of flats like an insurance salesman.
He got out when Julie pulled up behind him.

'I should have said I'll meet you in the pub,' he
said. 'That would have got you here quicker.'

'Been here long, sir?'

'I finished the crossword in the *Caledonian*,
wrote a book and wallpapered my lavvy wall while I
was waiting.'

'The crossword's easy, though, sir. A bairn could do it,' Elvis said.

'Really? Four-letter word. A new detective constable. Starts with D, ends with K.'

'Duck?'

'Close. Let's go. He's in, lives in the top flat. I already called.'

Miller pressed the buzzer button and a voice that may or may not have belonged to the Tin Man answered. *'Hello?'*

'DI Miller. We spoke on the phone.'

'Who? You're selling a phone, did you say?'

Miller looked at the others and stamped his feet. 'Police. We spoke earlier. I'd like to come up and talk with you.'

'Sake.'

The reply sounded further away, as if the man had turned away from the entry phone handset. But then it buzzed.

They walked in out of the cold and along to the lift.

'You alright there, Elvis?' Miller asked. 'You look a bit...' He turned to Julie. 'You sure you were at the mortuary and not the pub?'

'I had a foosty pie before we went in, sir,' Elvis

said, jumping in before Julie could throw him under the bus.

'You should stick to Greggs pies. At least you know they aren't filled with shite that's been shovelled off the floor.'

Elvis started his breathing exercises, practised regularly for such occasions as this.

The lift doors opened and they stepped in.

'What are you having for dinner tonight, Elvis? Hamburger?' Miller grinned.

'You told him, didn't you?' Elvis asked Julie.

'He asked,' Julie said in her own defence.

'I knew I should have worked in an office like my mother wanted. And not one that requires you to go and look at dead people.'

The lift doors opened and at once they saw the door to a flat on the corridor was already open. Miller looked at the other two. Now they were all on their guard.

'It's open!' a voice from within shouted. And in a lower voice, 'In case you're fucking blind.'

Miller barged in, pushing the door hard, his adrenaline kicking in now. He had walked into houses before where the occupant was waiting with a surprise, and it wasn't a group of people shouting 'Surprise!'.

Bingo was sitting on a chair in his living room, an ice pack on his head. The house looked like a fight had broken out in an off-licence.

'Grab somewhere,' he said, making a sweeping motion with his free hand.

'I'm DI Miller.'

'I know, you told me on the intercom. If you're a bunch of conmen – and -woman – your disguise is pretty good,' Bingo said.

'You're Eddie Shaw?'

'Correct. Everybody calls me Bingo. A nickname from high school.'

Miller looked at the empty cans on the settee.

'Just put them on the floor with the others,' Bingo said. 'As you can see, it was the housekeeper's day off.'

Miller hesitated, but Elvis had no such reservations and accepted the invitation to decorate the carpet with more empty tins, just had a quick look at the cushion to make sure there were no pish stains before sitting down. Julie looked around and saw an overturned folding chair next to the TV where it looked like it had been fighting with the big screen and lost. She picked it up and sat on it while Miller put a couple of cans on the floor.

'There was a party here last night?' he asked.

Like Elvis, he checked for any mess that could have escaped from a body cavity before sitting down. There was none visible to the human eye, so he risked it.

'What gave it away?' Bingo asked, swapping hands as no doubt the first one was starting to go numb with holding the cold bag.

'We need to ask you a few questions about your party last night,' Miller said.

'About not getting invited or...?'

'Or about a woman who was invited here and who is now missing,' Elvis said.

Bingo took the ice bag off his head and sat forward, which, judging by his wince, only served to make the pain worse. 'Who? What do you mean, missing?'

'Her name is Sharon Boyle,' Julie answered, 'and the second part is self-explanatory.'

Apparently, the second part wasn't as clear as Elvis had tried to make it.

'Missing?' Bingo said again. 'How is she missing?'

'We believe she was invited to the party here,' Miller said. 'Was she here?'

'Aye, she was here with her boyfriend, Ewan.'

'Ewan Gallagher?' Miller said.

Bingo looked at him before answering. 'Aye. How do you know Ewan?'

'We've been talking to him regarding another matter. You're saying she was here with Ewan. Did she leave with him?'

'I'm not sure. I was wasted. I sort of remember talking to them at one point, but as the night wore on, the drink took over and you know what it's like – alcohol is like anaesthesia. One minute you're having a good time, the next you wake up on the settee wearing only your underpants.'

None of the detectives were willing to admit that they did indeed know what this was like. Miller and Elvis looked at each other, wondering what end of the settee had had Bingo's underpants on it.

'Do Sharon and Ewan get along?' Julie asked.

Bingo narrowed one eye as he put the ice bag back on top of his head. 'Define "getting along",' he replied.

'Oh, come on, I'm sure I don't have to spell that out.'

Bingo nodded. 'Did they fight a lot, culminating in him making her disappear? I get it. But they were good together. Except Ewan was hesitating finishing it with the older woman. Cassidy. She and Sharon are both nurses at the Sick Kids'.

It's where Ewan met them. The problem is, the relationships were overlapping and that pissed off Sharon. To be honest, I was drunk and I think I was drinking too much, so I can't remember anybody leaving. You'd have to ask Ewan about that.'

'Oh, we will.' Miller looked at Bingo. 'My boss said you and Ewan work together?'

'We do. By Christ, I don't know how I made it into work today. A wing and a prayer, no doubt. But I took the bus, or buses, and that in itself was a sobering adventure. I also had a wee hair of the dog from a hip flask. Still, my headache seems to want to hang around and enjoy the festive period.'

'How do you get on with Sharon?' Elvis asked.

'I like her a lot. I wish Ewan would make up his mind and dump Cassidy. Don't get me wrong, Cassidy's nice, but I think she was just looking for company after her husband died.'

'Did Ewan talk to you about the husband dying?'

'It was all over the hospital, but yes, he did say he was there when it happened.'

'Was there anything going on between them before the husband died?' Miller asked.

Bingo made a face as if silently asking Miller if he was daft. 'Ewan making a move on Cassidy?

While Victor was around? No, no, that's not in his nature. He wouldn't break up somebody's marriage.'

'I'd like the names of the people who were at your party.'

'Christ, it was me, Ewan, Crawford Ingram, Sharon. And a bunch of people from the hospital. I don't know exactly who was here. Ewan invited some of them, or he mentioned I was having a party. I didn't invite half of them. It was a good time, though. My girlfriend, Lexi, was here, obviously. She's a nurse too. She's at work. I can give you her number. Some other woman I seem to remember dancing with, and when I use the word "dancing", I do use it loosely. It was more of a strange movement fuelled by alcohol. She was somebody else from work, but I'm buggered if I can remember her name.'

'We can start by you giving one of my team the names of the people who were here that you do remember.' Miller nodded to Julie, who was ready with her notebook.

'Give me the names again, please,' she said, and Bingo rattled them off.

Julie put the book away and they stood up, except Bingo, who remained seated.

'You won't mind if I don't see you out. I don't think my legs could carry me twice to the front door.'

'We'll leave you to whatever it is you're going to be doing now,' Miller said.

'Let me ask you,' Bingo said. 'Do you think something happened to Sharon, or do you think she's sobering up somewhere?'

'Her mother said she was supposed to be at work today, but she never showed up. She's not answering her phone and nobody knows where she is. Where could she be, Mr Shaw?'

Bingo slowly shook his head. 'I don't know,' he replied in a low voice.

'Work it out for yourself,' Miller said and then they left.

TWENTY-ONE

Evans put his bags of groceries on the kitchen counter top. Lillian put hers on the floor.

'I hope that wee bastard didn't spend all my money on booze and crisps?' Stewart said.

Lillian laughed. 'No, sir, we bought decent food.'

'By "decent", I hope you don't mean overpriced shite?'

'There's a box of doughnuts in there for you,' Evans answered. 'Just to keep the cliché going.'

'There you go with the French bollocks again,' Stewart said.

'It's very nice of Harry to lend us his flat for a bit,' Evans said.

'Now we just have to work out who gets what bedroom, since there's only two. And since Jimmy's away with Harry McNeil to talk to some bawbag, I suppose I'll have to decide for you both.'

'I have the feeling it'll be the settee for me,' Evans said.

'I don't give a rat's tadger who gets the spare room. You shaggers can fight over it. Share it if you like. But if you get up for a pish through the night and wander into the wrong room, it'll be the fucking last time.'

'I have an idea,' Lillian said. 'I live literally round the corner in the next street. I have two bedrooms. You could sleep there, Robbie. Save you breaking your back on Harry's couch, nice as it is.'

'Have you got scran in?' Stewart asked.

'I have. And beer.'

'There you go, Evans. But no bloody funny business. And you'll get paid for using your flat, Lily. I'll make sure of that.'

'Thank you, sir, but I'm not doing it for the money. It'll be nice to have somebody stay over for a change.'

'That's it settled then,' Stewart said. 'You can come back here later, Robbie, and get your bag with your manky skids in it and bugger off. Right now, I want to get moving. Harry said the traffic will be like a rabid badger.'

'Let's go,' Evans said.

'Hold your fucking horses. Get the dairy in the fridge and we can sort the other pish out later. I don't want to end up shitting my troosers 'cause you left the fucking milk oot and it went foosty.'

Evans put the milk and eggs away. 'There you go. No rank milk on your Rice Krispies in the morning.'

'Or we could go to the wee café round the corner,' Lillian suggested. 'Tattie Scones it's called.'

'Sounds good, Lily. You can show us where in the morning. Now, I'm starting to get antsy. Let's go and see what the wee scrote is like. I'll call Chance and update him.'

Jock Forrest sat back at his dining table and patted his stomach. 'That was a damn fine meal, Ruby. Thank you for doing that.' He sipped his glass of wine.

'Och, away. It's my pleasure.'

'I'll clear the dishes away if you put the kettle on. We'll have a coffee if you like.'

'Absolutely.'

They both got up from the table and Forrest

scraped the excess food off his plate and into the bin before putting the dishes into the dishwasher. Ruby switched the kettle on.

'You know, I was thinking. Maybe we could take our relationship to the next level,' Ruby said.

'You know I told you about getting my back injured at work. I told you from the outset that I might not be able to be anything other than a friend,' he said, smiling and touching her arm.

'I know. I thought you might have got some of those pills over Christmas and we could have tried.'

'Ruby, I think the world of you and I enjoy your company, and I know you have needs, but unfortunately I'm not the man to fulfil those needs.'

'Oh, don't be silly. I love being around you.'

Forrest blew out a breath. 'Maybe it's time for you to find another man, Ruby. One who *can* fulfil your sexual needs.'

'I'm in my sixties, Jock. I don't need it that badly. It would have been nice for us to take it to the next level, but we're not teenagers anymore.' She stepped forward and gave him a hug.

'I never thought I'd retire from the police force a cripple, but that's what I am. They give me a big pension, but I'm half the man I used to be.'

'You're all the man I need,' she said, hugging him tighter.

'Anyway, I think the kettle's about to go off.'

'We'll have the cuppa, then I'll pop round to see Cassidy. Brian's going out to his AA meeting tonight and she'll be all alone.'

'What about Ewan?' He gently prised her off him.

'When I spoke to her earlier, she said the police went to the hospital today and she called Ewan. They found Sioux's body, as I told you earlier, and Ewan came to the family room where they break bad news and he found out that Brian is staying with her. He wasn't happy, and later on he sent her a text telling her they were done.'

'Oh no. What is she going to do now?'

'She's up to high doe. First her husband dies, then her daughter goes missing, and now her boyfriend has dumped her.'

'He wasn't really her boyfriend, was he? He wormed his way into her affections and took advantage of her. She's better off without him.'

'She is, if he was going to discard her like a piece of rubbish when she needed him the most.'

'Good riddance. That's what I say.' He looked from the dining area through the archway that led into the living room and saw Brian McLean walking past his house, towards the short pathway that led to Baberton Mains Drive, the main road that circum-navigated the housing estate. It would be a fifteen-minute walk up to Juniper Green and his AA meeting.

'Decaf?' Ruby said.

'No, I'll have a full, please. I don't want to be nodding off in front of the TV later.'

Ruby busied herself with the mugs.

'I think I'll just stay with Cassidy for the rest of the evening, if you don't mind,' she said.

'Why would I mind?' He smiled at her.

'You're a good bloke, Jock Forrest. They broke the mould when they made you.'

'You're embarrassing me, woman. Just finish the coffee.'

They both laughed.

TWENTY-TWO

'I don't know about you, Harry, but I could go for some real scran right about now,' Jimmy Dunbar said.

'We can go back to my place after this,' Harry replied, slowing the car down as he turned into Baberton Crescent. 'Grab a fish supper.'

'What about Morgan? Won't she be there?'

'I didn't give her a key, but she'll be over later. It would be nice for you to meet her.'

Dunbar nodded. 'You okay with it all, mucker? Seeing another woman?'

'I am. I mean, I'll never forget Alex, of course. How could I? I have our daughter, and I'll never let Grace forget who her real mother was. But I feel good around Morgan. She's been a widow for ten years and I think she likes us being together.'

'That's good. If it works out, then I wish you all the best, my friend.'

The words felt genuine coming from the Glaswegian detective, a man Harry thought of as a friend.

'Right, let's go and talk to this joker,' Dunbar said, opening the door as Harry turned the engine off. Darkness had come down fast, and the sky was the colour of *This is going to hurt me more than it's going to hurt you.* More snow was coming, but right now it was hiding round the corner.

'This is a nice area, I can tell,' Dunbar said as Harry opened the gate. The bungalow was well kept and had an extension in the roof as well as one sticking out on the right-hand side. There was a light on in the room on the left, behind closed curtains.

Harry walked up to the front door and knocked. Dunbar clanked the gate closed behind him. A couple of minutes later, an older man opened the door.

'Yes?' he asked. The left-hand side of his body was hidden behind the door and it reminded Harry of Jock Forrest and the golf club.

They showed the man their warrant cards.

'I'm DCI McNeil. I called your son earlier.'

'Which one?'

'Ewan.'

'Oh, right. He's not done anything wrong, I hope.'

'We just want a wee word,' Dunbar said. *Before we freeze our tits off.*

'Come on then, before you let all the bloody heat out.' The man opened the door wider and they stepped inside, rubbing their boots on a thick mat.

'What's your name, sir?' Harry asked.

'Joc Gallagher,' the man replied. 'In here.'

They went into the living room, which was compact but well kept, and the detectives sat down on a couch that wouldn't have looked out of place in a show home.

Joe stood at the door for a second. 'Ewan!' He turned to the detectives. 'Normally, my son would ask you to take your boots off. What is it they call that?'

'OCD?' Dunbar offered.

'ADHD?' Harry said.

'Neat freak,' Joe said, snapping his fingers. 'But probably the other two thrown in for good measure. He's a wee bugger for getting the hoover out. I told him he should stick the handle of it up his arse and he could vacuum while he's walking about. He wanted me to get a duster out while he's at work. But with him, you have to get in every wee nook and cranny. I said, I don't think so. Bloody cleaning. I bet neither of you two do the bloody cleaning in your own house.'

'As a matter of fact, I do,' Harry said, quick to jump in.

'We're getting off-track here, Mr Gallagher,' Dunbar said.

Joe snapped his fingers. 'Here, don't I know you from somewhere? Let me think.' He put a finger and thumb on his chin, as if this simple act would jolt his memory. Harry thought a car battery would do the same.

'Pitlochry!' Joe said as the two detectives stood around wondering how long it was going to take the old boy. 'You were the polis who was first on the scene when that daft bastard went over the bridge. That wench's husband.'

'Wench?' Harry said.

'Look, son, I know you think you've been round the block once or twice, but I've not only been round the block, I bought it. I know what women like her are like: husband pops his clogs, and she's left with the mortgage and bills on top of everything.

Not the car payment, though, as that finished years ago and he was too tight to pull the trigger on buying a new one. He left a huge bank account, being frugal?' Joe made a face and shook his head. 'Her husband had a wee gee-gee problem. Liked a drink to himself too. We sat in the bar with the drunken sod the night before he departed and he talked about gambling and drinking. So there was nowt in the bank. And this is what Cassidy said, mind. This isn't hearsay. Well, technically it is, but this is the pish that she's been spouting to Ewan. And the silly bugger was falling for it. But I saw through her bollocks.'

He looked to the living room door. 'Ewan! Fuck's sake. Selective hearing with that boy.'

'You were telling us you saw through Cassidy's bollocks,' Dunbar said.

Joe looked back at him. 'Aye. She wants a meal ticket, son. Somebody to move in and pay her bills. Well, Ewan has enough responsibility helping with this place. This is my house, but he moved in with us after his wife fucked off.'

'You and his brother, Simon.'

'You called?' a voice said from the lobby and a figure walked in. Harry and Dunbar were immediately on their feet. The man standing before them was wearing an overcoat and a Fedora and holding a cigarette holder with an unlit cigarette in it.

'These men are police officers,' Joe said as if he was giving the other man a heads-up.

'Are they now?'

'Gentlemen, this is my other son, Simon.'

'The pleasure is all mine,' Simon said.

'Yes, I think it probably is,' Dunbar said to Harry in a low voice.

'I'm sorry, did you say something?' Simon said, and both detectives noticed a shift in him. A slight physical movement that mentally prepared them for getting in about him.

'I said, nice hat,' Dunbar said.

'Thank you. I always think that it was such a more civilised society when gentlemen wore hats, don't you think?' Simon smiled.

'Absolutely,' Dunbar agreed.

Simon waved at them. 'Sit, sit, please don't stand on my account. I thought Foghorn Leghorn here was calling for me.'

'I've told you about that pish,' Joe warned.

'Relax, Dad. I was just being nosey. I wanted to see who you had round. I thought it was the prostitutes again.'

'My son has a juvenile sense of humour, as you

can see.' Joe looked at Simon. 'Where's Ewan?'

'Upstairs.'

'Did he hear me shouting?'

'I think they heard you shouting in the Railway Arms.'

'Funny. Go and get him.'

'Manners,' Simon said, tilting his head slightly in anticipation. 'Anything else you want to add?'

'Now.'

Simon tutted and turned round to look back into the lobby. 'Ewan! Get down here! His Majesty requires your presence!'

He turned back into the living room and smiled, then walked across to the settee and sat down. Only then did the detectives sit down.

'You wrap that pish,' Joe said, but the admonishment fell on deaf ears.

Harry looked at Dunbar; apparently the guest was staying. Dunbar barely shrugged his shoulders.

'You were at Pitlochry, weren't you?' Simon asked Dunbar.

'I was. I didn't see you there.'

Simon sneered at him. 'I wasn't wearing my receiving attire up in the woods,' he said.

Just then, Ewan walked into the living room and stopped like somebody had taped shrink-wrap across the doorway. 'Sake,' he said. 'As much as I like you, Inspector, I was hoping that would be the last time I saw you when you were at my work. No offence.'

'None taken. But you see, that's our job; we talk to people, and sometimes we need to talk to them again.'

'Did you forget to ask me something?' Ewan still stood in the doorway like he was hedging his bets: stand and talk, or run. Neither men looked fit enough to catch him, but they could always call for back-up.

'Not forgot, no. But some more information came to light that we need to ask you about.'

Ewan sighed and apparently gave up all thoughts of doing a runner as he walked into the living room and sat beside his brother. 'You staying for the duration?'

'I wouldn't miss this for the world.'

'Something to tell Morgan when you next see her,' Ewan said.

'It's Dr Allan to you,' Simon replied, putting the cigarette holder in his mouth, then looking at his father. 'I'm not lighting it.'

'Damn straight you're not.'

Joe stood next to the fireplace, the gas fire

throwing out enough heat to make the occupants fall asleep if they were to have a few drams.

Harry looked at Simon more closely now. He wondered how long Simon had been going to see Morgan.

'We wanted to ask you about Sharon Boyle,' Harry said to Ewan.

'Who?'

'You know, your other girlfriend,' Dunbar said, immediately pissed off at Ewan.

The younger man looked at his father.

'What's going on with Cassidy?' Joe asked. 'I hope you're not messing that poor woman about?'

'Of course not. You said I should go and keep her company.'

'Obviously keeping a woman company in my day was a lot different than nowadays.'

'Aye, back then it meant trying not to rip her nylons as they weren't easy to come by.'

'Cheeky wee sod.'

'Anyway, Cassidy was never a serious thing, you know that. I work with her and she was lonely. It was never meant to go this far. I met Sharon at the hospital, we hit it off and now Cassidy's history. I broke it off with her.'

Joe shook his head. 'Poor cow. Her husband dies,

her daughter goes missing, and just when she needs you most, you dump her. Despicable.'

'Get over yourself. She's an older woman. I was hardly going to marry her.'

Harry jumped in. 'Was your relationship with Sharon serious?'

Ewan shrugged. 'I was hoping we could get more serious, but she was antsy about me getting rid of Cassidy.'

'How was she at the party last night?' Dunbar asked.

'How do you know about the party?'

'She's missing,' Harry said. 'You were with her at a party last night. Your pal Bingo told us you were there with Sharon when we spoke to him.'

'Missing? What do you mean, missing?' Ewan said. Harry could see the younger man had gone stiff.

'You admit you were at the party with her?'

'Yes! We were there together. She was pissed off that I hadn't broken it off with Cassidy. I was going to, and today, after I saw you in the family room, I sent Cassidy a text telling her she was on her own.' Ewan put his head in his hands for a moment. 'Missing. Jesus Christ.' Simon put a hand on his back. 'Get off me.'

'I'm here for you,' Simon said, keeping the

cigarette holder away from Ewan in case it should take his eye out.

'Really? You approved of me seeing Cassidy?' Ewan said, suddenly sitting up straight.

'Tell us about last night,' Dunbar said, his voice sharp now.

Ewan looked away from his brother. 'We were in the flat. There were a lot of people there. I went to the toilet, got talking to a bloke from work who's on the golf team. Then a woman told me that Sharon had left. I went after her, but when I got outside she was getting into a van.'

'What kind of van?' Harry asked.

'A white one. Like a Transit. The thing is, she said her ex-boyfriend had wished her a Merry Christmas and asked her if she fancied going out sometime. He's a builder. I thought then that maybe she had called him and he'd picked her up. That was enough for me. As soon as she stepped into that van, we were finished.'

'Anybody else see her get into the van?' Harry said.

Ewan nodded. 'A woman who was at the party came down and saw Sharon get into the van. I wasn't even near her.'

'What's this woman's name?' Dunbar asked.

'Denise. I don't know her last name. We walked round by the Malmaison hotel. There's a wee all-night café there. We sat and had a coffee.'

'What happened after that?' Joe asked as if he were part of the team.

'Alright, fucking Columbo.' Ewan looked at Harry. 'We shared a taxi. She got out in Dalry. She said if it didn't work out with Sharon, she wouldn't mind going out for a drink one night. We sat and talked in the café, that's all. I wasn't too pished and neither was she.'

'Christ, you're certainly getting around,' Joe said like he was in *The Sweeney*.

'I just said, nothing happened.'

'Had you told Sharon you were finished?' Harry asked. 'Like, called her or texted her?'

'Yes. I sent her a text. Just as soon as I got into that wee café. Officially, we were no longer seeing each other, so I wasn't cheating on her if that's what you're thinking.'

'Maybe it put Sharon over the edge,' Joe said. 'God knows why, but maybe she was upset about you giving her the old heave-ho.'

'Maybe she's just away somewhere sulking,' Ewan said.

Harry wanted to slap the man. 'Her mother says

she hasn't called, hasn't been home, didn't go to work and this never happens.'

Ewan looked back at him. 'Maybe she's not used to being dumped. It happens, you know.'

'You see the pattern here. You're seeing Cassidy McLean and her daughter disappears and her friend is found murdered. You're cheating on Mrs McLean, seeing Sharon, and that lassie goes missing too. You're the link in all of this.'

Ewan poked himself in the chest. 'Me? I haven't done anything. I was here on Christmas Day with Joe here –'

'It's Dad to you,' Joe said.

'– and Simon.' Ewan looked at his brother, who nodded.

'He was. We had a nice dinner, thanks for asking,' Simon confirmed. 'Joe dozed off, but Ewan and I watched *Die Hard* and had a wee drink to ourselves. He was only away for half an hour or so. I can confirm that.'

'What is it with you pair of sods and the lack of respect?' Joe said. He moved away from the fire.

'What do you mean, he went away for half an hour? Away where?' Dunbar said.

Ewan looked at Simon and shook his head.

'I went to give Cassidy a small gift,' Ewan said. 'I went down to her house and then came right back.'

Dunbar looked at him. 'Let me get this straight: you go down to your girlfriend's house on Christmas Day with a gift, and then scarper back up here to your dad and your brother. Sorry for being sceptical, pal, but if that was me, I would have expected to stay a bit longer and have some Christmas cheer.'

'Is that a euphemism for having sex with her?' Simon asked.

'Give over, Simon. It means having some eggnog. Get your mind out of the bloody gutter,' Ewan said.

'Excuse me. But it's your fault for watching that filth on TV.'

'*The Sound of Music* is not filth,' Joe interrupted. 'That's full of Christmas cheer.'

'So anyway...' Dunbar said. 'Before we get ahead of ourselves. Tell us more about Christmas Day.'

'What's to tell?' Ewan said. 'I went down, we had a quick drink and then she said, "I'll see you tomorrow." Which was Boxing Day. I went round on Boxing Day to spend the evening with her, then she told me about Moira going missing.'

'Moira was last seen on Christmas evening. What time did you say you went round?' Harry asked.

Ewan shrugged. 'Around six thirty. Would you say that's about right, Simon?'

'I don't know why you're asking me,' Simon replied.

'Because you're the one who brought it up.'

'It *is* about right,' Joe confirmed. 'We had our turkey dinner early, then I was going to make some salmon sandwiches, and Ewan said he wouldn't be long. By the time I got the can open and made them, he was back.'

'You saw Moira then?' Harry asked.

Ewan made a face like he'd licked a cobweb. 'No. She was upstairs in her room, painting her tongue or piercing herself or something. I don't know. But she didn't come downstairs, and I didn't see Sioux either. I don't even know if Sioux was round by that time. As I said, quick drink, then up the road.'

'Tell us about this party at your friend's house,' Dunbar said.

'I had gone round to Cassidy's, but I was going to tell her that we shouldn't see each other anymore. I couldn't do it on Christmas Day, but I thought Boxing Day wouldn't be so hard. But she was upset because Moira had gone out Christmas night and hadn't come back. I didn't want to be in that atmosphere, so I left and went to the party.'

'Where Sharon was,' Dunbar said.

'Yes. She was annoyed because I hadn't told Cassidy yet. Then Sharon buggered off from the party without me, jumped into a white van and scarpered, and a woman called Denise and I sat and chatted in a café for an hour or so.'

'That's why you looked like a half-shut knife this morning,' Joe said. 'I told you the drinking would catch up with you.'

'My point being, I have alibis that prove I didn't do anything wrong.'

'I want the contact details of this woman, Denise,' Harry said. 'Ask your pal Bingo if he knows her. When we talk to her, we'll decide if we need to bring you in for more questioning or not.'

'I'll ask him at work tomorrow,' said Ewan.

'If I was you,' Dunbar said, standing up, 'I'd stay around people for a while.'

Harry stood up and he and Dunbar made their way out into the cold night air.

'I think that wee bastard is just in the wrong place at the wrong time,' Dunbar said. 'Or he's the unluckiest bastard who ever lived.'

'I think you're right. Now let's get to the chippie. Then I need to call Morgan.'

They got in the car and Harry started the engine

and then pulled out his phone. He sent a text to Chance: *Call me later and let me know how you got on tonight.*

Moments later Chance sent him a thumbs-up emoji.

'Right, let's grab the chippie and I'll shoot Morgan a text. See if she wants to come round still. The babysitter is okay with Grace for a wee while longer.'

'Go for it, mucker.' Dunbar looked out the window. 'I just hope Stewart knows what the hell he's doing.'

TWENTY-THREE

The church hall was tacked on to the back of the church itself. It was warm as they sat on the chairs in a circle. Chance McNeil was one of the last ones in. He walked along the corridor and pulled the handle on one of the double doors and slipped into the hall. One woman said hello, while a few others nodded to him.

A man was sitting on a chair in the middle of the circle. He smiled at Chance.

Chance hesitated for a moment before stepping further in and letting the door close behind him. It smelled like the gym at his high school. Musty and needing fresh air brought in.

He looked at the man in the middle. He was maybe in his late thirties, with long flowing hair, like he was trying to be a hippie and not quite managing to pull it off. He didn't look like the church's minister.

Maybe a dozen people were already seated, including Brian McLean. Chance nodded and walked over to Brian. The younger man had purposely sat away from the others, so there were empty chairs on either side of him. Chance sat down on one of these chairs without saying a word to him.

There were several women, their ages ranging from twenties to forties. And several men. Two of them in their fifties, both of whom ignored him.

The meeting started with the chairperson reading the AA Preamble, then he led the Serenity Prayer before a couple of members of the group read sections from AA literature.

'Do we have any first-timers here tonight?' the chairperson asked.

One of the older blokes put his hand up.

'Would you like to introduce yourself?'

'I'm Charlie and I'm an alcoholic.'

'Welcome, Charlie,' the group said.

'My name's Oliver,' the chairperson said. 'Welcome, Charlie. Anybody else?'

The other older bloke put his hand up. 'I'm Calvin.'

'Welcome, Calvin,' they all said.

Then it was Chance's turn. 'I'm Robert and I'm an alcoholic.'

'Welcome, Robert,' Oliver said.

'Welcome,' they all chanted.

It had been Stewart's idea for Chance to use a false name, since he was undercover. He looked briefly at Stewart and Charlie Skellett. He hadn't known that Skellett was going to be here, but Stewart worked in mysterious ways.

'Karen!' Oliver said, smiling. 'Why don't you tell us what's been happening with you this week?'

A woman who looked to be in her late thirties started talking. Chance looked at his watch. Five minutes in and then the fireworks would start.

Then, as if on cue, the door burst open.

'You bastard!' shouted the young woman at the door. 'I knew you were creeping about. Who the fuck is she?'

Chance looked at Katie as she walked in.

Oliver was on his feet. 'I don't know what's going on, but this is a meeting –'

'Shut up!' Katie screamed. 'You! You're a fucking waste of space.'

Chance put an arm up to deflect the hand that

tried to slap him. Next to him, Brian cowered away as if he was going to be next.

'What are you looking at?' Katie shouted at him.

'N...nothing,' Brian stammered and pushed himself even further away from Chance.

'I'm going to have to ask you to leave,' Oliver said to Katie.

'I'm going. I just wanted this wanker to know that we're finished! Do you hear me? Finished! You won't cheat on me a second time!'

'We can talk about this later,' Chance/Robert said.

'Later? I don't think so! You had one last chance and you blew it! Bastard! Don't ever call me again, you little fuck!' She smacked his lifted arm one more time for good measure and stormed out.

Oliver looked pale behind his beard. 'Well, considering what just happened, I think it might be prudent for us to call it a night. Don't worry about cleaning up, I'll do it later.'

They all stood up, and most of them left quickly without saying another word.

'Are you okay?' Oliver asked Chance. 'I can call the police.'

'No, no, it's fine. This was a long time coming. I'll be fine.'

'If you're sure.'

'I am. Thank you for letting me join your group.'

'Every Monday evening, if you want to come next week,' Oliver said. 'You too, gentlemen,' he said to Stewart and Skellett.

'Fuck that for a game of soldiers,' Stewart said. 'You need to get this group under control, son. I've never seen such a fucking display in all my life.'

'Me neither,' Skellett said. 'You can shove this place up your arse. No offence, but I need a fucking pint after that. How about you, neighbour?'

'Aye. I need a wee dram just to stop my fucking hands shaking,' Stewart confirmed.

Chance wasn't sure where to look. Maybe at his feet or the floor. Were those cobwebs up in the corner? Please God.

'Please don't fall off the wagon because of one little incident,' Oliver said. 'This doesn't happen every time.'

'I'll bet it fucking doesn't,' Stewart said. 'I've seen fucking football casuals be less violent than that.'

He and Skellett walked out of the hall, Skellett's walking stick clunking on the wooden floor.

'Sorry about that, Oliver,' Chance said. 'I didn't know she was going to do that. My girlfriend is jealous and very possessive. Well, my ex-girlfriend now.'

'Not your fault,' Oliver said.

Chance left the hall behind Brian McLean, who had slipped out like a punter in a strip club who'd just run out of singles.

'Do me a favour, pal,' Chance said to Brian. 'Make sure she's not hiding round the corner.'

Brian hesitated for a moment. He opened his mouth to say something, then thought better of it. Then he walked down the rest of the pathway to the pavement on the side road, Chance following him, and walked to the main road. Brian waved the all-clear.

'Thanks. Boy, that was some first meeting. But I don't think I'll be seeing her again.'

'I don't blame you.'

'My name's Robert,' Chance said, holding his hand out.

'I know,' Brian said. He looked down at the outstretched hand as if debating whether Chance had been to the toilet and not washed his hands afterwards. Then he rolled the dice and shook it. 'Brian.'

'Good to meet you, Brian. I've just moved from

Glasgow through to Edinburgh. I don't know anybody here.'

They started walking along the main road.

'What made you come here to live?' Brian said.

'Work. I'm in IT with a bank, and this job was a promotion. I've only been with them for a year, but they said I have the potential to move right up, so I took the chance. What about you?'

'I don't work. I'm in between jobs just now. There's a lot of things going on in my personal life. I just can't concentrate on things. Plus my folks kicked me out. I'm staying with my aunt down in Baberton.'

'Sorry to hear that.'

'Don't be. My dad's an arse and my mum's an alcoholic. My dad made me come here because I was drunk one night. He thinks I'm going to turn out like my mum. I only come along to appease him.'

'You got a girlfriend, Brian?'

'Not at the moment. I asked out a friend of my cousin's, but she said no.'

'Don't give up, mate.'

'It's not as easy as that. I mean...she was murdered.'

Chance stopped and Brian kept on walking for a moment before he too stopped and turned round.

'Murdered?' Chance asked.

Brian nodded. 'Somebody took my cousin and her friend and killed them.'

'Your cousin is dead too?'

Brian shrugged his shoulders. 'I mean, if he killed her friend, he's probably going to kill my cousin. It makes me feel sick that I'm staying there and couldn't do a thing to stop it. My aunt Cassidy is going mental. She doesn't know what to do. I was thinking of going home, but I want to stay with her and protect her if somebody comes for her. You should maybe go back to Glasgow, pal.'

'It's not an option.'

'You fancy coming back down the road to my aunt's for a beer?'

'A beer?' Chance asked.

'Yeah, why not? I mean, I'm not going to AA for help, just to keep my old man from kicking the crap out of me. How about you?'

Chance shrugged. 'Why not? My car's parked down here a bit. I can't get pished, but I can have a couple.'

'Great.'

'To be honest, I only joined an AA meeting to shut her up, my girlfriend. She's been going on about my drinking. I'm not an alkie, I'm just a sociable drinker.'

'Me too,' Brian said.

They walked along in the cold, talking about football and cars. And when Brian brought it up, Chance tried to assure his new friend that there wasn't much possibility of his girlfriend waiting for him.

'You live locally then?' Brian asked.

'Nah. I'm renting a place down in Stockbridge.'

'How come you came all the way to Juniper Green to go to that AA meeting?'

'A pal at work told me about it. He said that anybody can go to any of them. He had been going but fell off the wagon. I thought I would give it a try. But to be honest, I thought if I didn't like it, my girl-friend wouldn't just happen to be waiting for me outside to see if I was really there.'

Brian looked at him for a moment. 'She might be following you now.'

'She drives a little red Audi. Sticks out like a sore thumb. Trust me, I would see her car.'

Chance unlocked the unmarked police car he'd driven here in. The vehicle had been gone over to make sure there were no signs that it was anything other than an old scrapper belonging to a young man who couldn't afford much else.

'Fucking car stinks,' Chance said as the driver's door hinges creaked.

'Is this a police car?' Brian asked.

Chance paused for a second, preparing himself for a fight. 'What makes you ask that?'

'The holes in the dash. Like a radio mike was held there or something.'

'It was used as a private hire, the guy who sold me it said.'

'At least it still runs,' Brian said, putting his seat-belt on.

'Right. I know the way down to Baberton, then you can guide me from there.'

'No problem.'

Chance drove along to Gillespie crossroads and took a left towards the roundabout and then turned into Baberton Mains.

'Round the drive, down to the right,' Brian said.

Chance drove round and then Brian shouted out, 'Stop!' Chance jumped on the brakes, thinking that somebody had run out in front of him and he hadn't seen it.

'Here'll be fine,' Brian said. 'Just park on the main road and we'll walk through that wee pathway across there.'

Chance turned the engine off and they got out into the cold. They crossed over the road and went down a short pathway that led into a cul-de-sac. Brian stopped for a moment. The man who lived next door to Cassidy McLean was pulling his garage door down.

'Hello, Mr Forrest,' Brian said quickly, keeping his head down.

'Hello, son. How's things?'

'Not bad, thanks.' Brian didn't make eye contact and carried on walking towards his aunt's door, Chance right behind.

Inside, the house was empty. 'I think my aunt's away out with my dad's sister, Ruby. Cassidy is going off her head looking for Moira,' Brian said, going through to the fridge and grabbing a couple of beers.

'Where do you think she is? Moira, I mean,' Chance asked, looking around the room.

'She's weird, and mad at the world because her dad died. But he didn't die.'

Chance looked puzzled. 'I thought he died in Pitlochry?'

'He did. But he didn't just die; he was murdered. I should know, I was there.'

Chance felt the hairs on his neck stand up. 'Who murdered him?'

'I don't know.' Then Brian stared Chance in the eyes. 'How did you know Victor died in Pitlochry?'

Chance thought for a second. 'They mentioned it on the news when they reported Moira missing. They were speculating that she might be depressed over his death. They mentioned he died in Pitlochry last summer. Why? Isn't that true?'

Brian kept eye contact with him for a moment. 'Sorry. I thought you were a reporter for a minute.' He clapped his hand on Chance's arm. 'They would bug the hell out of us when Victor died. Even the old bastard next door looks at me funny.'

'You were saying about Victor being murdered.'

Brian took a swig of beer out of his bottle. 'He was. I saw it happen.'

Chance didn't drink the beer but held the bottle at his side, ready to use it as a weapon. 'Really? Who killed him?'

Brian shook his head and walked around the kitchen. 'Nobody would believe me if I told them.'

Chance risked a quick drink. 'I would.'

Brian shook his head. 'Jesus, I've only just met you. I shouldn't be talking like this.'

Chance laughed and Brian looked sharply at him. 'I've never felt so relaxed with somebody I've just met. You know how you bump into somebody in the boozer and you just click? I felt that way with you. If you want to tell me who it was, fire away. If not, no problems, mate. I'm just hoping you and I could hit the pub one night and have a wee –'

'It was the boyfriend,' Brian said, then put the bottle to his lips. 'Now you have to go. Christ, I shouldn't have said it. But I can't keep it bottled up anymore. I mean, I came to live here not realising who he was or how close to Cassidy he was. Then in he walks one night. I was petrified. I'm shaking right now.'

Chance could see the young man was close to panicking. 'Calm down, mate.'

'Can I come crash at your place? Just as a mate? They think I'm weird, but I'm not.'

'Listen, pal, my girlfriend will be there. I'll have to find a place for myself. Look, I'll give you a call tomorrow. Give me your number.' He took out his phone and Brian looked up his number. 'Who remembers their own phone number, eh?'

Brian told Chance the number.

'I might have a friend who would let me crash at his. Maybe he'll let the two of us. I'll call you tomorrow.'

'Thanks, Robert.'

Chance looked puzzled for a second before smiling, remembering his new name.

He put the beer bottle down, hardly touched, and stepped out of Cassidy McLean's house knowing who the murderer was.

Ewan Gallagher.

TWENTY-FOUR

Dunbar dropped Harry off and took the pool car.

'I'll meet Morgan sometime soon, pal, but I would feel like a third wheel.'

'If you're sure.'

'I am. I'll take my fish supper down the road, though.'

'Catch you tomorrow, Jimmy.'

Harry walked up the steps to his pathway and stopped. The night air was cold and had a dampness to it that was almost palpable. He couldn't spot the babysitter, Maria's, car. A Nissan something-or-other. It wasn't on the street. He'd called her after he'd spoken to Morgan and told her he'd be home soon.

He saw Morgan's car parked further along. He'd

called her mobile phone, so he'd assumed that she
was at home. What if she was already here? What if
she'd told Maria that she was here to take care of
Grace? What if –

The door opened and Maria was standing there.
'Hi, Harry!' she said, beaming at him. 'I was
watching for you. Grace is in bed and your friend
Morgan's here. My husband has dinner waiting.
Probably a microwave meal, but bless his heart.'

'Thank you so much for staying, Maria. Tell Tim
I said hi. I'll get him a bottle of his favourite Scotch.'

'He'll love that. See you tomorrow morning,
bright and early.' She laughed as she went past him
and he watched as she walked along the pavement
and rounded the corner. That's why he hadn't seen
her car.

Inside, his house was warm. He took his coat and
jacket off and hung them on the rack in the hallway
and carried his fish supper in. Morgan was in the
living room.

'Hi, Harry,' she said, smiling. 'I hope you don't
mind, but I was standing outside your house and
Maria saw me. She recognised me and told me to
come in. We had a quick cuppa.'

'I don't mind at all.'

She stood up and walked over to him. 'I missed

you today. I was looking forward to you coming home.'

'I was looking forward to you coming over. Sorry things ran a bit late.'

She smiled and stepped closer, giving him a kiss. 'Don't worry about it. I was used to that with David. And I promise I won't keep comparing, but I just want you to know that I understand you don't have a nine-to-five. Is that the fish supper you told me you were getting?'

Harry held up the paper bundle. 'You should be a detective.' He smiled at her.

'I'll put the kettle on, Dr Watson.'

They went through to the kitchen, where Morgan turned the kettle on.

'Decaf tea? Or coffee with a bit of zazz?'

'By zazz, you mean caffeine?'

'Yeah, caffeine, but zazz sounds better.'

'It does. I'll go for the zazz. You want half of this lot? I'm not that hungry now.'

'Okay. I just nibbled at dinner.'

'Right, if you could split it up, I'll just pop my head in to look at Grace.'

'Okay.'

He left the kitchen and made his way upstairs to the wide landing and along to his daughter's room.

Her baby monitor was on and he could see she was sleeping peacefully with the toy giraffe Morgan had bought her on the shelf close by. She moved slightly as if she knew he was there, so he gently pulled the door closed and went back downstairs.

'Is she okay?' Morgan asked.

'She's sleeping.'

Morgan had split the fish and chips onto two plates, and they took them through to the living room, put the plates on the coffee table and sat back to eat and watch TV.

'How was your day?' he asked her as they watched a documentary about ancient civilisations and how aliens had built them.

'The usual. Talking to people and letting them pour their heart out so I can help them through their day. Same stuff, different day. I started to get distracted at times, thinking of coming here tonight.' She laughed. 'Listen to me, you'd think I'm turning twenty instead of forty.'

'It's good to look forward to coming home to a familiar face.'

'I haven't had that in a very long time. Close once or twice, but it wasn't meant to be.'

'You worked in the Royal Infirmary along with David, you said?'

Morgan nodded. 'Yes. He was an Accident and Emergency doctor, while I was in the psychology department.'

'You ever hear of a man called Ewan Gallagher?'

She paused with her fork on the way to her mouth, then carried on. She ate for a few seconds as if the fish and chips would be a diversionary tactic. She washed the mouthful down with her tea.

'Yes. He works there, in the Sick Kids' lab. Why?'

'Then you'll know his brother, Simon.'

Morgan nodded. 'Is this an interrogation?' There was a slight smile playing on her lips, as if she was more than ready to go into psychological battle with Harry knowing only too well that he wouldn't win.

'Oh God, no. Sorry, I didn't mean to give you that impression.' He put a hand on hers. 'It's just that Jimmy Dunbar and I were interviewing Ewan. I had already spoke to him in connection with the case I'm working on and then we went to Ewan's house and his father and brother were there. Simon was dressed in a Fedora and holding a cigarette in a holder. They both mentioned your name, that's all.'

'He's a patient of mine,' Morgan said. 'Simon, I mean, not Joe. But I'm sorry, Harry, I can't talk about his case.'

'I know you can't and I wouldn't ask you to, but I can ask your opinion of a former colleague?'

She drank more tea. 'Yes, there's no harm in that.'

'I hate to bring work home, but there's a young girl missing, her friend was found murdered and Ewan has been seeing the missing girl's mother.'

'You think he murdered the girl?' Morgan asked him, her eyes going a bit wider.

'I'm not sure. It's early days, but there's another woman missing too. A few years older than Moira, and she's Ewan's girlfriend.'

Morgan seemed to have lost her appetite but held on to the cup of tea like it was a life vest. 'I thought you said he was seeing the mother?'

'Cassidy McLean is Moira's mother. Ewan befriended her, but I think it might have been more serious in her eyes than his. He started seeing another woman. Sharon and Cassidy are both nurses at the Royal. They know each other, and they both obviously know Ewan. So Ewan was starting to see Sharon, and apparently she wasn't happy that Ewan hadn't called it a day yet with Cassidy, and she stormed off from a party that she and Ewan were at. Then she got into a van that Ewan says belongs to her ex-boyfriend, who apparently is still interested in Sharon.'

'I didn't think Ewan would be like that. I mean, it's been a long time since I worked with him, but he seemed a decent man. I didn't see him as a cheater.'

'I think it was just a casual fling for him with Cassidy after her husband's death. He's already kicked her into touch.'

'Oh no.'

'Please keep this to yourself. Professional courtesy and all that.'

'I will, Harry. I never see Ewan nowadays anyway. I don't discuss anything with Simon either. But do you think Ewan's other girlfriend found out about Cassidy and dumped him?'

Harry shook his head. 'No, she knew about Cassidy but still wanted to go out with Ewan after he told her it was a casual thing.'

'You think her going missing is connected to the murdered girl?'

'Ewan's the connection, that's the problem.' He looked at her. 'But enough shop talk. What else is on your mind?'

She leaned in and kissed him. 'Let me go brush my teeth and we can have an early night. Unless you have other ideas?'

'As a matter of fact, I do feel a bit tired.'

She laughed. 'Fun now. Sleep later.'

TWENTY-FIVE

Chance McNeil pulled up in Katie's street, off Queensferry Road, and let his head hit the headrest for a few seconds. A young man who had been in this very car had told him who had murdered Victor McLean.

Ewan Gallagher.

The man whom Calvin Stewart and Jimmy Dunbar had spoken about before Jimmy went off to talk to him along with Chance's dad. Chance wanted to talk to his dad so badly, but he didn't want to appear immature. He took in a breath and let it out slowly before getting out of the car.

The car that had been following him pulled in behind him.

Calvin Stewart got out from behind the wheel

246

JOHN CARSON

and stood on the pavement while the passenger took his time getting out.

'Come on, Charlie, for fuck's sake. I'm freezing my nuts off out here.'

'I'm coming, Calvin. Just haud yer wheesht for a minute.'

'I've seen a tortoise moving quicker than that, and it was deid.'

'Fucking leg. Jesus, maybe one day those arse-holes will fix my back.'

'That's a poor excuse, son, if you don't mind me saying. You're making it look like you're pished.'

Chance watched as Charlie extricated himself from the car, leaning on his walking stick. He gathered that Charlie knew Calvin well to be so familiar with him. They looked like drinking buddies rather than two detectives.

Katie opened the door and light from her lobby spilled out onto the pathway, cutting through the dark.

'Anybody ready for a cuppa?' she said.

'I could do with a wee dram,' Charlie said, hobbling up the path and trying not to fall on his arse. He'd already told Stewart on the way down that it would be 'a right bastard' if he fell.

'Well, I'm not putting my own fucking back out

lifting you on your feet, fat bastard,' Stewart had informed him in the car. 'You're lucky I'm fucking driving.'

Skellett was making his way towards Katie.

'You're having fuck-all drams,' Stewart told Skellett. 'The lassie's no' operating a knocking shop here. Or a distillery. Get the kettle on, love,' he said to Katie, who smiled at Chance and disappeared into the house.

Stewart turned to Chance. 'Keep your eye on the drinks cabinet, son. Fucking Moonshine Charlie's back in town.'

'I hope *you* think you're fucking funny, because nobody else does,' Skellett informed him.

Inside Katie's house, it was nice and warm. She led them through to the living room, which was spotless.

'I could do with a coffee, if you have any,' Stewart said.

'No problem, boss. And you, sir?' she asked Skellett.

'Aye, coffee, Katie. Thanks, hen.'

Katie laughed and nodded to Chance. 'You can help me if you like.'

Stewart looked at her. 'Uh-oh, you'd better do as

you're told, son. We've seen you get a fucking skelping off her.'

'That was all acting, sir.'

'Aye, sure it was. Away and find us a Hobnob while you're at it, ya wee fucking Jessie.'

'That's not fair, sir,' Katie said, laughing.

'Aye, it is. I wish I'd filmed it. His old man would be pissing himself if he'd seen that. Getting a belting off his girlfriend.'

'It was like a fight between two stunt people,' Chance said, but Stewart raised his hand.

'Stop talking shite and go and get the biscuits.'

Chance and Katie left the room, heading off to the kitchen.

Skellett was sitting down, rubbing his leg. 'This bastard brace makes my leg itch like nothing.'

'Just drop troo and have at it then,' Stewart suggested. 'The lovebirds will be a little while yet.'

'You think so?'

'Aye. Nash and I'll keep shotie.'

Skellett stood up, put his walking stick to one side of the chair and undid his belt before dropping his trousers. He bent over in front of Stewart.

'Easy, fuck. I meant sit down and do it.'

'It's no' easy scratching my leg when I'm sitting.'

'Well, away and hide behind the fucking chair then.'

'You told me to drop my fucking troosers right here.'

'I didn't say swing your ding-dong all over the place. Just hurry up and scratch.'

Skellett hobbled round the chair with his trousers round his ankles.

'Aw, that looks fucking barry, eh? You're making a fucking meal of this. The sun will be coming up by the time you've fucked about with that thing. And I'm talking about the leg brace.'

Stewart heard the Velcro coming apart as Skellett took his brace off. 'Oh, that's good,' he said.

'Keep it down, Charlie, for God's sake.'

'I cannae help it. It's so good. I need to rub it harder.'

'I swear to God, I'll boot you in the fucking bollocks if you keep that up.' Stewart shook his head and tutted. 'Fuck's sake, my ex-wife could shave both her legs quicker than you're scratching yours.'

'I'm almost finished,' Skellett said, just as Katie walked in with a tea tray. She stopped for a second and looked at both men. Skellett stood up straight as Chance walked in.

'This isn't what it looks like,' he explained to the

younger officers. He quickly attached his brace as Katie put the tray on the coffee table.

'What you do in your own time is your business, sir,' she said with a grin.

'Aw, here, none o' that talk,' Stewart said. 'Charlie's married and I'm seeing a woman. Charlie was just –'

'There's no need to explain, sir,' Chance said. 'We're off the clock.'

'I'll give you "off the clock" in a minute.' Stewart turned to Skellett. 'You got your fucking troosers on yet?'

'They were never off. Don't be saying things like that in front of those two.'

'"They were never off,"' Chance said, using air quotes.

'Enough of your bloody lip,' Stewart said, walking away now that Skellett had his trousers up and fastened again. The two senior officers sat down on the couch.

'Sit on a chair, Charlie, for fuck's sake,' Stewart complained.

'Oh aye. Right enough. Tongues are wagging already.'

'Stop talking.'

Charlie moved chairs like they were playing their own version of musical chairs.

'Right, laddie, let's go over what happened tonight, and I mean earlier, at the meeting in the church.'

Chance looked at Katie as they each grabbed their drink. 'That was a hard smack,' he said to her.

'It was meant to look authentic,' she said, smiling.

'Mission accomplished,' Stewart said. 'I nearly shat myself. I thought she'd popped something before she came in and she was going to have a go at us as well, just for good measure.'

Chance drank some of his tea. 'Outside, Brian and I got talking. Then we drove down to his aunt's house, where he got us a beer.'

'I'm really surprised,' Stewart said. 'From what Jimmy said, that laddie's lift doesn't go all the way to the top floor.'

'He's just shy, I think. He said his dad makes him go to AA just because he likes a beer, and he doesn't want Brian turning out like his mum, who's an actual alcoholic. So Brian goes, just to show his face. Anyway, then we started talking about Pitlochry and his uncle's death.'

'Oh aye?' Stewart said. 'Did he give you a full confession?'

Chance shook his head. 'No. He told me who did it.'

The sound of a pin dropping exploded around the room as they waited.

'Ewan Gallagher,' Chance said.

More silence.

'Bastard,' Stewart said. 'That makes sense. He's been after Mrs McLean for a while, Jimmy told me. Get the husband out of the way, then move in.'

'Right now, it's just hearsay,' Skellett said.

'We should get him in for an interview tomorrow. Chance? You can stick around in Edinburgh in case we need you again. Both you and Katie can come along to the MIT incident room and observe.'

'Great, sir,' Chance said.

'However, it's going in my report that you didn't bring the Hobnobs through with my coffee.'

'It's not like you need any more biscuits,' Skellett said.

'I think you've done enough damage tonight, Charlie,' Stewart replied. 'That lassie will have to go and get her eyes checked out. You nearly blinded her, parading about in your fucking skids.'

'Like I'll ever listen to you again. I should have just gone to the lav and done it.'

Stewart shook his head. 'That's the thanks I get.'

TWENTY-SIX

Joe Gallagher zipped up his jacket, making sure his scarf didn't get caught in the zip. 'You sure you don't want to come round to the golf club for a pint?' he asked Ewan.

'I've had enough beer to last me a lifetime. Or at least until the weekend. I'll just stay in my room and watch TV.'

'You sure? Some of the boys are going to be there,' Joe said.

'Don't you think I've been pished enough these past couple of days?'

'I suppose so. Take your liver out and put it in the dryer. Give the poor bastard a chance.' Joe left the living room. 'Don't wait up!' He went out.

Then Ewan heard the front door open again. 'You forget something?' he said.

'No,' came the terse reply. It wasn't Joe. Simon walked into the living room, his face looking like a well-skelped arse.

'I didn't realise you had gone out,' Ewan said to his brother.

'I just slipped out the back way.'

Since their garden was on a slope, there were stairs at the back of the extension that led out to the back door. Simon had come down his stairs and carried on down the back. Creeping about like a bloody housebreaker.

'Where did you go?' Ewan asked.

'I went for a walk. I felt I needed some cold air to clear the cobwebs.'

Oh, the porno store still open this late? Ewan thought, keeping it to himself.

'Right. What you doing now?'

Simon looked dishevelled; something wasn't quite right about him, like he'd been running for a bus just as the driver pulled away from the stop, laughing.

'I'm just going up to my room. I don't want to be disturbed.'

'When do we ever disturb you?'

'I'm just saying.' He walked through to the back of the house where the stairway led up to his bedroom.

When Ewan heard the door close, he put his jacket on and left the house, closing the door quietly.

He started the car and thought that it was warmer outside than it was in here. The streets were wet with the remnants of the previous snowfall lurking about like a bad rash.

The drive down to Cassidy's house didn't take long and he took it easy going round the main road. He parked near the short pathway that led into Cassidy's cul-de-sac and locked the car before going through.

He looked over to Jock Forrest's living room window and saw it was in darkness. Then he stood and looked at Cassidy's window. Same result. Darkness. She was either upstairs sobbing her heart out after their split or she was out on the lash with her pals.

He cursed himself. How could he have got himself involved with her? Why had he thought it was a good idea to pursue her? Because she was available? Vulnerable? That meant he had taken advantage of her. Though when he thought back, he recalled her kissing him first. True, he had put himself in front of her, but he hadn't forced her to do anything.

Still, he admitted, he was a lousy bastard.

He was about to turn away when he saw her front door was ajar. Had she gone in and forgot to push it shut behind her? Maybe she'd brought a man home and they had been in such a hurry to get upstairs that they hadn't pushed the door all the way closed.

Ewan felt his blood rush. He had no right to be jealous, he knew that, but he was here to tell her he wanted to give it another go. Maybe she would slam the door in his face, finally closing it properly. Or maybe she would throw herself at him. Or throw *something* at him.

He'd never know if he didn't tell her how he felt.

Which was what exactly? he asked himself. *This isn't the time to be nit-picking.*

He walked up her path and climbed the couple of steps to the front door and listened for a moment. No sounds of two human beings cavorting upstairs. No TV, no kettle boiling. No sound at all.

He gently pushed the door open. It glided open silently, and he stepped in, ready with his line about worrying about her. If he came face to face with a hairy-arsed biker running about starkers, he would pretend he was a Jehovah's Witness, the first one in history to make it over the threshold. Then he'd give him a lecture about the sin of fornication. Maybe. If the bastard was carrying a knife – although why he would be carrying a knife when he was in the scud didn't figure in Ewan's thought process – he would turn around, tell him that he was forgiven and then run like fuck back to the car.

But there were no bikers in the house, hairy-arsed or otherwise. One thing Ewan *did* notice was that the house was bloody freezing. He stood in the small hallway, debating whether he should close the front door or not. It would keep the heat in if he did but would hinder his escape if said biker was waiting in the kitchen to belt him with a frying pan. Better to think of fighting a man with a frying pan than one with a carving knife.

He closed the door. From what he knew of Cassidy's tastes, he didn't think she was into bikers. If she did have a boyfriend, then he might be in with a fighting chance if her dead husband was anything to go by. Thin and weedy with a big mouth.

Ewan walked into the living room. There wasn't a sound coming from anywhere. No lights, no TV playing, no music, no nothing. Even the tray table had scarpered.

He carried on through to the small dining area and the kitchen on the right, and then he saw the back door leading into the garden was open. It was the wind making itself known. It wasn't a hurricane, but it was coming in gusts, flapping a newspaper that had been left on the counter top.

Where was Brian? He thought he heard a noise behind him and spun round, all thoughts of a fight out the window. This would definitely be flight. He liked Cassidy, but she wasn't worth having his face rearranged for.

He walked over to the kitchen door. There was another door that led back into the hallway, but the door that caught his eye was tacked on to the side of the detached garage outside. The gate that joined the garage to the house at the driveway was banging. With one last look into the house like a man about to jump overboard, Ewan stepped out onto the concrete steps that led onto the paved patio. He walked across to the gate and clicked it shut.

That was when he noticed the garage door was slightly ajar. Was Brian in there watching instructional videos? How to disembowel your aunt's boyfriend?

Ewan reached over and unlatched the garden gate again, just in case. Then he stuck the toe of his boot into the crack between the garage door and the frame. It moved open, and now that he'd started rolling the snowball down the side of the mountain, there was no stopping it.

Quietly poke his head in or shock and awe? No, the first one. No point in giving the bastard a heads-up. He opened the door wider, fully expecting to see Brian up to no good.

He stepped into the darkness.

TWENTY-SEVEN

'It's only been a couple of weeks,' Dr Kate Murphy said.

'Look, love, no offence, but you're a pathologist. Your job is to deal with punters after they've had their last hurrah,' said her live-in boyfriend, DS Andy Watt. He was in his fifties and had been stuck at sergeant level for years because of his runaway mouth.

'Cheeky sod. And offence taken. I'm still a bloody doctor. And I'm all for you going out with your pals again, but I'm advising you to take it easy. Take a taxi there and back, no dancing on the tables, no taking wee hoors home.'

Watt laughed at her London accent. 'You shouldn't use the word "hoors", honey. It just isn't right. Besides, you're the only...' He stopped when he saw her staring at him. '...woman for me.'

'I'd better be, Andy Watt.'

'Don't be talking like that. Look, I'm meeting Frank for a few beers. There's going to be an empty seat that would have been filled by Paddy Gibb, so we're going to toast him a bit.'

'Andy, you were run down by a bloody maniac and almost killed. If it hadn't been for our neighbour coming round the corner, that car would have reversed over you and finished the job.'

He laughed. 'I know. God didn't want me upstairs yet. Probably thinking, *I'm going to leave you down there for a while, you fat bastard. Piss off a lot more people yet before I come for you.*'

Watt was silent for a moment. He knew he had a long way to go, not just physically but mentally. Knowing who it was who had tried to kill him had taken its toll.

'At least that bastard had the decency to do what he did.' It was the millionth time he had mentioned the fact that one of his would-be killers had hanged himself in prison while he was awaiting trial. The other one was still languishing inside, getting fed three meals a day, and didn't have any broken bones. Which Watt would have remedied if he could.

'Now we have to concentrate on you getting better. You're lucky you didn't need surgery on your broken wrist or femur. Not to mention your fractured ribs.'

'Let's not forget the dislocated shoulder,' Watt said. 'That bastard ended my police career prematurely.'

'You're getting a nice pension. Time for you to be taking it easy.'

'God knows what I'm going to be doing with my day.'

'You could always read a book,' Kate suggested.

'Can you honestly see me reading a book?'

Kate dismissed the idea as ridiculous. 'How could I be so absurd?'

'Listen, lady, I've read books before.'

'They're called police manuals.'

'Anyway, as much as I'd love to stay and chat, my friend is coming down in a fast black and we're going for a pint.'

'I could drive you,' Kate said. 'I would sit in the corner of the pub and mind my own business.'

'As much as I love you, you'd have to pour me through the sunroof and toss my crutches in afterwards. How you would ever get me out is another matter.'

'Just promise me you'll be careful, Andy.'

He hobbled over to her on his crutches. 'I will. I'll be fine.' He kissed her gently. 'It's just a couple of pints.'

'Right. I'll come down with you.'

'No, you won't, Kate. I have to do this on my own.' Watt had had nightmares where the car had driven right over him. He had woken up in a sweat many a night.

Kate saw him to the door of their flat and opened it for him. He took a few tentative steps into the corridor and hobbled along to the lift. He pushed the button and waited for it to arrive. Then the doors slid open and he walked inside.

It was only when the lift was going down that he took out the little get-well card that had been tucked inside his pocket. It was dog-eared now that he had read it over and over a thousand times.

He read it one more, then put it back inside his jacket, the words rattling around inside his head: *You won't be so lucky next time.*

TWENTY-EIGHT

DI Frank Miller loved his wife, Kim, more than anything, and his daughter, Annie, and his stepdaughter, Emma. His whole family. But it didn't stop him thinking *What if?* sometimes. Like today, when he had told his wife he was going in early to the office. Technically, it wasn't a lie. He would end up in the office early, but he wanted to do a quick detour first.

He stopped at Tesco on Broughton Road and bought a bunch of flowers. He didn't know what the bunch consisted of, but they had nice colours to them. He knew two types of flowers, three if you included the thistle. Sunflowers and roses were a snap, but what were all these other things? He had no clue. Just like when he was reading a book and the writer was mentioning trees. First of all, who gave a shit? And second, how did they find out what trees grow where and what they look like? He hated padding in books. His father, Jack, was living with an American writer, Samantha Willis, and she wrote fast-paced thrillers with very little crap in there.

He was standing waiting to pay for the flowers, knowing he was hesitating. *Why?* he asked himself. *You should be excited, not nervous.* Was it because he was lying to Kim?

Of course not. He was a free man. He could do what he liked. Sort of. Kim might have a different opinion on that, but he didn't answer to anybody.

'Sir?' The female cashier was smiling at him, a gesture that might not be there at the end of her shift when the Mr and Mrs Nobodys had come through her checkout lane and pretended they were royalty, giving her guff.

'Good morning,' he said, keeping hold of the bouquet and letting the girl scan the barcode with her hand-held scanner.

'Good morning. Are those for me?' she said, her smile wider.

'Alas, I have to say no. Another time and place, they certainly would be, but today I have to give them to another lady.'

'Aw. Maybe next time. They're beautiful. Very festive. I see rose, chrysanthemum, carnation, gypsophilia, statice and ornamental cabbage. They do a great job with the bouquets at this time of year. She's very lucky. She must be worth it.'

'I certainly think so.'

She rang him up and smiled as he left. Maybe he wouldn't be all alone if Kim kicked him to the kerb, he thought, but then focused on what was at hand.

He got back in the car and drove round the one-way system. He had forgotten there was a Lidl on Logie Green Road now, where an old furniture warehouse used to stand. It was incredible the changes going on in Edinburgh now. Round the corner from Lidl was a whole bunch of new flats sitting on what was once B&Q. Which were next to flats that sat on ground that used to be occupied by Powderhall Stadium.

He knew his mind was racing now, and he could feel the nerves in his gut going. Visiting another woman, some would say. Cheating on your wife, others might think. They would all be wrong.

He drove round to Canonmills and headed up the main road to Inverleith and turned into Warriston Gardens. He slowed down at the cemetery gates, driving past the house just inside the entrance, then turned left.

The grass was covered with the remnants of the last snowfall. He turned off the engine, got out and walked down the track towards the grave he was looking for.

He stopped in front of it and gently laid the bouquet down in front of the stone marker. He read the names for what seemed like the millionth time. Carol Miller, his first wife. Harry, his unborn baby son.

'I'm sorry I'm late this year, sweetheart. Things were busy. Paddy Gibb died. It's a long story and I'll tell it to you when it's warmer. Andy Watt got badly hurt and he'll take a while to mend, and his career's finished. He's out on medical retirement. I'm part of a new MIT since Paddy is gone. It's led by Harry McNeil. They're a good bunch. We've moved to Fettes now that the old High Street building is up for sale. All departments will move now. Annie's doing great. You would have loved her. Like I would have loved our little boy. I know I'm married to Kim now, but I miss you. I wish we could have spent the rest of our lives together. I hate the way you left. I wish it could be different.'

He stood in silence as the wind cut through the

cemetery like a knife. He felt his nose getting red and he took a cotton hankie out and wiped it.

'I'll be back soon. Love you.' He heard a distant *Love you too*, but maybe it was just in his mind.

He turned away from the gravestone and trudged back over the grass to his car. What would Kim say if she knew he was coming down here? He didn't care. Carol had died in the line of duty and she had been a spectacular detective. She and Miller had worked together, working with his father, Jack, when his old man had been a DCI.

He got back in the car and drove round in a square, heading back out of the cemetery.

He drove along Inverleith to the Fettes Station at Comely Bank. He was way early, but that didn't matter. He had things to think about.

Like who still wanted Andy Watt dead.

TWENTY-NINE

Harry was rapidly thinking of giving himself the nickname *The Magician*. It perfectly described how he was learning to juggle life in his house. Get breakfast started for himself and Grace, get her ready for the day and try to fit in time to eat the toast and drink his coffee.

Morgan came downstairs, dressed for work.

'Morning,' he said.

'Good morning.' She leaned in and kissed him.

'I didn't want to disturb you, so I showered in the main bathroom.'

'You could have woken me up for that,' she said, grinning. 'But at least let me make the coffee.'

'Already made. I wasn't sure what you would

want to eat. I usually have toast or cereal. I'm not a big breakfast eater.'

'Thank you.'

'If the coffee's cold, you can put it in the microwave to heat it up a bit.'

'I just love your gourmet kitchen,' she said, taking a sip of the coffee he'd put out for her. 'It's just right.'

'Just right, or you don't know how to use my microwave?' he said, smiling at her.

'Just right, smarty-pants.'

'I aim to please.'

Morgan smiled at Grace and waved her fingers at her as Harry finished giving her breakfast. 'Maria will be round shortly, then I have to get into the office.'

'Busy day ahead?' she said, then gently slapped her forehead. 'Of course it is. You have a murder on your hands and a missing girl to find.'

'It does keep us on our toes,' he said, hoping it didn't come across as sarcastic, but it did. If she noticed, Morgan didn't say anything. 'What about you?'

'First one will be there at nine on the dot.'

'Are there any days when you don't have any patients to see?' he said.

Morgan shook her head. 'No. I'm fully booked. I could maybe squeeze in one or two new patients if need be, but I have a pretty full book, as it were.' She sipped more coffee and looked Harry in the eyes. 'It's Lizzie Armstrong. I'm only mentioning it as she's the daughter of...well, you know.'

'How is she doing? Are you allowed to tell me?'

'I can't go into specifics, but she's a voluntary patient at the hospital. She doesn't feel safe, Harry. Every shadow has a hidden killer in it. Every noise makes her jump. She's a nervous wreck after what happened.'

'Will she ever improve?'

'That's up to her mind and how much it will allow her to improve. Everybody's different. It's only been a few weeks, but I see her three times a week. She'll get there, slowly. She can come and go as she pleases, but she doesn't leave often. She feels secure in there. She went Christmas shopping, though. That was a step in the right direction. She smiled when she found out one of her abductors hanged himself in his prison cell. It was a weird comfort, knowing he won't be able to hurt her again.'

'Can she be sectioned?'

'We'd only keep her there against her will if we

thought she was a danger to others or herself, but Lizzie presents no signs of either.'

Harry looked at Morgan for a moment, his mind drifting back only a few short weeks. A lot of things had happened to him personally, and to people he knew.

'I hope she can work through it all,' he said. 'She deserves it.'

'I'll help her all I can.' She drank some of her coffee. 'Can I talk to you about something?'

'Of course you can.'

Just as she was about to speak, the doorbell rang. 'Hold that thought. That will be Maria.' He left the kitchen and answered the door. A minute later, he came back with the babysitter.

'Hello, Morgan,' Maria said.

'Hi, Maria. Would you like a coffee?'

Maria laughed and tilted her head sideways at Morgan. 'Listen to her. Coffee. I don't have time for that.'

'Maybe next time.'

'I'd love that, but young miss here has a busy day ahead of her. Don't you, sweetheart?' Maria smiled at Grace and got her giggling. She lifted the baby out of her chair and started fussing, getting her dressed. 'Uncle Tim is off today and we're going to the park for a wee while. So we'll be well wrapped up, won't we, my little chook?'

Grace laughed as she put a bunny's ear in her mouth.

'Right. We'll be off. Just let me know if you'll be working late, Harry.'

'I'll be here,' Morgan said.

'Righty-ho.'

Harry walked out with Maria and watched her walk to her car with his daughter before closing the door.

'Now, more coffee, or do you want to have some more fun?' Morgan said.

'Neither, sweetheart,' Harry said, looking at his watch. 'I have to get going. Oh, you wanted to talk to me about something.'

'It can wait.'

'No, it can't. I have time for a quick chat.'

'It's about my ex-husband. David.'

He was going to ask her how many ex-husbands she had but kept his mouth shut. 'Okay, I'm listening.'

She looked down at the floor for a second before lifting her chin. 'I wasn't completely honest with you.'

Several things went through his mind all at once.

Was he really dead? Was he still around and in her life?

'I think that a relationship is built on trust and that trust has to be built on honesty. I've nothing to hide, and I don't want you hiding things from me. If you want to be honest about something, now's the time to do it.'

'David didn't go for a bottle of Coke on that Christmas Day ten years ago. He was going to see his girlfriend.'

That wasn't the answer Harry was expecting. He had to stay quiet for a few seconds while he processed the information. 'His girlfriend?'

Morgan nodded. 'He was cheating on me. I knew about it. I'd caught him out in a lie a couple of months before and he promised me it would stop. I believed him, but he just got cleverer.'

'How did you know he was going to see this girl-friend at Christmas?'

'Because he told me.'

Harry blew out a breath. 'Was your marriage over at that point?'

'Not before that. Christmas was ruined, but he didn't care. Apparently, he even bragged about her at the golf club. So that night, he went to see her. He took his car and they had a drink, and they were going to leave together. Her husband had left. He had found out about the affair and had left her. Now all David had to do was come back for his stuff and move in with her. But the drink was too much. It had impaired him and he hit the bridge at Colinton.'

He reached out and put his hands on her arms. 'I appreciate you telling me that.'

'That's not all,' she said and Harry let go.

'Okay.'

'The woman he was going to see? His girlfriend? They worked together. *We* worked together. She was a nurse in the hospital. Still is. Her name is Cassidy McLean. I just thought you should know this. I didn't want it to come back and bite me later on if you found out and I hadn't told you.'

'I appreciate that.'

She smiled at him. 'That was the real reason I left the Infirmary and went to the Royal Edinburgh.' She slowly shook her head, as if thinking back to that time and where she would have been now had her husband chosen a different path to go down.

'Not all men are alike,' Harry told her. 'Is that why you were asking me those questions when we met in the pub all those times?'

'Not at first. It was just conversation. But then I

was starting to really like you, so I asked some probing questions. I was worried.'

'You don't have to worry anymore.'

'I'm glad.' She kissed him. 'Tonight?'

'See you after work,' he said, and then they left together.

THIRTY

DCI Tony Burns was standing by the passenger door of the pool car when DS Craig Benini decided to show himself.

'Naw, that's alright, son. I'll just stand here drinking my coffee and freezing my tits off waiting for you to finish your phone call to whatever wee floozy you're calling.'

'Floozy? What's that, boss?'

'You fine well know what I'm talking about. Get the shagging car open before my coffee turns into iced coffee.'

'For your information –'

'Car open!'

' – I was calling somebody on another matter altogether.' Benini unlocked the car and they got in.

'This bastard's freezing. They need to be in a garage, not sitting about outside like this.'

'Maybe when we move they'll have our cars inside.' Benini grinned at his boss.

'Don't talk shite. We're going down to Fettes to be near Harry McNeil and his crew. And all the other specialist departments.'

'Don't they have an underground car park there?'

'Aye. And they have valet parking too.' Burns shook his head. 'Maybe they have flying cars so we can land on the roof. Have a robot park it for us.'

'You've taken that too far.' Benini started the car.

'It's you. Fucking gibbering. I think I have hypothermia, I was waiting that long. When I said, I'll see you downstairs, I stupidly thought you would be behind me thirty seconds later, not dialling a porno line.' Burns sipped his coffee.

'Where did you say we were going?'

'Fuck's sake. Attention span of a badger's bellend. Down to Fettes. Not for the move, to speak to Harry McNeil. Maybe you should have called a fucking hearing aid hotline.'

'You could have just called him,' Benini said, reversing out of the parking spot.

'Since when did you start making the decisions?'

Benini looked away and made a mee-mee-mee-mee-mee sound, pulling a face to go with it.

'I heard that,' Burns said, trying not to put his coffee about himself. 'This is why I get extra milk. So it won't take my face off when you have the fucking car upside down.'

'Still need to bring an extra pair of Y's when I'm driving, sir?'

'Don't be a smartarse. I'm sure I hear you in the broom cupboard, chanting and waving incense about just to help with your driving skills.'

'Don't forget my wee voodoo doll. If you feel a pain in your arse, that's me.'

'Don't be talking like that in front of anybody, for God's sake.'

Benini laughed as he headed down towards Fettes Station at Comely Bank. Burns sat back in his seat and tried not to think about Benini's driving being like a roller coaster, but it was hard.

THIRTY-ONE

Ewan Gallagher lay back in bed and wondered how soft the prison mattress would be compared to this. Would he be on the top bunk or the bottom bunk, where a gang of rampaging killers would storm in and fight over who got to go first?

Harry McNeil was a complete bastard, he just knew it. And forget about that weegie radge, Dunbar. Ewan could just tell the man was itching to bring out his baton and have at it. No matter what way he looked at it, Ewan thought he was fucked.

So far this morning, there had been no sound of car doors being closed, or the front door being blootered off its hinges before polis with machine guns stormed the house.

He wanted to call Cassidy, ask her if they could

talk, but he knew there would be screaming and crying and hysterical gibbering. And that was just him. If she'd got home and seen what he'd seen, then half of Police Scotland would be at his door already. So why weren't they?

Ewan suddenly sat up in bed. He knew why: she wasn't home yet. She had stayed out overnight and she would be coming home today to find the horror show in her garage. But what if she hadn't gone in there? Of course she had. He had left the house just the way he had found it, with the back door and garage side door open. His fingerprints? *Yes, of course they were in the house, Officer. I was her boyfriend.* Semen? Well, they had slept together, but he had hardly sprayed it about the bedroom walls. Fingerprints in the garage? No way. He had eased the door open with his boot and hadn't touched anything after he saw what was lying there. He'd watched too many true-crime shows to be stupid about it. On shows like *Law and Order*, the detectives kept their hands in their pockets, so that's what he had done. That and stood stock still, not because he didn't want to leave a DNA trail but because he had nearly shat himself.

At that point in time, he had expected to see blue flashing lights and hear shouts of 'Don't move, ya bastard!' from some big burly sergeant with a baton and a radge Alsatian.

But nothing came, so he had taken the opportunity to once again utilise his steel toecaps and open the unlatched gate and sneak out along Cassidy's driveway, only stopping briefly, at the edge of the house, to make sure the coast was clear. As he walked up the pathway towards the main road, he felt like he had a huge target on his back, but no shouts, screams or threats came his way.

He had never felt so relieved in his life to get in his car. He had driven like an old granny going to church, just slipping over the speed limit. He didn't want any following police patrol to think he was dead on the speed limit because he was pished.

But he had got home in one piece and gone to his room. The only sound after that was Simon going up to his room and banging about up there like he had suddenly got it into his head to buy a Punch BOB freestanding kick dummy and was beating the crap out of it with a piece of furniture.

Then his father had come home the worse for wear, singing and banging into things as he tried to take his jacket off. He was the reason they couldn't have nice things.

After that the house had gone quiet. Simulating

prison after lights out. This was what Ewan imagined a cell would be like, except he hadn't woken up with a sore arse.

He got out of bed and showered in his en-suite bathroom.

There was nobody in the kitchen. He looked at the stairs that led up to Simon's room and the stairs leading down to the garage. They were filthy. Christ, Simon might be daft, but he wasn't that daft he couldn't use a brush. He'd have a talk with him later on.

Meanwhile, Ewan would call Cassidy on his way to work. He'd call in the car because he would get more privacy there, and he could tell her she was breaking up if things got out of hand and then end the call and just not answer if she called back.

He had a cup of coffee and left the house.

———

'Is he gone?' Brian McLean asked, sitting on the edge of the bed.

Simon Gallagher was lying on the floor with his ear to the carpet. 'I'm not sure. I think so.'

'Why don't you use a glass to listen?'

Simon lifted his head and looked at him. 'Is that what you do?'

'No. I'm just saying.'

Simon shook his head and put it back down on the carpet.

'Right,' he said, getting up. 'I heard the front door close. Ewan's gone to work.'

'What about your dad?'

'I heard him singing last night so he was well wasted. He won't surface anytime soon.'

'For a drunk man, he could play a good game of chess. I lost three pounds twenty to him.'

'At least you still have the shirt on your back.'

'So how do we solve this problem?'

'We figure it out later. Meantime, I have to go and see somebody.'

THIRTY-TWO

'Where is that wee bawbag?' Calvin Stewart said. 'I hope he's not been up to his usual carry-on with Lillian, or else Vern will take his baws off with a chainsaw.'

'I'm sure he's minding his P's and Q's,' Dunbar said.

They were walking into the incident room at Fettes. Frank Miller was at a desk, sitting with a coffee.

'A'right, Frank, son?'

'Doing well this morning, sir, thanks.'

'Where's Hairy-baws?'

Both Miller and Dunbar looked puzzled as to which member of the team had that new nickname. With their powers of deduction, Lillian and Julie were ruled out, but anybody else was fair game – Elvis, Skellett, Harry or Evans.

Harry walked into the incident room. 'Morning, sir,' he said to Stewart. 'Jimmy.'

'Morning, son. Where's Hairy-baws?'

Harry looked puzzled.

Dunbar exchanged a look with Miller. Elvis or Skellett?

'Elvis is in the canteen getting a roll.'

'Is he now? That's fabulous. Maybe if he feels like it, he could join us later.'

'He's been in since six,' Miller said.

'Really?' Stewart said. 'Nobody likes a show-off. That just leaves Hairy-baws.'

'Charlie,' Harry, Dunbar and Miller said at the same time.

'How do you know he's got hairy baws?' Elvis said, coming into the incident room and holding the door open.

'You missed the bit when I said nobody likes a fucking show-off. Add smartarse to that remark. I was generalising. And shut that door, you're letting the heat out.'

'There's heat in the corridor as well,' Elvis said. 'And I'm keeping it open for DI Skellett.'

A few seconds later, Skellett hobbled in. 'Thanks, son.'

'Why are you sweating like a paedo?' Stewart said.

'Hello? Walking stick alert,' Skellett answered, shaking his stick. 'You should try walking with this bastard and watch the bus driver laugh at you as he fucks off.'

'Aye, well, I just hope you didn't have your troosers round your fucking ankles on the back seat of the bus.'

Robbie Evans and Lillian O'Shea walked in.

'Here's wee Hairy-baws now,' Stewart said, solving the mystery.

'I like the new nickname, sir, but can we just stick to Lily instead?' Lillian said to him.

'That's funny, but it might come back round to bite you in the arse. And glad you could join us, by the way.'

'We've been here with DI Miller, sir,' Evans said. 'We just stopped for a quick coffee. Been here since six.'

'You, early? That'll be a first.'

'It's true, sir,' Miller said. 'Julie and I were in early.'

Julie nodded her agreement. 'Bright and early, sir.'

'Right then, laddie, stop fucking faffing about like you're a greeter in Asda and get the kettle on.'

'Coming right up,' Evans said.

'Oh, by the way, Tony Burns and his partner are coming in from Standards,' Harry said. 'I just want him to check –'

Stewart held up a hand. 'No need to explain to me, Harry, son. This is your show. We're here in a back-up capacity. If Jimmy there hadn't been at the scene of Victor McLean's death, we wouldn't be here at all. Just do what you have to do. Then we can go over what young Chance and Katie were talking to us about last night. Where are they, anyway?'

'Canteen. Waiting for you to turn up. They were in early too.'

'If I was Chance, I would have been rolling over for a bit of a cuddle, if you know what I mean.'

'Aye, well, we're no' all machines like you, Calvin,' Skellett said.

'This is true.' Stewart looked at Harry. 'When are you talking to Burns?'

'He sent me a text. He should be here in about five minutes.'

'Right. I'll be sitting at a desk waiting for my

coffee. If Evans pulls his finger out of his hole, I might get it by lunchtime.'

Chance and Katie came in, swelling the MIT crowd.

'Morning, son,' Harry said. 'Hi, Katie.'

'Morning, sir,' they both said.

'Right, lad,' Stewart said. 'Tell DCI McNeil what Jack the Ripper told you last night.' He looked at Harry. 'That's Brian McLean, in case you didn't get it.'

'Thanks for clarifying.'

'Nae bother. Right, Chance, the floor's yours.'

Chance looked around at the other faces in the room, then explained what had happened at the AA meeting the night before. 'Then Brian told me something: Ewan Gallagher killed Victor McLean.'

'Is that exactly what he said?' Harry said.

'He didn't name him, but he said "her boyfriend" killed Victor. As far as we're aware, Cassidy McLean only has one boyfriend.'

'Not anymore,' Harry said. 'He jacked her in.'

'Okay. But Gallagher wasn't her boyfriend last summer when Cassidy McLean's husband died. Maybe Gallagher wanted the husband out of the way, so he killed him.'

Harry nodded as Evans came across with the coffee for Stewart.

'Thanks, son,' he said.

'DCI Burns is coming down here. They're starting to close down the High Street Station and there's a lot going on there, with moving things, so he asked to come down here for a bit of peace when he's working on the project.'

'Spill the beans then, Harry,' Stewart said, sipping his coffee.

'I talked to a neighbour of Cassidy's, Jock Forrest. He said he used to be in the job. I just wanted some background on him.'

'Okay. Keep us in the loop on that. Meantime, let's pick Brian McLean's life apart, then somebody go and get him and bring him in for questioning,' Stewart said.

Dunbar took a step forward. 'We also need a follow-up for the CCTV footage in Leith to see if we can spot the van that Sharon Boyle got into.'

'We need a timeline for Moira McLean and her pal too,' Skellett said. 'If they were out and about, we need to find somebody who saw them.'

'Moira was a drinker,' Miller said. 'Only turned eighteen but already into spirits as well as beer.

Maybe we can find somebody who supplied her and Sioux.'

Just then, the incident room door opened and Burns and Benini walked in. 'Good God, it's like a football game just got out.'

'Aye, we were all brainstorming while you were out gallivanting getting a coffee, Tony,' Stewart said.

'It's High Street Station pish, sir.'

'Right, get on with what you have to do.' Stewart seemed to have forgotten what he'd just said about this being Harry's show; his seniority just kicked in. 'I want somebody to find this ex-boyfriend of Sharon Boyle's. Bring him in if need be.'

Harry took Tony Burns aside as Craig Benini gravitated towards Robbie Evans and Lillian. They went into Harry's office before Stewart could claim it.

'Thanks for coming down, Tony.'

'Any time, Harry. What is it you want me to access?'

'Have a seat.' Harry pointed to his own chair at the desk, facing the computer. Burns sat down after taking his overcoat off.

'I want you to look up the record of a retired officer. Nothing specific, I was just interested in what sort of an officer he was.'

'Do you know where he was based?'

'No.'

'When he retired?'

'No.'

'What rank he was?'

'No.'

Burns looked at him. 'Please tell me you know his name.'

Harry laughed. 'Of course I do. It's Jock Forrest.'

'Jock Forrest? You sure?'

'Yes. You know him?'

'Know him? Yes, I know him alright.'

'What kind of officer was he?' Harry asked.

'He was one of those know-it-all types. A bit strong-handed; that's why he got some complaints against him. It's the reason he couldn't become a regular.'

'What do you mean, couldn't become a regular?'

'Just what I said, Harry. He wanted to become a regular, but his record showed he wasn't fit for anything other than a special.'

'He never mentioned that part obviously.'

Burns looked at the computer screen. 'Nope. He was eventually booted out after being heavy-handed again. It says here that he worked in the Sick Kids' hospital.'

'Alongside Ewan Gallagher.'

'If you say so, squire.' Burns sipped his now cold coffee, made a face, then put it back on the desk.

'Ewan's the young man we got a tip about,' Harry explained. 'I've already spoken to him twice about this case. His name keeps cropping up. He's been trying to tell us that Cassidy McLean's nephew is a psycho, and it was starting to sound like it after we spoke to a few people. But what if he's just weird? What if Gallagher's involved in all of this but was trying to divert our attention? That would make much more sense.'

'You should go and bring him in, mucker.'

'I think we'll go and lift him in front of all his workmates. Just to put a bit of pressure on him.'

Burns stood up and grabbed his coat, and Harry shook his hand. 'Thanks for going through your system.'

'Any time, pal. Get a pint soon?'

'Count on it.'

Harry appreciated his friend accessing the Professional Standards intranet, which only team members of Standards could get into, for obvious reasons.

They went back into the incident room.

'Come on, DS Benini,' Burns said to his

colleague. Benini was standing chatting to Robbie Evans about a party in Glasgow on Hogmanay.

'I'll be there. I put in for time off the following day,' Benini said to Evans.

'Good man. You and your girlfriend can stay at my place.'

Burns and Benini left the room just as Dunbar walked up to Evans. 'Stay at your place? You live with your old maw.'

'I meant Vern's place. We can all crash there.'

'You'd better hope, son.'

Evans grinned. 'She won't be able to resist my charm.'

'If I was a betting man...'

Lillian held up a piece of paper. 'I have an address for Sharon Boyle's ex-boyfriend. I got it from Sharon's mother.'

Harry looked at her. 'Go with young Robbie and have a word with him. If he's not at home, find out where he works. Apparently, he's a builder.'

Harry joined Frank Miller and Charlie Skellett at the whiteboard.

'Let's see. Ewan Gallagher is in the middle of all this. He goes hiking with his father and brother to Pitlochry last summer and Cassidy's husband dies. Ewan's there, as DCI Dunbar witnessed. Then he starts to become friendlier with Cassidy, because he works beside her in the hospital. Not in the same department, because she's a nurse, but in the same building. He eventually takes it to the next level with her, and then he starts seeing another nurse, Sharon Boyle, who works beside Cassidy. Suddenly, Cassidy's daughter goes missing with her friend, and the friend, Sioux, is found murdered. Anybody else see a pattern here?'

Elvis stepped up. 'When this Gallagher guy is finished with Cassidy, he wants to end it with her, and divert the attention away from that, he abducts the daughter and the daughter's friend and kills the friend. Now Cassidy is hysterical, and even if he hasn't told her yet, he's preparing to, and when she's at her lowest ebb, he dumps her. By text message. But the other nurse, Sharon, isn't happy with him not telling Cassidy it's over, so she revs him up. Maybe he thinks that she isn't the one after all and abducts her too.'

Harry looked at him. 'Good thinking. But also, I have it on good authority from a source that Cassidy had an affair ten years ago.'

Calvin Stewart walked up. 'Maybe this Gallagher spoon got wind of it and thought he wasn't so much the golden boy as he thought he was and got pissed off at Cassidy and decided to punish her by taking her daughter.'

'Could be,' Elvis said.

Chance and Katie were sitting at desks, observing. 'I can't wait to get into MIT,' Chance said.

'CID first, son,' Stewart said. 'But it won't be long for you both.'

'Thank you, sir.'

'Just because I'll be away to pastures new, doesn't mean I won't still be in touch.'

'I appreciate it,' Katie said.

Harry stepped away from the board. 'Right, let's get going. I can take Jimmy and Frank to go and lift Ewan Gallagher. Lillian, go and talk to the ex-boyfriend. While we're at it, let's bring Brian McLean in under the guise of him helping us with our enquiries. We'll do that before we bring in Gallagher. You never know, he might crack and give us a confession. Or tell us he's been working with Ewan Gallagher all along.'

'I can go with Elvis and Lillian,' Stewart said. 'You wouldn't mind that, eh, son?'

'I'm supposed to say no at this point?'

'You're picking it up quickly. Lillian, you can drive since the wee man here is still recovering from his battered ribs.'

'I'm on the mend now, sir. Ninety per cent. I can drive.'

'Come back when you're a hundred per cent. I don't want to end up under a fucking bus.'

'I'm not that wee,' Elvis said, turning away from Stewart.

'I can call you Knob-end instead of Wee Man, if you like?'

'No need to start throwing the knob word about, sir.'

'Right, get your coats. You're going for a ride with Uncle Calvin.'

'Well, that doesn't make you sound like a paedo,' Elvis said in a lower voice to Lillian.

'I'm no' fucking deef, ya wee midget bastard.'

Lillian laughed as she put her coat on. 'You did poke the bear,' she told Elvis on their way out.

'I'll stay here with DI Skellett,' Robbie said.

'Good lad,' Dunbar said. 'I'll go with Harry to Baberton, then to the hospital.'

'Right then, let's get going. Busy day ahead,' Stewart said. And they went their separate ways.

THIRTY-THREE

'Hi, honey,' Ruby said to Jock Forrest as she stepped over the threshold.

'Hi. I thought you would have been round sooner,' Forrest said, stepping back to let his friend in. She turned to kiss him, but he turned away from her.

'I stayed at my own place last night and Cassidy stayed with me. She's just shaken up.'

They went through to the living room.

'That was a bit silly, wasn't it? I mean, what if Moira came home, hurt and scared? She could have come to me, but that's not the point. That was a bit irresponsible, wasn't it?'

'I didn't think of it that way, Jock.'

'You really need to screw the nut. I found that

out in the polis. You didn't get to where I was by not screwing the nut.'

Ruby put a hand on her chest and took a breath. 'I honestly didn't think.'

'At times like these, you need to think, Ruby. But anyway, I want to have a word with you.'

'What is it, love?'

'Sit down first.'

Ruby sat down in a chair. 'Is there something wrong? Is this the "it's not you, it's me" speech?' she said, giving a nervous little laugh.

'Of course not.' *Not quite.* 'I've been thinking about things, Ruby. I've had a good time, I really have, but I'm going to sell up and move to Spain. I'm retiring soon and I don't want to spend my twilight years in the cold. I'd rather be burning my bum in a warmer climate.'

'That's great, Jock! I can come with you,' Ruby said, jumping to her feet. 'We can do whatever we like, whenever we like. Have drinks in the sunset. Walk on the beach –'

Forrest held up a hand. 'Whoa there, Ruby. I'm not denying that we've had a good time together, but you're talking about spending the rest of our lives together.'

'I know! It's exciting, isn't it?'

'Not exactly. Listen, I'm going on my own. It's been fun, but I think we should call it a day. I'm selling my house and then I'm out of here.'

'Oh, come on, Jock. I know you can't get it up...'

'Jesus.'

'...but sex isn't everything.'

Maybe I just can't get it up for an ugly old boot like you! He kept the thought to himself. 'I'm sorry, Ruby, but I've made up my mind.'

Her face fell, and a different version of her came out. The real one. 'Well, you can fuck right off then!'

And there we have it, he thought. *Would the real Ruby McLean step into the room?*

'Look, Ruby –'

'Don't you fucking "look, Ruby" me! You've just been using me!'

'Using you for what? We were friends. That was it.'

'You make me sick.'

Forrest smiled inside as she stormed out. She couldn't accuse him of using her for sex, since they'd never had any. He just didn't want to be around her anymore since it wasn't going anywhere. He only wished he'd done it before Christmas so he hadn't had to buy her a present. Still, Argos jewellery wasn't that expensive.

He watched her walk out his front door without closing it.

He smiled. One part of his plan complete. Now to move on to the next part.

THIRTY-FOUR

Andy Watt had enjoyed the pint with his old boss last night. He'd always admired Frank Miller, since back when he and his future wife, Carol, had joined CID. Watt knew the young copper had what it took to be a detective. Both he and Carol had been superb detectives.

Then Carol had been killed in a ransom drop gone wrong.

It had shaken the whole team. Miller's father, Jack, had been the DCI in charge at the time, and it was something he never forgot. Watt missed Carol too. It had been like losing a daughter.

Being on crutches made Watt feel like less of a man, not to mention more vulnerable. He had thought about telling somebody about the flowers and the threatening card that had come with them, but he hadn't. He had told Kate that they were from the office and she had no reason to doubt him. After all, the person who had tried to kill him was in prison now, awaiting trial. The accomplice was dead. Why should Kate worry if there were no threats?

He came out of the stairway's main door, thinking that a circus acrobat couldn't do any better. Holding the door open while trying to get his crutches round was no easy feat.

He had talked to Dr Burke up at the Royal Edinburgh about the feeling he had when he stepped out of the safety of the apartment building. At first, Watt hadn't been happy about going to see the shrink, but it was a requirement of the force now that after such a trauma with an attacker an officer had to have a mental well-being session. Or as many as he or she wanted.

Watt had been three times. Today was his fourth.

He wanted to be able to walk out into the cold light of day without wondering if somebody was going to kill him. When he was on the force, he'd had so many threats that if he had written them all down, he'd have been able to wallpaper his lavvy wall with them. It was different back then. He had a team behind him, he was fit, he carried a warrant card and a baton. Now he had none of those things. He was on crutches, as helpless as a toddler.

He was damned if he was going to live his life in fear.

Kate had said that he should get a taxi up to the Royal Edinburgh and he had agreed, but it was a waste of money. He would get buses, then he would have a couple of pints to himself in the Canny Man's on Morningside Road before getting a taxi home.

He stood in the cold at the side of the building on Hutton Road, where the accident had happened. No, where the attempted murder had taken place. Let's call it what it really was. He heard a car rev up on the main road and he froze for a second. Crap. He'd thought he was getting over this, tensing up whenever he heard a car's engine getting louder. It was something Dr Burke was helping him with.

Watt kept telling himself that his attacker was in prison.

Then who wrote the card?

He hadn't received anything else while he was in hospital or in the mail. Maybe it was some nutter.

Another thought had come to him: what if they hadn't got all the members of the group who were killing people? One dead, two in prison, and one of those two had now taken his own life. That left one still in prison. But what if they had missed one? Another member of the group who was hiding in plain sight?

He had been going to mention it to Frank, but he didn't want to come across as being some conspiracy nut.

He shook his head. Maybe he had been reading too many crime novels recently. Besides, this was daytime. It was light, a time the night crawlers didn't like.

The street was a wide lane between his building and the hotel next door. Plenty of room for a small van to gather speed in a short amount of time.

Watt heard the engine revving, but there were always vans round here, drivers delivering goods to the hotel or workmen doing maintenance or some such thing.

He didn't figure on a killer sitting behind the wheel of one.

Didn't figure on that killer sitting waiting for him.

He hobbled on his crutches, walking in the middle of the road, heading for the pavement. He was careful because the cobbles were slick and wet.

He was concentrating so hard, he didn't see the van coming towards him from behind.

Didn't hear the engine revving hard. Not at first. Just at the last minute, when he turned round and saw the vehicle bearing down on him.

He hobbled more, looking round, his heart exploding in his chest. He knew, he just knew in that instant that the person who had sent him the flowers with the threatening card had come back to finish the job.

He looked at the driver through the windscreen, at the smiling face, and knew he had been right all along. Except he would never be able to tell Frank, or Kate, or anybody else.

The van hit him with full force, throwing him through the air. He landed with a sickening thud, his crutches scattering.

The pain was incredible, like nothing he'd ever experienced. But he was alive. *Hold on, Andy,* he told himself. *Hold on.*

Then the van's reverse lights came on.

THIRTY-FIVE

Harry pulled in to the side of the road, blocking Cassidy McLean's driveway. The patrol car pulled in behind him and parked and he watched the two uniforms get out.

'Fuck you!' a woman shouted, coming out of Jock Forrest's house next door. 'And what do you fucking want?' she asked Harry.

'Nothing that concerns you,' he said, walking up the path and ignoring her. He knocked on the door.

'You forget your key?' Cassidy asked, yanking the door open. 'Oh.'

'Mrs McLean, you know who I am. This is DCI Dunbar.'

'How do,' Dunbar said as the two uniforms stood back.

'Can we come in and have a talk with you?' Harry asked. 'Privately?'

'Yes, of course.'

'I'll be right out here,' Ruby said, 'freezing my tits off, but never mind.'

'Go home, Ruby. I'll be fine,' Cassidy said.

'Right, I will. But when that wee bastard chops your head off, don't come running to me.' Ruby stormed off, sticking up two fingers in the direction of Jock Forrest's house as a parting shot. She got in her car and booted it away.

'Ruby's just had a lot on her mind,' Cassidy said. 'It doesn't look like her relationship with Jock is going to make it through Hogmanay.'

They entered the house, Harry instructing one of the uniforms to stand by the front door, the other by the back door.

'Would you like a coffee?' she asked.

'Thank you, no.'

She led them to the living room, where there was an array of magazines lying about the place. 'Grab a seat,' she said.

Just like in Bingo's flat, Harry had some cleaning to do before he could sit down on the couch. He saw a folding TV tray table in a corner with a towel draped over it. The towel looked like it had been used to dry a pig that had been wrestling in mud. What part of the pig's anatomy it had touched he didn't want to think about.

He and Dunbar shared the chore of moving the magazines onto the floor before sitting down. Cassidy sat on a chair.

'Did you find her?' she asked, tears starting to come down her cheeks. 'Is she dead?'

'We haven't found your daughter,' Mrs McLean,' Dunbar said. 'We were hoping Brian could help us with our enquiries.'

'Brian? How would Brian be able to help you?'

'We have information that indicates he might know something connected to the case,' Harry said.

Cassidy sniffed and looked at him. 'Know something? You don't think he was involved in Moira disappearing, do you?'

'We just need to talk to him. Is he in?'

'I literally got home a few minutes ago. I haven't been upstairs.' She stood up and walked past them to the bottom of the stairs. 'Brian! You up yet?'

Harry and Dunbar stood up.

'I thought you told me he sleeps on the couch?' Harry said, remembering their conversation at the hospital.

'He did. He's been sleeping upstairs in Moira's

room. Let me go and see if he's up yet.' She barged past the uniform and thudded up the stairs.

'That's convenient,' Dunbar said.

Then an ear-splitting scream shattered the quiet. The uniform was fast, Harry would give him that, thudding up the stairs and taking his baton out, followed by the older boys, who weren't quite as lithe.

Harry wished he worked out more, while Dunbar wished the bloody woman had a stairlift.

The other uniform left his post and stood at the bottom of the stairs, either to fend off any attackers or run like fuck.

When Harry and Dunbar got to the top of the stairs, Cassidy was standing in her bedroom doorway, her hands lifted to her face. The uniform had gone in to have a look. He'd go far, as long as he wasn't touching stuff.

'Holy fuck,' Harry heard the man say, then he came back out, hand over mouth in the classic pose of police officers everywhere. He went into the toilet and closed the door, all thoughts of not transferring his fingerprints gone out the window.

Harry gently moved Cassidy to one side and looked at what she had screamed at. Her daughter was lying on Cassidy's bed, what remained of her face a bloody mess. Harry assumed it was Moira McLean, but he would defer opinion until the pathologist confirmed it.

The young girl's face was exactly like Sioux's had been, smashed in beyond any recognition of it being human. As lacking in medical qualifications as he was, Harry could tell she hadn't been murdered here, due to lack of blood, but some remnants of her face and head were lingering about on the bedroom carpet.

Cassidy was screaming into her hands as she slid down, back to the bedroom door. 'Oh no, God, no,' she kept repeating as she hit the floor.

'Come on, Mrs McLean, we need to get you downstairs,' Harry said as they heard the toilet flushing. The uniform came out with bloodshot eyes and water still on his chin from when he'd rinsed and spat.

'Sorry,' he mumbled.

Dunbar put a hand on his shoulder. 'I need you to keep an eye on things with your partner down there. Secure the scene for us, pal. Can you do that?'

The man nodded gratefully. Dunbar had been there, done that. He got on his phone and called it in. Control would spring into action, alerting everybody who needed to be alerted.

'Leave me alone,' Cassidy said, shrugging off Harry's hand.

'What's going on?' Jock Forrest said from the front doorway, trying to get past the uniforms, who were barring entry.

Harry left Cassidy and let Dunbar have a go at convincing the woman she needed to move. He went downstairs to talk to Forrest.

'Do you know who I am, son?' he heard Forrest say. 'I was on the force. I'm one of you lot. That's my girlf...friend in there.'

Harry came into view as he reached the bottom of the stairs.

'Harry McNeil. He'll vouch for me. What's going on in there?'

'I can't discuss the situation, but I'd like a word anyway,' Harry said, moving between the two uniforms.

Forrest stepped back on the path. 'What's wrong up there?' he said in a lower voice, as if Harry had just put on a show so he could tell Forrest what was really going on. 'So, what's up?'

'I meant it when I said I couldn't discuss things,' Harry replied.

'You know I was on the force, son. It's not like I'm one of those awful plebs.'

'You were a special constable.'

Forrest looked affronted. 'A special?'

'Come on, Jock. It's all on record.'

'I know it is. I was just agreeing with you. But being a special meant doing the job just like a regular. I was part of a team.'

'Until you got booted out.'

Forrest tutted and shook his head. 'Because some moaning bastard complained that I hit him. I fell on the guy, that's all.'

'You didn't tell me you worked beside Cassidy. Or Ewan Gallagher.'

'You didn't ask.'

Harry mentally kicked himself. It was true; he had assumed that Forrest was retired.

'Anyway, we have an ongoing incident that I can't talk to civilians about,' Harry said, turning to walk away.

'Fine. You won't want to hear about who I saw lurking about here last night.'

Harry turned back to him. 'I'm all ears.'

'Now you're all ears. Well, maybe it's left my mind now.'

Harry stepped in closer to the older man. 'You were on the force. You know how it works. I can make your fucking life a living hell. Have random patrol cars pull you over. Have a wee drink at Baberton golf club then drive home? It's not far, but between there and here, you'll be running the gauntlet. And I will damn well make sure there's an increase in patrols up there after we get a tip-off about drunk drivers leaving the club –'

Forrest held up his hand. 'I said "maybe", but now I find that isn't the case. You see, Harry – you don't mind me calling you Harry, do you? – I don't want to get anybody into trouble. Especially somebody I know.'

'Jock, if you know something and you're keeping it back, it's not going to end well for you.'

'I know, you just said. Let me finish. I happened to look out of my living room window last evening. I sit with just an LED light on. One of those RGB bulbs you can put low colours on. Because it's easier on my eyes, not because I'm a...'

Nosey old bastard.

'...curtain-twitcher, but I think more along the lines of being security conscious. And there he was, standing outside of Cassidy's house.'

'Who?'

Forrest hesitated for a moment. 'Ewan Gallagher.'

'What time was this?'

'Eighteen oh six.' He looked at Harry. 'PM,' he added, in case Harry hadn't connected the evening part with the time. 'Skulking about outside her house he was. I watched him go in, and then about five minutes or so later, he was back out.'

Harry turned round at the sound of more police vehicles coming into the cul-de-sac, fast.

'Did you see any weapons on him?' he asked, turning back to Forrest.

'Nothing obvious. How did she die?'

Harry didn't say anything for a moment. 'I can't discuss that.' *How did you know it was a 'she'?*

'Thanks, Jock, you've been a great help.'

'Keep me in the loop, Harry.'

'I will.' *Fuck you.*

He turned to the uniformed sergeant who had got out the lead car from Wester Hailes.

'DCI McNeil, MIT. Inside is DCI Dunbar, Glasgow Division. There's been a murder. We're not sure if she was dumped here or not, but it's more than likely. Get a door-to-door started, see if anybody saw anything. It's a working day, so there might not be many people about.'

'Yes, sir,' the man said, and Harry turned once again to see Jock Forrest stop on his top step and lift a fist in solidarity.

He saw Dunbar come down the stairs with Cassidy. Harry told one of the uniforms to go in with her and the other one to make tea.

'Sir,' said one of the uniforms guarding the door, 'I was standing guard at the back door before we ran upstairs, and it looks like it had been muddy then wiped up. Then I saw that towel draped over the tray table.'

'Show me.' Harry followed the uniform in through the other kitchen door from the hallway.

'Is the back door locked?'

'Sorry, I didn't try it.'

'No problem.'

Harry pulled on a nitrile glove and tried the handle. It was unlocked. He stepped out into the garden, which he imagined would be a little suntrap in the summer but was just another square of Balticness right now. If that was a word. He saw the garage door was ajar and stepped forward. He nudged it with his foot and opened it.

And stepped into the abattoir.

THIRTY-SIX

'Change of plan,' Calvin Stewart said. 'Pull over to the side of the road.' He was on the phone and sat in the back listening. 'Fuck me. Right, I'll get right onto that.' He disconnected the call.

'That was Charlie Skellett. He's running the incident room. He got a call from Harry McNeil. Cassidy McLean's daughter, Moira, has just been found bludgeoned to death.'

'Whereabouts, sir?' Lillian asked, keeping the car in neutral.

'In her mother's bed. Somebody planted her there. Charlie and Robbie Evans have been doing some background research for us as we head to see Sharon Boyle's ex-boyfriend. Guess what?'

'What?' Elvis said.

'Fucking guess.'

'The ex is dead.'

'How did you know that?' Stewart asked.

'Robbie just texted me.'

'Wee bastard. I hate that. Somebody beats you to the punchline. Well, if you're such a fucking know-it-all, what else?'

'We need to find Ewan Gallagher, but he isn't at work. Chance sent me a text.'

'Just drive, Lillian, before I blow a fucking stack here.'

'You did ask,' Elvis said in his own defence.

'Elvis, son, if you were on my team in Glasgow, you'd be responsible for rinsing fucking mugs oot.' Stewart looked at Lillian. 'Get the ice cream van music going, Lily. Baberton Crescent. Unless you know any better, fucking show-off?'

Elvis shook his head. 'I'm all out of useless trivia. Except for one thing,' he said as Lillian booted it with the sirens and lights on.

Elvis kept looking at Stewart.

'Sake. Go on then, let's pass the time by listening to drivel,' Stewart said.

'How many senior detectives does it take to screw in a lightbulb?'

'Shut the fuck up,' Stewart said.

'I don't know,' Lillian said, smiling.

'Don't bloody encourage him.'

'Six. Five to screw it in and one to shout, "Hurry up, ya bunch of lazy bastards!"'

Lillian laughed.

'You just made that up, ya wee bastard,' Stewart said. 'I'm going to kick you square in the fucking nuts when we stop this car.'

THIRTY-SEVEN

Charlie Skellett sat back in his chair and debated whether to take his trousers down and get the leg brace off for a quick scratch or not. There was only one lassie in the office, young Katie, but he thought he could bribe her and Chance to go to the canteen to give him time to get his breeks down, then whip them up again. Bob's your uncle.

The only drawback was, those raging psycho bastards in the drug squad wouldn't take it too kindly if one of their female officers walked in and he had his troosers round his ankles again. Mind you, Katie had already seen him do that, but her gaff was different from the office. He didn't want her to think he was some kind of deviant. Right, lavvy it was.

'Who wants to make a phone call?' he asked.

Chance put up a hand.

'It's no' a prank call,' Skellett elaborated.

Chance put his hand down and Katie put her hand up.

'Magic. I need to go to the lav and adjust my leg brace.'

'Who do you want me to call?'

'Sick Kids',' Skellett answered.

'And tell them what?'

'The hospital, Katie, the hospital. Ask if Ewan Gallagher is working today. If he is, tell him we need to speak to him and to make himself available.'

'Won't that alert him, sir?' Chance asked.

'Son, they just found his girlfriend's daughter mangled in her house. I don't think a phone call from us is going to spook him. If he's not already running, he should be. But if he is in, tell him we'd like a word. Then we'll go in with armed response in case he takes a benny.'

'I'll get right on it, sir.'

Katie made the phone call and eventually got through to Ewan Gallagher's lab.

'He's not in today,' Bingo told him. 'He's on holiday. Lucky sod. He and some other members of staff play golf, so they're going to their golf club to plan some golfing trip. You a friend of his?'

'Fine. Thanks,' Chance said, not wanting to get into a big conversation over it. He turned to tell Skellett, but the DI had left the incident room.

'Call Calvin,' Katie said.

'Good idea.'

THIRTY-EIGHT

Julie was driving when Frank Miller got the phone call.

'Sir, it's Sergeant Dickson from the station. I think you'd better come down to Holyrood. There's been a fatal accident.'

'Who is it?' Miller said.

'I'd rather you come and make a positive ID, sir. But be warned, it's a nasty one.'

'Give me your exact location. We'll be there in ten.'

'Bottom of Holyrood Road, sir. Next to the hotel, in the alleyway.'

Miller hung up and he felt his heart racing. 'Julie, give it the biscuit. There's been an accident down at the bottom of Holyrood Road.'

'Holyrood? Where Andy lives?'

Miller could only nod as Julie put her foot down.

Weaving through the traffic, they saw the group of police vehicles and ambulances at the bottom of the road, with a uniform directing traffic. Miller got out into the biting cold and walked across to the sergeant who had called him.

'Tell me,' he said to the man, who had been walking towards him but then turned to keep pace with Miller.

'I thought you would want to know right away, sir.'

'Just tell me, for fuck's sake,' Miller said in a low voice, looking at the blankets that were covering the still form in the lane.

'It's DS Watt, sir. He was run over again. This time it was fatal.'

Miller stopped for a second, feeling like he had been punched in the gut and all the air had left him. The whole world spun, and he thought for a moment that he was going to be the next one lying on the road. He felt a strong hand grab his arm.

'I've got you, boss.'

Miller took a few deep breaths and nodded. Only then did the sergeant let go. If anybody else noticed, they didn't say. They were all too busy.

Tarps were being held up by firefighters who had attended.

Julie sidled up to Miller's side and stood close to him. She looked at the uniformed sergeant and nodded. Team work.

'You're sure it's him?' Miller said, his voice gruff.

'Ninety per cent, but as I said, I wanted you to be the one who formally identified him, sir. Unless you prefer for me to make that call.'

'No, no, I'll do it. He was a friend to me. A good friend.'

'It's messy.'

Miller walked round the firefighters and looked at the ambulance crew standing near the body. He walked forward and one of them lifted the blanket covering Watt's face. Miller noticed the crutches Watt had been using were lying some way away from him.

'Take it off all the way,' he told the paramedic. He could see there were other sheets and blankets under the grey one the man was holding. The paramedic and his partner then took the other coverings off.

The scene was like something out of a horror movie. There were tyre marks on Watt's shirt where a vehicle had run right over the top of him. Blood was everywhere and Watt's eyes were open, as if staring at Miller, saying goodbye. Julie stood slightly behind her boss.

The uniformed sergeant walked over. 'Witnesses say the van knocked him down and then reversed over him before driving forward over him. We went through the pockets to see if we could find ID, and he had a wallet. We also found a card in his pocket. This is where it gets creepy.'

Miller noticed the sergeant was holding a polythene evidence bag with a card in it. The sergeant held it up for Miller to read: *You won't be so lucky next time.*

'Jesus. I had a pint with him last night and he didn't say a thing. Why couldn't he have told me if his life was in danger?' Miller looked at Julie.

'Andy was a proud man. Maybe he thought that he could work it out on his own.'

'Aye, he was a stubborn old bastard.' He took his phone out and took a photo of the card through the polythene and nodded to the sergeant.

'I'll have to go and talk to Kate Murphy, his girl-friend, at the mortuary.' He turned to Julie. 'Would you mind staying here?'

'Not at all. Do what you've got to do, sir.' Julie couldn't hold her tears back any longer.

THIRTY-NINE

Dunbar cut the call from Calvin Stewart. 'Harry, this is your show. Stewart's been diverted to Ewan Gallagher's house. Sharon Boyle's ex-boyfriend's been dead for six months.'

'She was spinning Ewan Gallagher a line then?'

'Looks like it. Using a wee bit of psychology: if you don't want me then my ex will take me back. I'm not sure if she knew he was dead, but I presume so. Ewan Gallagher's not at work, so Stewart's going to his house up in Baberton with Elvis and Lillian. He wants you there too. I'll keep an eye on things here. Wait for forensics and the pathologist.'

'Thanks, pal.'

'Nae bother, son. You would do the same for me.'

'Just keep an eye on that old bastard next door. I don't trust him.'

'Will do.'

Harry walked back to his car, turned it around and headed back out to the main road. He drove north, cutting out at Wester Hailes before going up to Baberton itself.

His phone rang.

'Hello?' he said through the car's speakers.

'Harry, it's Frank. Andy Watt's dead. They ran him over again, but this time they finished the job.'

Harry was silent for a moment. Two huge pieces of information were shooting towards him at once. 'Andy Watt. Jesus. Whereabouts?'

'Down where he lives. In the lane next to his flat. He's a right fucking mess, Harry.'

'Christ. How do you know it wasn't an accident?'

'There was a small card in his inside pocket, like you get with a bunch of flowers. It read, "You won't be so lucky next time." It looks like the card wasn't new, as it was a bit dog-eared. I think somebody sent him a bunch of flowers in hospital and he didn't tell anybody about the card.'

'Christ almighty, I can't believe it.'

'Harry, it means that we might have missed some-body. We thought we'd got all the members of the

group, but we didn't. Somebody's hiding in plain sight. We need to watch our backs. Somebody's maybe trying to finish the job that was started.'

'You think from prison?'

'That's what I'm thinking. They had contact with a lot of bad people, so it wouldn't be too much of a stretch to try and get to us, even while they're in there.'

'Well, only one now, Frank.'

'This could have been arranged before the other one died. We could be looking at a hitman. A professional.'

'Christ, that's all I need in my life.'

'You and me both. Just watch your back. I'll see you later back at the station.'

'Take care, Frank.'

Harry drove a short distance along Lanark Road before turning right into Baberton Crescent where Stewart and an armed response team were waiting.

Harry pulled up alongside Stewart and wound his front window down. 'Hi, Lillian. Sir. I have some bad news: Andy Watt was murdered this morning. He was run over again, in the same spot outside his building.'

'What? Bloody hell. Do you think the mastermind is pulling the strings from prison?'

'That's what Frank thinks. Andy had a card in his pocket from a florist. There was a threat on it, and he probably got it in the hospital but didn't tell anybody.'

'Christ, we could have all protected him if he'd let us know,' Elvis said from the back.

'Anyway, let's go and see if Ewan Gallagher has killed anybody else.' Harry took off and the other vehicles followed.

FORTY

Frank Miller had been to the mortuary many times before, but never for something like this. The wind felt colder and sharper as he pressed the buzzer at the side of the receiving door.

Gus Weaver smiled as he unlocked the door and stood back to let Miller in. 'Come away in, Frank. I'm back doing mornings just to help out around here. I jumped at the chance, considering I was sitting at home twiddling my thumbs. Retirement...' Weaver stopped for a moment. 'You okay?'

'I need to speak with Kate, Gus.'

'She's in her office. Will I tell her you're here?'

Miller shook his head and walked away across the receiving area. Through the glass window, he saw Kate standing up from her desk.

'Frank! If you're coming to see me, it'll have to wait. I just got called out to a scene down the road.'

'Let Jake deal with it. I need to talk to you.'

'Wait, what's going on? You're scaring me.' Her London accent was thicker now.

'This is the worst part of my job, so I'll do it quickly. Kate, I'm sorry to tell you that Andy was killed earlier this morning.'

The scream would have brought the house down had Miller not reached forward and grabbed hold of her. She held on tightly, sobbing so hard her whole body was shaking. Miller didn't know how long she held on like that, but it felt like hours.

When she finally pulled away from him, her face was red and puffy, her eyes bloodshot. 'How...how did it happen?'

'This is hard, but you need to hear it. He was run over. This time witnesses saw the van reverse over him.'

Kate's breath caught in her throat. 'You think... you think the job was finished? They actually had the balls to finish the job they started?'

'I think they did. Even from inside prison. We'll leave no stone unturned in this, Kate. If they were responsible, then we'll find out.'

'There's only one left, I thought.'

'This job could have been rolling before they went to prison. Somebody on the outside paid to take Andy out.'

'Oh God. I can't believe it. How do you know it wasn't somebody else with a grudge?'

'There was a florist's card inside his jacket pocket with a threat written on it. It looked like it had been read over and over; it had the usual creases like when somebody puts one away in a pocket. From the hospital, I think – unless you know of him getting flowers since he got home?'

'No, he didn't. Only in hospital.' She started sobbing again. 'Oh, Frank, what am I going to do?'

'You're going to be strong for Andy. And you're going to take extra care. I can have Neil McGovern have a bodyguard follow you. Even better, you can be taken to a safe house outside of Edinburgh. Just in case. I know there's one in Fife where you'll be safe.'

Neil McGovern was in charge of a government witness protection office, and was Miller's father-in-law. Kate Murphy hadn't always been Kate Murphy, and now she was in witness protection.

'I know Neil will insist on me having a body-guard and I won't fight him on that, but I don't think I'm a target, Frank. I think you are. Their plan went sideways, so they might be pissed off at you and Harry McNeil. Enough to come after you.'

'I thought the same thing. We're going to have to be vigilant.' *Or draw the bastard out.*

First of all, a call had to be made to the prison.

FORTY-ONE

'What're you doing home?' Joe Gallagher asked his son.

'I just decided to take another day's holiday. I know I keep that place running, but I need to recharge my batteries.'

'For somebody who's on holiday, you look like somebody pissed in your cornflakes.'

'There's something wrong, Dad. I'm scared as hell.'

'You know you can talk to me about anything, son.'

'I know. The thing is, I saw something that I might get the blame for and it wasn't me. I know I should have reported it to the police, but if I'd made the phone call, I wouldn't have been able to talk my way out of it.'

'Well, maybe you can talk to them now,' Joe said, looking out of the living room window. 'I wouldn't be lippy to the boys with the guns, though.'

'What? Oh fuck, no. Christ, I told you they would think I murdered her.'

'What? Murdered that lassie Sioux?'

'And Cassidy's daughter, Moira.'

Ewan hung his head and walked along the corridor to the front door and opened it before one of the uniformed patrol could smash it off its hinges.

'Morning, cock,' Calvin Stewart said. 'I would make introductions, but you already know Harry McNeil. For the record, I'm DSup Calvin Stewart. A nice, friendly copper who goes by the rule book. Or your worst fucking enemy if you yank my fucking chain. And if you think you can batter us with a putter, go ahead and grab it. These guys are Red Alpha Victor, which in polis slang means wee bits of metal are already in there and they'll take your knob right off. Now get back in the fucking hoose.'

'Oh, please come in,' Ewan said sarcastically, turning and leading the posse into his house.

Stewart, Harry, Elvis and Lillian followed to the

living room, while the uniforms stood guard outside. The ARU team went in behind the detectives.

'You can't just come bursting in here like this!' Joe said, putting on his best indignant tone.

'Hardly bursting in,' Harry said. 'Your son just invited us in.'

'Did you?' Joe looked at Ewan.

'Yes.'

'Oh. Okay then. Anybody for a cuppa?'

Nobody took up the offer.

'Oh well, just me then. Unless it was me you came to see?'

Stewart shook his head, either dismissing the old man or showing his displeasure.

'Right, Ewan, sit down and relax. We want to ask you some questions. And keep your hands where we can see them, son. I'm no' saying the boys have itchy trigger fingers, but if you come at us, you'll no' be writing postcards home from prison,' Stewart said.

Ewan sat down without complaining. 'I know why you're here,' he said.

'Go ahead and tell us,' Harry said, sensing there was no more threat. He indicated for the ARU men to wait outside. Elvis and Lillian stood in the doorway, Elvis keeping an eye out in case Joe went berserk.

'It's about Moira, isn't it?'

'Is it?' Stewart said, and he and Harry sat down, keeping their distance.

'It is. She's dead.'

Harry and Stewart exchanged a look.

'How do you know that, Ewan?' Harry said.

'I saw her lying in the garage, dead.'

'In the garage?' Stewart said.

'Yes. She was lying there in the dark. With...no face.' Ewan shook his head and tears ran down his face.

'What were you doing round there?' Harry asked.

'I went down to see if Cassidy would give me another chance. There were no lights on. The front door was ajar, so I went in. The back door was open. So was the garage door. I went in and this...thing...was lying there, holding a putter. It wasn't Moira anymore.'

'If you couldn't recognise her, how could you tell it was Moira?'

'I assumed. I didn't get close and I didn't stay long. I knew if somebody saw me, you would think I killed her.'

'Somebody did see you,' Harry said. 'Cassidy's neighbour, Jock. Your workmate.'

Ewan looked at Harry. 'Bastard. We all get on like a house on fire, and he would drop me in it. Christ, we're all on the work golf team, we're members of Baberton. We socialise down there, even though he's a bit older than us.'

'Us?' Stewart said.

'Me and Crawford Ingram. He lives down in Baberton Mains too. We work in the same lab, all three of us. But Crawford and I have known each other for the longest time. We're best buds, in and out of work.'

'Wait...you said a putter was in Moira's hands? If it is indeed Moira,' Harry said.

'Yes, a putter.'

Harry looked at Stewart before looking back at Ewan. 'She wasn't found in the garage, and there wasn't any putter.'

'Then maybe Brian moved her,' Ewan said.

'No, he didn't,' Joe said from the hallway. He took a sip of the coffee he'd made for himself.

'What?' Ewan said a half second before Harry and Stewart said it.

'Come here, you two.' Joe stepped aside and two men came into view, Brian McLean and Ewan's brother, Simon.

'What's he doing here?' Ewan said, standing up and pointing to Brian.

'He's been staying here,' Joe said.

'Are you joking?'

'Nope. He was supposed to be staying at Cassidy's, but it got uncomfortable. He stayed one night, but that was it.'

Ewan put a hand on his face for a moment. 'How? How did Brian...? How did this happen?'

'We're friends,' Simon said. Gone was the Fedora and the cigarette holder. 'We met up at Pitlochry and got talking about chess. So we constantly play matches. We became friends. Brian's kipping on the couch in my room.'

'It's a big room,' Joe explained. 'Attic conversion. The two lads were here all last night. I played a game with Brian before I went to the golf club. And when I came back.'

'And when you got back?' Stewart asked.

'We had another game. The boys had a surprise waiting for me. A new chess set. I'd had a couple of beers, but I wasn't drunk. Luckily for me, Ewan's pal Crawford was at the golf club, and he wasn't drinking so he gave me a lift home. He's a good lad.'

'I met him at the lab,' Harry said, eager not to let go of the story from Brian and Simon. 'You know,

Brian, some people think you could easily have killed your cousin.'

'It's because I'm quiet.'

'You told one of our officers that Cassidy's boyfriend killed Victor McLean in Pitlochry.'

'No, I didn't. I haven't spoken to any police officer.'

'Robert from AA,' Harry said.

'Oh. He was a police officer? I never would have guessed.' Brian shrugged his shoulders and stared at the carpet for a second before looking up again. 'Oh yes, I remember. I think Jock Forrest killed Victor. Ruby's boyfriend, not Cassidy's. Not Ewan. Jock Forrest.'

'How come you were down at Cassidy's house with our officer if you were living here?' Stewart said.

'I was just there to get my *Star Wars* chess set. I phoned Simon and he was waiting in the car round on the main road.'

'I was. Brian was only a few minutes. He brought the chess set out and we came back here to play.'

'You went upstairs to get your chess set,' Stewart said.

Brian shook his head. 'No, my chess set was in the living room. Thank goodness nobody had touched it.'

Harry was getting a bad feeling about this whole situation. 'If she was in the garage and was moved, either of you could have done it today.'

'I was playing chess with Simon with the new set. Simon had to go out to his therapist again. He wanted to see her today as he won't be going again until after New Year. You can ask her if you like. Dr Morgan Allan is her name.'

'I will,' Harry said. *And sooner than you think.* 'Why didn't you call us, Ewan?'

'This! All these police officers in the house! Can you imagine how it would have looked if I'd called and said I'd found the dead body of my ex-girl-friend's daughter?'

Harry's phone rang. He looked at the screen: Jimmy Dunbar. 'Sorry, I have to take this.' He moved into the hall.

'Kitchen's through that way, son,' Joe said. 'If you want some privacy.'

'Thanks.' Harry answered it and walked into the kitchen and shut the door behind him. 'Jimmy.'

'Harry, we got an ID on the female after the pathologist arrived and had a good look at her. She had an identifying mark on her. A birthmark. It's Sharon Boyle, not Moira McLean.'

'There's no good news there, pal.'

'*I don't know if it makes that laddie more guilty or not.*'

Harry looked around to make sure he was still alone and walked to the other side of the kitchen and lowered his voice. 'Ewan has an alibi for when Sharon got into that van. Somebody vouches for him. I don't think he killed her. It appears that when Brian said the boyfriend killed Victor McLean in Pitlochry, he was talking about his aunt's boyfriend, Jock Forrest, not Ewan.'

'*I think we should bring Forrest in for questioning, Harry.*'

'Go ahead. We can talk to him when I get back.'

'*I can't right now, mucker. He left with a friend of his. He was hovering about outside and I told him to bugger off, but he said he was waiting to be picked up by his friend.*'

'Who was this friend?'

'*Somebody from work. Crawford, I heard him say when he opened the car door. He was being a smartarse so he said it loud enough for me to hear.*'

'Crawford Ingram. They work together with Ewan.'

'*That explains a lot.*'

'Cheers, Jimmy. I'll see you later.' Harry hung up and went back to the living room. 'Jock Forrest was picked up by Crawford Ingram. They work and golf together.'

'We play down at Baberton. Jock's going to Florida with the work team, so I heard,' Ewan said.

Stewart stood up. 'That might just be a cover story.'

'No, they're really going,' Ewan said. 'Me and Crawford didn't get chosen. Well, me, not at first. Crawford, not at all.'

'Forrest could be using this excuse to take off,' Harry said. 'Do you know if they're going to the club?'

'We were meeting at Crawford's house, then going to the club later. Crawford lives alone, so his house is quieter.'

'Where does he live, son?' Stewart said. 'And turn that fucking fire down a bar or two. My skids have gone up my arse they're that sweaty. Do you own a fucking power station or something?'

'We manage to pay the bills.'

'Aye, well, some old pensioner might not be able to and you're wasting it.'

'I'll go and get a pad and write down Crawford's address. It's down in Baberton Mains too.' Ewan turned the bulb off in the fire but kept the central heating on.

He gave Harry the piece of paper.

'Mr Gallagher, I'd like you to go to the station with my two colleagues to make a formal statement.'

'Anything you want. I just need to get a coat.' Ewan walked out of the living room and turned as his brother followed. 'Chess? Seriously?'

'It's a game of skill,' Simon said.

Ewan just looked at Brian and walked on past.

'Sir, I think we should go down and check on this Crawford Ingram,' said Harry. 'He might be in danger.'

'You think this Forrest guy is a nut job?'

'I think he might be. I think he had the opportunity to move the body from the garage to the bedroom undetected.'

Stewart went outside and spoke to the ARU. 'You lads follow us. Behave yourselves and we might let you have some fun with those machine guns.'

FORTY-TWO

The drive back down to Baberton Mains didn't take long. The house they were looking for was at the top of the estate in a cul-de-sac. The houses in this street had been built on a hill and each house was stepped up from the last one. Crawford Ingram's house was on the top corner. There was a short driveway in front of a garage, and a dark hatchback car was parked here. Another driveway led off at an angle to the back garden. It was in this driveway that a white van sat.

Harry parked in front of the driveway and the ARU pulled in behind.

'He's a sick bastard, right enough,' Stewart said again. 'Good call on not telling Ewan Gallagher that it wasn't Moira in there but his girlfriend Sharon.'

'He'll find out soon enough.'

They got out of the car and went up to the front door. By comparing the front of this house to similar ones in the street, Harry could tell this one had an extension on the front.

They heard shouting coming from inside and the sound of crashing furniture.

'Christ, Forrest is killing this Ingram guy. Get the fucking door in, you two,' Stewart said to the ARU men.

Harry reached out and tried the handle. It moved and the door opened.

'Nobody likes a smartarse, Harry,' Stewart said as the four of them entered the house.

There was a scream from further inside and they rushed through into a living room. Jock Forrest was standing over Crawford Ingram, who was on his front with an arm behind him sticking up straight. Forrest was holding a knife.

'Let him go, Jock. It's over. We know what you did,' Harry said.

'Get him off me!' Ingram shouted. 'He's going to kill me.'

Harry walked forward slowly, his hand out. 'Give me the knife, Jock.'

'Aye, right. As soon as I let him go, he's going to try and kill me. Like he killed those lassies.'

'I didn't kill them!' Ingram said. 'He did!'

'Just like he was going to kill Moira,' Forrest said. 'She's through in the garage. Alive. Go and see for yourself.' He nodded to the hallway, where there was a door to the garage.

Harry walked slowly towards the door and pushed it open. Moira squealed behind the gag in her mouth. She was sitting down, her hands and feet tied. Harry rushed over and pulled the gag down.

'Who did this to you?' he asked.

'He did,' she said.

FORTY-THREE

Harry walked along the corridor towards the interview room. He and Dunbar were sitting in on the interview, with Stewart and Charlie Skellett watching through the one-way mirror.

They'd been at it for a couple of hours, getting him formally booked in and setting up the interview. Harry walked into the room where Dunbar was already sitting. He prepared the tapes and indicated that the camera was recording.

'Now, Mr Ingram, why don't we start from the beginning?' Harry said.

'You've got the wrong man! It was Forrest who did this. That lassie is wrong!'

His solicitor was sitting next to him. Crawford Ingram had maintained his innocence even though they had been told by Moira that he was the one who had abducted her, and not Forrest.

For the first twenty minutes of the interview they went back and forth, and Harry thought that Stewart must have been champing at the bit to come in and kick Ingram in the bollocks.

'If you help us, we can ask for leniency with the Crown Office,' Dunbar said.

'I've seen all the TV shows where they say that.' Ingram sat quietly for a moment. Then he looked at his lawyer for confirmation, and the man nodded.

'What does it matter now anyway?' Ingram said. 'I did it to save my best friend.'

'Who are we talking about here, Mr Ingram?' Harry said.

'Ewan, of course. He made a huge mistake getting involved with that stupid bitch Cassidy. He was falling for her after her husband died. I couldn't believe it. Sometimes we'd arrange to go for a pint, then he'd cancel to go out with her. I mean, I've worked with him for years, we golf together, we go drinking together. He's like a brother. Cassidy was going to spoil it all.'

'Did you kill Victor McLean?'

'Yes, I did.'

'Somebody else thought it was Jock Forrest.'

Ingram shrugged. 'We had the same golf club jacket and jeans on. From behind, it would've been easy to confuse us.'

'Why did you kill Victor McLean?' Dunbar asked.

'He was a horrible bastard. He said something to me that day. He made a derogatory remark about Ewan. My best friend. We were there enjoying our day of hiking, and he had to be the big fucking cheese. "My photos are better than your photos." When his family group were up ahead, I just happened to come across him standing on that bridge, taking photos. I told him to be careful, and you know what he said? He told me to fuck off and mind my own business. So I shoved him off the bridge, then I scarpered, and came back when I saw there was a commotion. That's when Ewan got interested in Cassidy.'

'Why did you take the girls?' Dunbar asked.

'I wanted to absolutely devastate Cassidy's life so she wouldn't have any time for Ewan. I was going to kill Moira and leave her in the garage, but then I thought it would be better if I killed Sharon and left her there instead. You people might think it was Cassidy who killed her, then she would go to prison. You know, out of jealousy. Then you would think that she killed Sioux for getting Moira drunk and buying her drink.'

'What about Jock Forrest?'

'We were just going to go round to the golf club for a beer. He said he would walk round to my house, but I didn't want that. So I suggested I pick him up. I drove back and all he was supposed to do was sit in the car. But he came in, looking for a toilet. Then he heard Moira making a noise, even with the gag in her mouth. He opened the door and saw her. I thought I could batter him, but he got the better of me, and that's when you came in.'

'You killed Sioux and Sharon just to keep your friend for yourself, is that right?' Dunbar said.

'Yes. Ewan and I have been having a laugh for years. We do everything together. I didn't want Cassidy to stop that. I've seen the way she flirts with men in the hospital when she's working. I knew it wouldn't last long with Ewan. I had to stop her, so my life could carry on the way it was. I didn't want anybody to change my life.'

'Guess what?' Dunbar said. 'You've changed it all on your own.'

FORTY-FOUR

Harry was exhausted by the time he pulled into his street and parked. Stewart, Dunbar and the rest were having a pint and staying one more night before heading back to Glasgow, and they'd invited him along, but he was on the fence. Maria had had a long day with Grace and he didn't want to take advantage. Besides, it didn't feel right now that Andy Watt had died in a horrible fashion.

He'd thought about a hitman taking them all out, one by one. What if they were all in one place? That would make the hitman's job easier, if he was armed.

There were no lights on in Harry's house except the Christmas tree in the living room window. Maria had said that she had to drop Grace off a little bit early but Morgan was there. Did he want her to leave Grace with Morgan?

Harry had debated, but then relented. Morgan was good with Grace, and he trusted her. He had told Maria that would be fine but he wouldn't be that much longer anyway.

He climbed the steps to his pathway and walked along to the front door. It was ajar.

He looked around again, but once more couldn't see Maria's car. Darkness had come down to envelop the late afternoon and all the dark cars looked alike. Had she parked round the corner again? There were spaces now, but that didn't mean there had been spaces when Maria pulled up.

He wasn't going to rush in. That's how people got killed. His training kicked in and he gently nudged the door open. He thought about drawing his baton, but swinging a baton in close quarters wasn't the best way to fight. Plus, what good was a baton if the hitman had a gun? Somehow he didn't think that would be the case, though. Why run Andy Watt down if he had a gun and could have shot him?

Harry wished Robbie Evans was here. Younger, fitter and an ex-boxer. However, Harry was here alone, so he had to deal with this. His daughter was inside and he needed to see her now.

There were no lights on in the house except the Christmas tree lights. They cast a dull glow that was coming through the living room doorway. He walked quietly along towards it. He knew every inch of this house in the dark, which gave him an advantage.

He reached the living room and pushed the door, looking over his shoulder in the wide, square hallway first in case it was a trap. Then he moved inside.

Morgan was sitting on a chair, holding Grace in her arms. His daughter looked to be sleeping. Then he saw the knife Morgan was holding. It was large, with blood dripping off the end. There was no sign of Maria.

'Morgan, listen, please don't do anything silly.' Harry held up both hands.

'Harry, this is not what it looks like,' Morgan said, looking at him. She seemed out of breath, like she'd just run a marathon.

'Harry!' he heard a voice shout from behind. He spun round and saw Maria rushing out of the kitchen with what looked like a wet towel.

'Christ, Maria, what's going on?'

'I need to take care of Morgan's wound. We were attacked. Her arm's been slashed. I've called treble nine.'

He looked at Maria's face and saw blood coming

out of her nose. 'What? What the hell happened? Is Grace okay?' He didn't want to rush at Morgan just this second but kept his eyes on her.

Maria rushed by him and went to Morgan. 'You can put the knife down now, honey. She's not going anywhere.'

'What's happening?' Harry said, moving closer. He picked up Grace as Maria tended to Morgan's wound.

'Look over the couch, Harry,' Maria said.

Harry did and his breath was taken away for a second. The so-called hitman was lying on the floor, hog-tied with electrical cord, duct tape wound round the head to cover the mouth.

It was Lizzie Armstrong. She wasn't moving.

'It was my fault, Harry,' Morgan said. 'Maria had just come in with Grace, and then Lizzie came to the door, and I was surprised. You know she's a voluntary patient at the hospital and can leave any time after filling out a request form, so it wasn't unusual, but she was in such a state. Lizzie barged in, then went mad, talking about having to kill you and the others before you killed her. She's been telling me that her mother has been feeding her this information for years, how you and the others were all killers and you were coming for her. She's a lot more psychotic than we thought.'

'Is she dead?' he asked, then realised that they wouldn't have hog-tied her if she was.

'No. She punched Maria and grabbed Grace. When I went to grab the little one, Lizzie pulled out a knife. I'm sorry, but I didn't hesitate. There's no way she was going to get near the baby with that knife. Lizzie slashed my arm, then I grabbed the knife arm and headbutted her. Twice. Then I got Grace and Maria got up and struggled with Lizzie. Then I turned Grace away and stabbed Lizzie. After she fell, Maria tied her up. I don't think it's a serious wound, but I don't care.'

'Christ, you could have died,' Harry said.

'I wasn't going to stand by and let anything happen to the little one. I just acted on instinct. I've dealt with patients who have got violent before and have had to physically restrain them, and this was no different. I used to do kick-boxing. I would have died before I let her harm Grace.'

Harry looked at her and smiled. Then he took his phone out. 'Frank? It's Harry. It's over, son.'

FORTY-FIVE

The following day, Harry's dining room looked like a McDonald's.

'Great tattie scones, son,' Calvin Stewart said.

'I made them myself,' Harry replied.

Stewart raised his eyebrows. 'Let's no' end the year with you gibbering a load of pish, now.'

'This is a great fry-up anyway, pal,' Dunbar said.

Miller, Skellett, Dunbar and Evans sat across the table from Stewart, who was sitting next to Morgan, Chance and Katie. They all had orange juice, and Harry grabbed a glass as he sat on the other side of Morgan. Grace was in her high chair, playing with her food.

'Yesterday was a hell of a day,' Harry said. 'Lizzie Armstrong came here to kill me, because of her mental issues, which her mother had compounded. She's in a secure unit now and is no longer a voluntary patient. She'll get the help she needs, though it's too late for Andy Watt. Now, I'd like to make a toast to Morgan who without a single care for her own safety put herself in danger to protect my daughter. Here's to Morgan.'

'To Morgan!' they all chanted. Then got wired into breakfast.

'Let's not forget that Calvin's last day will be on Hogmanay,' Dunbar said. 'I'd like to raise a toast to him and wish him the best in his retirement. To Calvin!'

'To Calvin!'

'This is great scran, Harry,' Skellett said. 'My dug would love these tattie scones.'

'Listen to you,' Stewart said. 'Wasting tattie scones on your fucking dug? It must be this Edinburgh air.'

'Sir Hugo loves his tattie scones.'

'We're still talking about the dug?'

'Naw, he's my butler. Of course the dug. He loves them.'

'That's a bloody illness with you. Feeding your dug good scran.'

'He likes tuna pizza as well.'

Stewart speared a piece of tattie scone and held it on his fork, pointing it at Skellett. 'See when you look up "boggin' bastard" in the dictionary, it's got your photo there.'

Skellett laughed.

'What are you doing for Hogmanay?' Harry asked Morgan, leaning in close.

'I think I'll find myself a nice policeman to kiss at midnight.'

'Got anyone in mind?'

'Well, there's nobody else available, so I think it's going to be you.' She smiled at him and he gave her a quick kiss.

'I can live with that.'

AFTERWORD

And that just leaves me to thank a few people before I go. So here goes – thank you to Jacqueline Beard for her tremendous work and keen eye for detail. To my niece Stacey Mitchell, for all baby-related advice. To Ruth, as always. Rosie Burgon at scottishcutflowers.-co.uk. for her advice on Christmas bouquets. And to Eve Bell for the help with my research.

To my brilliant editor, Charlie Wilson. Stuntmen from the 1920s had an easier job than she does. She grabs on, holds on tight and doesn't let go until the book is finished.

Thanks also to my niece, Lynn McKenzie.

A huge thank you to the real Charlie Skellett and Carol Allardyce. This is just the beginning.

Finally, a huge thanks to you, the reader, who

makes this all possible. If you could see your way to leaving a review or a rating, I'd greatly appreciate it.

Stay safe, my friends.

John Carson
July 2022
New York

Printed in Great Britain
by Amazon